love letters from memphis

B. LOVE

PROLIFIC PEN PUSHER

Copyright © 2023 by B. Love

All rights reserved.

No part of this book may be reproduced in any form or by any electronic or mechanical means, including information storage and retrieval systems, without written permission from the author, except for the use of brief quotations in a book review.

note:

True lovers of B. Love, continue swiping after you reach *The End* for details on how you can receive exclusive, limited-edition copies of books and B. Love merch.

preface

Please note: Though this is a dual point of view book, the first 15,000 words or so are told from the main female character's point of view only. Don't worry... Londen is worth the wait.

Very briefly, suicide is mentioned in chapter six. Please skip that chapter if necessary for healthy reading.

introduction

Between Memphis and Rose Valley Hills... there are the good and the gritty—both have stories to tell.

one

STANDING DIRECTLY in front of the six-foot-tall mirror, Royalty looked herself over. She was no blushing bride. In fact, she had to constantly remind herself not to frown. The silver crown that set atop her elegant updo was slightly crooked. Inhaling a deep breath, Royalty's eyes lowered down the silk gown that fit against her frame perfectly.

"Are you ready, baby?" Royalty's mother, Jennifer, asked.

Blinking slowly, Royalty nodded. "As ready as I will ever be."

Jennifer chuckled. "You don't sound too enthusiastic about marrying Steven. Are you getting cold feet?"

Royalty was glad her mother waited until it was just the two of them in the room before she asked that. This wasn't a conversation she wanted to have in front of several people. Her parents, Jennifer and Marcus, treated her differently since the birth of her sister, Regal. The two were five years apart, and from the beginning, Royalty felt the effects of being the older sibling.

While her parents hadn't outright forgotten about her, she was no longer their sole priority. The older Royalty got, the less her parents focused on her and gave their younger daughter their attention. As an adult, Royalty could tell herself that was the natural order of things, but the damage had already been done by that point. She rebelled heavily throughout her teenaged years to regain her parents' attention and priority.

And it worked, but the attention and priority weren't given in love. They yelled more than anything else. Punished her more than they rewarded her. Disapproved of her actions more than they validated. But she was the center of their eyes again, and in that moment, that was all that mattered.

By the time Royalty left for college, she'd received the nickname of Troublemaker. Her parents had all but washed their hands of her, practically forcing her to live on campus while she was in college and paying for her apartment when she graduated. Eventually, Royalty's desire for them turned into resentment. In her mind, her parents should have known she was acting out to get their attention, but that had never been the case.

Now, as a twenty-six-year-old woman, Royalty had gotten used to the lack of her parents in her life. Regal was still living at home, in college, making them proud. Her eyes rolled just at the thought. As much as Royalty wanted to open up to her mother about what she was thinking and feeling, Royalty felt it was pointless. She didn't think Jennifer would care either way. However, Royalty couldn't hide her physical reaction to her mother's question.

Did she have cold feet?

At that point... they were frozen.

"I just have a few last-minute feelings I need to work through, but I'll be fine."

Turning Royalty toward her, Jennifer cupped her arms and looked directly into her oldest daughter's eyes.

"If you need to talk or hold off on the wedding, now's the time, Royalty. Is everything okay?"

Royalty scoffed, unable to hold it in as she removed her arms from her mother's grip.

"Please, don't act like you care. You're glad a man is marrying me. That keeps you and Daddy from being at the top of my emergency list."

Jennifer's expression shifted from surprise to sadness. "How can you say that, Royalty? Your father and I love you. We will always be here for you. If you're marrying Steven because you think otherwise..."

"How can you stand there and say you will be there for me when you kicked me out the house as soon as you possibly could? I don't really have anyone except my friends, so if I did need to talk to someone about how I was feeling, it would be to Destiny or Simone."

Jennifer's mouth opened and snapped shut before she spoke. "Where is this coming from? I don't understand why you're speaking to me this way."

Royalty's head shook as she passed her mother in search of her heels. "It doesn't matter, Ma. I'm good."

"No, you aren't. And obviously we aren't either. We need to discuss this."

"There's nothing to discuss," Royalty grumbled, stepping into her shoes. "I have bigger issues to process besides you and Daddy shoving me to the side when Regal came."

"Oh." Jennifer chuckled. "So *that's* what this is about? It's your wedding day and you're still allowing your jealousy of your sister to—"

"I am *not* jealous of her!" Royalty almost screamed, slamming her hand down on the makeup tray that was next to her and causing all the contents to topple over. "Like always, you're completely missing the point because you're focused on surface level things. I said you shoved me to the side. And even right now, you're shoving my words and feelings to the side. I literally told you what the problem is, and it went completely over your head."

There was a soft tap on the door before Destiny asked, "Are you okay, Royalty?"

"Stellar," she replied under her breath with a shake of her head.

"They're ready for you."

Nodding, Royalty released a shaky breath. If she was to be honest with herself, she wasn't really angry with her mother... Not in that moment.

As Royalty headed to the door, her mother called out to her. "I really would like for us to finish this conversation."

Head hung and hand on the doorknob, Royalty smiled softly. "We don't have to, Ma. In fact, I apologize. I'm irritated and I'm about to take it out on you if I don't get out of here."

"It's your wedding day, baby," Jennifer reminded softly, as if Royalty didn't know. "This should be the happiest day of your life."

Royalty's eyes watered. "Yeah, it should."

"Why is it not?"

Gritting her teeth, Royalty kept the words from coming out. If she told her mother what she knew, Jennifer would call the wedding off, and that was the last thing Royalty wanted. Licking her lips, Royalty swallowed hard and inhaled a deep breath.

"Everything will be fine, okay?" Royalty looked back at her mother. "I love you."

"I-I love you too. But, Royalty, I really think we should talk..."

Ignoring her mother, Royalty left the room and wrapped her arm around her father's. He placed a kiss to her temple and looked down at her with a smile.

"Are you ready, baby girl?"

Nodding, Royalty inhaled a deep breath. "Yeah. Take me to my fiancé."

two

MARCUS PLACED a kiss on Royalty's forehead then placed her hand inside of Steven's. Steven smiled widely as he looked into his bride's eyes. The longer she looked at him, the more hurt and angrier she became.

As soon as the pastor said, "Dearly Beloved," Royalty pulled her hand out of his.

"Pastor Jones," she called softly, gaining everyone's attention. "Before we get started, I prepared a video montage for my fiancé."

Pastor Jones nodded in agreement, as if he had much of a choice. Looking back at her younger sister, Royalty gave her a genuine smile before her attention shifted to her best friend, Simone. With one bob of her head, Royalty gave Simone permission to play the video that crushed her soul when she received it last night.

"What is this about?" Steven asked quietly.

"You're about to see."

The video began to play on the projectors behind them, and as soon as Steven and Regal came into view, gasps and whispers filled the room. Pictures of them together, videos of them kissing, screenshots of their conversations, all quickly flew against the screen.

"Maybe we should cut this off so you and Steven can discuss this in private," Pastor Jones suggested to which Royalty shook her head.

"No. I want everyone to see what my baby sister and fiancé have been up to."

Turned out, Regal's best friend had more loyalty toward Royalty than her own sister did. Last night, Bridgette called Royalty and told her she couldn't keep Regal's secret anymore. Apparently, Regal and Steven had been sleeping together for the past six months—half the amount of time Royalty and Steven had been engaged. Royalty wasn't sure what hurt worse—the fact that her sister slept with Steven, or the fact that she'd convinced herself that letting them still get married was okay.

According to Bridgette, Regal cried over the affair ending because of the wedding and how a part of her wanted to tell her sister just so she could have him. To make matters worse, Regal was pregnant, and Steven had no idea. Once the video stopped, Royalty turned to face her sister while their parents charged over to them.

Regal's eyes were wide, mouth slightly ajar.

"Sis..."

"The only reason I'm not beating your ass is because you're pregnant."

"Pregnant?" Steven roared, walking over to Regal. "You're pregnant? Why didn't you tell me?"

The whispers grew louder but nothing was louder than the beating of Royalty's heart.

"I didn't want to mess up your relationship with my sister."

"That's not true," Royalty replied. "You want to be with him. Don't you?"

Regal's head shook as she struggled to find her words, and before Royalty could stop herself, she was punching Regal in the eye. The only thing that stopped her from hitting Regal again was Steven grabbing her, but that only angered Royalty more. She elbowed him in the eye before spitting on him.

"All right, that's enough!" Marcus yelled, picking her up and quickly carrying her down the aisle.

"You both better stay the hell away from me!" Royalty yelled as tears poured. But these weren't sad tears; they were angry tears, and her sister knew her well enough to know she meant business.

"So this is what you were angry about?" Jennifer asked, running behind them. "Why didn't you just *say* something, Royalty?"

"Why! So you could protect Regal and make excuses for her like you always do? She deserved that embarrassment and a hell of a lot more!"

"You didn't just embarrass her, Royalty," Marcus reasoned, placing her on her feet outside of the event venue. "You embarrassed yourself and us too."

"I don't give a fuck about either one of you right now. This doesn't have anything to do with you. This is about the man I love cheating on me with my sister. This is about my sister being pregnant with my fiancé's child. I can't believe you have the audacity to stand here and make this about you!"

Destiny and Simone made their way out, acting as her saving grace as always. Before her parents could say another word, Destiny was grabbing her hand and quickly pulling her away.

"We need to talk about this!" Jennifer yelled, causing Royalty to chuckle.

"At this point, I don't want to talk to any of you."

"Look, we're sorry, okay?" Marcus said, grabbing her hand and stopping her movement. "You're right, this isn't about us. You have every right to feel how you feel. While I might not like the way you handled this, it's your right."

His admission softened Royalty slightly, but the sight of Steven and Regal filled her with anger all over again.

"Can we please talk, Royalty?" Steven asked, heading in her direction.

"Daddy, I need you to handle him. And, Mama, unless you want me to beat your daughter's ass, you need to keep her the hell away from me."

"Let's go, Royalty," Simone said. "Now."

With her best friends on both sides of her, Royalty quickly made her way to Destiny's car. She slipped inside of the back seat... shaking. Her breath trembled as her head shook. Even though she'd had all night and all morning to process this, Royalty couldn't. In fact, her mind wouldn't allow her to understand how they could betray her. Sure, she could say Regal was spoiled and used to getting everything she wanted, but never in a million years did Royalty think that would include her man.

It seemed the more Royalty acted out for her parents' attention, the more they spoiled Regal for being the *good daughter*. It shouldn't have surprised her that they would care more about her actions than Regal's. Royalty didn't even have it in her to be upset about that. Her heart was broken enough over Steven and Regal sleeping together.

"A baby," she muttered before chuckling as tears slipped down her cheeks.

She hadn't been the emotional type, but this was taking her to a depth of pain Royalty wasn't used to.

"Where do you want to go?" Destiny asked. "What can we do?"

A part of Royalty wanted to numb herself with alcohol or drugs so she wouldn't have to feel or think about anything. The other part of her wanted to feel everything so she could get those emotions out.

"I don't know," Royalty admitted. "I don't have my phone or purse. Any clothes."

"I'll call Danny and tell him to bring your things in my car," Simone offered. "We can just go to my place for now. Give you some time to figure out your next move. Whatever you want to do, we're here for you every step of the way."

"No doubt," Destiny added.

Nodding, Royalty closed her eyes as more tears fell. So much of her life was about to change, and Royalty had a feeling she'd feel less and less in control as the days went by.

three

IT TOOK three days before Royalty was ready to go home to her apartment. Three days of smoking, drinking, and staring at the ceiling of Simone's guest room. Though she ate and kept herself up, Royalty didn't speak to anyone about the situation. That was the only way she felt like she'd be able to maintain control.

All cried out, Royalty felt numb more than anything else. It didn't matter how much she tried to reason and process, the betrayal was too profound to make sense. Royalty figured it would be one of those things she would have to simply accept without understanding.

"If you need me, call me," Simone said before hugging Royalty's neck.

Royalty nodded and gave her a quick, quiet thanks before getting out of the car. She grabbed her bag from the back seat, then headed up to the second floor. Releasing a long breath, Royalty tried to mentally prepare to step inside of her home. Between the memories she'd created there with Steven and the fact that's where she received the news, Royalty had been in no rush to return.

She stepped inside, clutching her chest at the sight of the wrinkled sheets and pillow on the couch. That's where she'd slept instead of her bed the night everything went down.

Slowly, Royalty made her way down the hall toward her bedroom. When she walked in and saw Steven sitting on her bed, she chuckled.

"I've been waiting for you," he announced.

"You're an intruder. If I shot you, it would be justified."

With a long sigh, Steven tilted his head and stood. He was dressed in a loose-fitting navy-blue shirt and blue basketball shorts. From his scruffy beard, it looked like he'd been at her place for days, like he said. Royalty wasn't sure why. As far as she was concerned, they didn't have anything to talk about.

"I know you're angry, but can we please talk?"

Her eyes stayed on his. She looked his features over, unsure how she missed the signs of his cheating. Then again, a liar would do whatever they could to hide the truth.

"I don't have anything to say to you."

"Then will you listen and let me explain?" Steven requested calmly.

"I saw everything. I don't need an explanation."

"I just... want to tell you why."

Royalty chuckled and shook her head, crossing her arms over her chest. "The why doesn't matter. I'm not like the women of your past, Steven. I don't care what sorry ass excuse you plan to give me. You cheated, and you lost—me. Now get the hell out."

Steven walked over to her, and when their bodies were just inches apart, she held her hands up to keep him from getting any closer.

"Let me apologize," he demanded, softly but with a stern tone.

"That's not for me, Steven." Her chin trembled and eyes watered as she took a step away from him. "That's for yourself. To make you feel less guilty about what you did to me. To give you closure so you can move on with a clear conscience. I'm not giving that to you."

"I'm not denying that all of that is true, but I also want to do this for you." Steven grabbed her and pulled her close. As much as she wanted to fight against him, Royalty couldn't. She looked up and into his hazel eyes. "You can act hard like you don't care, but I know this hurt you. I know it's eating you up. I know you have issues with your sister, and I don't want this to be yet another thing that makes you feel as if she's the better version of you. Let me explain. Please."

Royalty considered his request for a few seconds. As

much as she didn't want to talk to him, maybe his words would help her process everything. She nibbled her cheek before nodding and agreeing with, "Fine."

They left her bedroom and went to the dining area. Sitting across from each other at the dark brown table, Royalty avoided his eyes. They had been her favorite part of his face, along with his pink lips.

"Have you really been with her for the past six months?"

She saw him shake his head out of the corner of her eye. "No. Not the way she made it seem. I told you that the temp agency sent her to my office. As soon as she got there six months ago, she started flirting. At first, I let it ride because I didn't want to believe she was flirting. When I couldn't deny it anymore, I called her out on it, and she pretty much got even more relentless with it."

"Why didn't you tell me?"

"You two already had issues. I didn't want to make it worse."

Royalty nodded. "How long did it take you to cave?"

Running his hand down his neck, Steven breathed deeply. "Three months. It became an everyday routine. She's funny as hell, you know that. We started eating together and shit and just hanging out at work. I was able to ignore the flirting and we talked like friends. I started to enjoy her company."

Royalty locked eyes with him. "You started to enjoy her company?"

Steven looked away briefly. "Yeah. So we started hanging out outside of work. She asked me not to tell you to keep the peace, so I agreed. One night I was out with the guys, and she called. I told her where I was, but I didn't expect her to pop up. But she did." He swallowed hard. "We were drinking a lot and... I did some shit I wouldn't have done sober. We had sex in the bathroom."

She nodded. "How many times did you have sex with her?"

"One."

"Don't lie to me," she said after laughing.

"Fine. It was more than once, but I was with her because I felt like I would lose you when you found out." He scratched his head and sighed. "I was securing something with her because I planned to tell you before the wedding. I decided not to tell you because I didn't want to hurt you. I felt like if I just kept it from you and treated you even better to make up for it, that things would be okay between us."

"Did you honestly not know she was pregnant?"

"Not at all. We stopped having sex and I cut her off. I asked that we get a new temp in, which is why she had to go to a different office before her assignment was up. She was calling and texting a lot, telling me she was in love with me and wanted to be with me..."

"And that's why you randomly changed your number?"

He nodded before muttering, "Yeah," quietly. "She cornered me when we did a family dinner at your parents' house demanding an explanation or she would tell you, so I told her the truth. I told her I was dumb as hell and chose not to practice discipline but I regretted it immediately. And I told her I didn't want to hurt you or lose you. It took a little persuading, but I eventually got her to see you were most important in this situation. I told her if she cared about you at all that she would let me go and she had. We talked after everything went down and she told me finding out about the baby is what made her want me, but she knew I wasn't going to choose to ever leave you, Royalty, that's why she hadn't said anything about it."

Royalty released a soft chuckle as her leg shook under the table. His words hadn't brought her solace—they only confirmed what she'd been feeling about her sister all along. She cared less about Steven's cheating and more about the fact that her sister seemingly always wanted her spot, or what belonged to her. There was always a competition between them that started with their parents love and attention.

"This thing between my sister and I... that's not anything new. I didn't think you were a weak man, unable to control your desires, but that was my fault."

"Royalty..."

"I've always said Regal wants everything that I've had or that belongs to me. That was a subject I confided in you about. And you give her *you*?" She scoffed. "Because you enjoyed her company?"

"Baby..."

"Just get out, Steven. Everything that belongs to you here will be dropped off within the next few days. Please don't come here or reach out to me again."

"So that's it?" He sat up in his seat. "You're not even going to give me a chance to fix this?"

Royalty laughed. "You slept with my sister and got her pregnant, Steven. There's nothing you can do to fix that."

His head shook. "But I want to be with you..."

"Then you shouldn't have fucked my sister!" she roared, slamming her hand down on the table. Royalty shot up from her seat, shaking with anger. "I want you to leave, Steven. Get out!"

He stood, holding her eyes for a few seconds before leaving with a hung head. As soon as the door closed behind him, Royalty ran her fingers through her hair and released a whimper. She'd get over losing him soon enough. One thing Royalty couldn't deny was her ability to detach from things and people quickly. But there was no doubt in her mind that her heart would hurt deeply until she got to that point.

four

AT THE SOUND of beating against her door, Royalty stirred in bed. She'd spent all day yesterday looking up apartments in Memphis, only to decide she wanted to move to a completely different city. Not only did she want to avoid the risk of Steven popping up on her, but Royalty wanted to get away from her family as well. Royalty could admit that a lot of toxicity between her and her family came from her wild child era.

Unable to communicate in that moment, she acted out, creating a cycle between her and her parents that she still suffered the effects of today. It didn't matter how many times she told herself it was her parents' responsibility to identify the problem within her and create a solution, Royalty was also aware of the fact that she could only take responsibility for her own actions.

What started as neglect turned into rebellion and simmered into outright resentment toward her parents. She'd tried to establish a healthy relationship with her sister out of guilt, even going as far as asking Regal to be her maid of honor. Royalty felt as if they missed out on a lot of time to bond throughout their childhood because they were pitted against one another. Now, Royalty was convinced she didn't know her sister at all.

Sitting up in bed, Royalty looked around the room. She had no idea what time it was, but the sun was out. Her phone vibrated on the nightstand, and Royalty assumed whoever it was, was at her door. Sitting on the edge of the bed, Royalty grabbed her phone and rolled her eyes at the sight of her mother's name.

"Hello?" she answered with sleep thick in her voice.

"Come open the door."

Not bothering to vocally agree, Royalty disconnected the call. Groggily, Royalty made her way to the door, opening it to find both of her parents standing on the other side. They both smiled at the sight of her, and Jennifer immediately pulled her daughter into her arms. Hugging her back softly, Royalty closed her eyes.

Once they were inside of her home, Royalty motioned toward the couch for them to be seated.

"Let me freshen up and I'll be right back," she said, heading down the hall.

In her bathroom, Royalty stared at her reflection for a few seconds before washing her face and brushing her teeth. She used the bathroom, then made her way back out into the living room. It didn't surprise her to find her mother in the kitchen making a pot of coffee. When it was done, Jennifer fixed them all a cup. They sat at the dining room table, where her father was the first to speak.

"How are you, baby girl?"

"I'm good, actually. I got a lot of clarity and peace last night."

"That's good to hear," Jennifer said. "We've been worried about you. You haven't been answering any of our calls…"

"I apologize for that," Royalty interrupted to say. "I planned to call you today, though."

"We wanted to stop by and apologize ourselves," her father said. "After the wedding, your mom shared with me the brief talk the two of you had. She said it felt like you had a lot of resentment toward us. That you feel as if you're alone or that we aren't there for you." He looked over at Jennifer. "That we shoved you to the side."

The fact that her mother had used her exact words in conversation with her father meant more to Royalty than she imagined it could. Her eyes closed briefly as she inhaled a deep breath.

"Can we please talk about that?"

Royalty took a small sip of her coffee. "When Regal was born, you both started treating me differently. Maybe I was spoiled and took not having all of your attention anymore hard because I was a five-year-old child. Whatever the reason, I felt like you all weren't there for me as much as you used to be when you had her. The older she got, the more it felt like a competition between us. You made her do everything I did but you were prouder of her for it. From dance to art to playing an instrument. She literally followed in the same footsteps as me, yet you all praised her more and stopped caring about my interests and activities. I felt alone and ignored, and that's why I started acting out. I was angry and thought since being good didn't get your attention, maybe being bad would."

Royalty laughed quietly. Her head hung and shook as she sighed. "When I started acting out, you two treated me like I was the biggest burden. Like I was an inconvenience. Then I told you I wanted to stay home for school, but you forced me to stay on campus. I felt like you didn't want me around so you could give all your focus and love to Regal. I got my shit together in college and thought maybe things could turn around between us after that, then you put me up in this apartment and offered to pay my bills just to keep me out of your house. I just..."

Royalty shrugged as she avoided their eyes. "I just feel like having me was a mistake. Like she was the daughter you two feel like you got it right with. In my mind, I believe you don't love me or care about me anymore, though I know that's not true in my heart. It's difficult for me to rationalize and say you love me just because you say you do, when ever since I was five, your actions have said the opposite."

Neither of her parents replied right away. While Jennifer wiped away fallen tears, Marcus squeezed his closed eyes.

"We're not going to try to justify why we treated you the way we did with excuses," Marcus said. "But I want to make extremely clear that there was never a competition with you and your sister. We have never loved either of you more than the other. You have never been a burden or a mistake, Royalty."

"I'm sorry, but I can't." Jennifer chuckled, but quickly stopped. "We might not have done everything right, and I won't deny that we may not have divided our time properly, but I also can't let you sit here and make it seem as if we were horrible parents who tossed you to the side when we had a second baby."

Royalty's head tilted as she stared at her mother. "But you did."

"Jen," Marcus called softly. "You can't argue with her feelings or perception of things. If that's how she felt, she's entitled to that. Whether it's true or false, whether you agree or not, that's how *she* felt. That's all that matters right now. And to be honest, your response is a prime example of why she feels the way she does." Marcus turned slightly in his seat. "When Regal was born, we did focus on Royalty less. It was hard on us to raise a newborn with just one child. I can honestly say we dropped the ball with Roy when Regal was born. To me, I felt like she was old enough to not need as much attention. I can admit that and that it was wrong. Can you?"

Jennifer's head lowered and she remained silent, causing Royalty to chuckle.

"You just... refuse to admit that you were wrong. You refuse to say you dropped the ball with me. It's fine, Ma. You don't have to."

Royalty's head shook as she shifted her attention to her father. "Thank you for finally acknowledging that. I can say now that I'm sure juggling your jobs and two kids, plus your relationship, was probably really tough. Did it hurt to feel neglected and ignored? Yeah, but I get it. It happens.

Some kids handle it gracefully and not let it shape them. That wasn't the case for me. I'm finally at a point in my life now where I want to take complete control, which is why I planned to call and talk to both of you."

Pausing, Royalty tried to prepare for their reactions to what she was about to say. She knew her mother would speak negatively about her choice while her father tried to play referee. That had always been the case.

"I need a fresh start. Steven cheating on me with Regal hit me in a place that still hurts and probably will for a while. There are too many memories in this apartment, this city, for me to heal and focus on myself. Last night, I booked a hotel room in Coronado."

"California?" Marcus confirmed.

Royalty nodded. "Yes. I'm going to stay there and at Mission Beach for a while until I come up with my next plan. I have enough money saved to not worry about working for at least six months. So..." She shrugged. "My flight leaves Wednesday morning."

"Whatever is best for you," he agreed while Jennifer shook her head.

"Running is not going to solve this family's issues. You need to stay here so we can work on this. No matter who the father is, you will have a niece or nephew soon. This issue needs to be resolved before the baby gets here."

With a chuckle, Royalty sat up in her seat. "I don't plan to be in Regal or that baby's life, and there's literally nothing you can say or do to change my mind."

"The baby is innocent..."

"And that's exactly why I'm staying away." She stood. "My mind is made up. You can leave when you're ready. I have a lot of packing to do before I go."

"Royalty..."

"Leave it be, Jennifer," Marcus said, causing her to chuckle.

"You always do this. You always side with her and make me out to be the bad guy." Jennifer's eyes shifted to Royalty. "*That's* why we wanted you out of the house—to save our marriage! Dealing with your antics almost led to us divorcing. Getting you out felt like the only way to keep you and Regal from killing each other and making us divorce because we were always fighting over you."

Nibbling her cheek, Royalty ran her fingers through her hair as her eyes watered. Sighing, she allowed the feeling of defeat to settle within the pit of her. She was so tired. Tired of this cycle. Tired of this same fight. Tired of trying to figure out what the hell happened between her and her mother that created this tension between them. Even with all the responsibility she tried to take, it still didn't make sense.

"I give up with you," she muttered as her father stood. "I'm standing here telling you what I'm going to do for myself, and you make it about you and her. Even after what she did to me, you still talk to me with so little love and respect. You still expect me to put my feelings and needs aside to accommodate her. She slept with my fiancé and will be having his baby, and that means nothing to you. Yet again, all you give a fuck about is Regal. How dare you sit there and demand I fix something that I didn't break? This is Regal and Steven's fault. Not mine!"

"If we keep this up, we're not going to progress," Marcus said. "Jen, why don't you go wait outside in the car?"

Scoffing, Jennifer walked around the table and headed for the door. After it slammed, Marcus walked over to Royalty and pulled her into his arms. She didn't realize how much she needed the love until she had it. Royalty crumbled in his arms and sobbed.

"Why does she hate me so much? What did I do to her, Daddy?"

"Shh." Marcus kissed the top of her head and held her tighter. "She doesn't matter right now. You're all that matters to me."

Clinging to the back of her father's shirt, Royalty cried even harder. She cried until she physically couldn't stand anymore. Cried for her mother, her father, her sister. The five-year-old girl who felt replaced and unloved. Unwanted. Neglected. Cried for the ending of her marriage before it even began. Cried for her bleeding heart.

Marcus helped her into bed, promising to stay until she no longer needed him to. Royalty insisted he leave but she wouldn't force him to. She found comfort in his desire to be there for her. To put her first. To see to her needs. Her father went outside, and after a few minutes, he returned to let her know Jennifer had left. That fact had given her even more peace. As her eyelids grew heavy, her father told her to rest and that they could talk when she woke up...

five

"I DON'T KNOW where to start," Marcus confessed.

A few hours had passed. Royalty had napped, showered, and cooked... though she didn't have much of an appetite. They had just finished eating barbecued drumsticks, mashed potatoes, and asparagus. While Marcus sat on one end of the couch, Corona in hand, Royalty was on the other sipping a glass of Port. The TV was on *One Tree Hill*, the last show Royalty had started to binge on Hulu, but neither of them were paying it much attention.

"The beginning is always a good place to start," Royalty stated softly.

Surprisingly, she felt soft and safe with her father, and she hadn't felt that way in a while.

"Okay, but before I begin, I need you to promise me you will hear me out completely before you talk. Listen to receive and understand, not reply."

That request began to unnerve Royalty, but it also made her want to know more.

"I promise."

Nodding, Marcus took a long swig of his beer before setting it on the small table next to the couch.

"Before you were born, Jen and I tried to have a baby for years. It put a huge strain on our marriage. I cheated and the woman got pregnant. Upon learning this, I made the decision to divorce Jen. It felt selfish to ask her to stay with me while I raised my baby with someone else, knowing how desperately she wanted a child herself." He paused and took in a deep breath. "I was honest with Jennifer, and she agreed to the divorce. We didn't want to part ways, but I didn't want my selfish choice to make us both suffer for the rest of our lives." Marcus squeezed the back of his neck and looked away briefly. "Unfortunately, Cashmere died while giving birth to our child. When Jen found out, she came back to me and offered to help. Eventually, we decided to get back together and agreed that Jen would raise the baby as her own."

As his confession began to loop around in her mind, Royalty's heart raced.

"Are you saying Jennifer is not my birth mother? That the woman who gave birth to me died?"

"Yes, baby girl. That's exactly what I'm saying."

"Wow," she muttered, chuckling nervously.

Her leg began to shake as she stared into the distance. Marcus continued.

"We didn't think she would have a child, so when she had Regal, it was like a miracle. I can admit that she treated Regal differently because she'd actually given birth to her. With Regal, you became just a reminder of my infidelity. With Regal, Jen began to act as if she didn't need you anymore. I called her out on it and reminded her she promised to treat you as if you were her own child, and she would always throw me cheating up in my face. I felt bad about breaking our vows and hurting her, so when we had those fights, I'd often give in and let her have her way."

"Why are you telling me this now?"

"Because I convinced myself that you were too young to notice that she treated you differently. I was in denial, telling myself you acting out had nothing to do with it. After the things you said today, I couldn't hold the truth back any longer. I knew it would free you from the way you were treated. You didn't deserve that, at all, and I'm so sorry I didn't protect you better."

All she could do was nod. When she learned the truth about Regal and Steven, Royalty didn't think things could get any worse. Now... that was a lie.

"Roy," Marcus called softly. "How do you feel?"

Her eyes blinked rapidly. Body heavy, she slowly turned her head in his direction.

"Tired. Can you go? I just really want to sleep."

"Yes, of course. But..."

"Please, Daddy," she whispered through trembling lips as her eyes watered. "Please go."

Marcus stood and made his way over to her side of the couch. He dropped a kiss to the top of her head, then told her he loved her and was only a call away. She couldn't even force her head to nod or her mouth to reply. As her tears streamed, Royalty laughed. All this time, everyone tried to make her feel as if she was losing her mind. She knew things had changed when Regal was born and that her parents, especially her mother, treated her differently. For twenty-one-years, she'd dealt with this cycle and believed she was the one insane, only to learn her parents deceit was the cause of her pain.

Standing, Royalty slowly made her way to her bedroom. She closed the shades before plopping down on her bed, face down. Royalty thought she'd cry even harder, but as she laid there, all she could do was laugh.

♥♥♥

Royalty missed her flight, and at that point, she didn't even care. Before learning the truth, Royalty was prepared to leave Memphis and start anew. But for the past three days, she'd been home in her room with her thoughts. The only reason she shared the truth with her friends was because she didn't want them worried about her. Apparently, Marcus told Jennifer that she knew the truth because Jennifer had been calling and stopping by every day. Every day, Royalty told her the same thing—she didn't want anything to do with her when Regal was born, and now that was about to happen.

Twice that day, Royalty tried to eat, but she didn't have the energy. She didn't have the energy to do anything for that matter. Unlike Steven and Regal's betrayal, this one seemed to have left her paralyzed. As if she'd thought him up, Steven called her from his mother's phone. The day of the wedding, she'd blocked him on everything but overlooked his parents' numbers.

"What?" she answered, surprised to hear her own voice.

"I was just calling to check on you."

She chuckled and turned onto her side in bed. "I don't have the strength to stomach your faux concern."

"Whether you want to believe it or not, I really do love and care about you."

Sighing, Royalty breathed deeply. "I don't know what you want me to say to that, Steven."

"I want you to say you believe me."

"I don't. Will you please leave me alone? Believe it or not, your cheating is the least of my worries right now."

"Something else happened? Is there anything I can do?"

"You can leave me alone, like I asked. That's all I need from you."

"Fine," Steven surrendered. "But if you ever need—"

Disconnecting the call, Royalty powered her phone off before tossing it to the corner of her room and going back to sleep.

six

Royalty

SEVEN DAYS.

For seven days straight, someone popped up at Royalty's home to check on her.

For seven days straight, she didn't talk to them or let anyone in.

For seven days straight, Royalty tried to find a reason

for this season of her life. Hell, her life in general. She couldn't find a reason for her mother's death. She couldn't find a reason for Jennifer to agree to raise her, knowing she had ill intentions. She couldn't find a reason for Marcus to stay with Jennifer, knowing she treated their daughters differently. She couldn't find a reason for the man she loved to cheat on her, with her sister no less.

Nothing made sense.

Nothing mattered anymore.

Seven days.

That's how long it took Royalty to decide her life wasn't worth living anymore.

All that day, she packed her things and wrote letters to everyone she loved. She hadn't decided how she planned to end her life, but it would be something clean for the sake of her best friends. Though Royalty was sure they would mourn her forever, she didn't want images of her with cut wrists or gunshot wounds haunting them.

For a while, Royalty tried to convince herself that she didn't want to die—that she just wanted her life to get better—but that was a hard concept to accept as true. Because as far back as she could remember, her life had always felt unnecessarily painful or difficult, and it seemed like the same people were always the cause. As she looked through the pills in her medicine cabinet, Royalty considered ending their lives instead of hers. They were the cause of her pain. But as horrible as they'd treated her at times, she couldn't stomach causing any of them permanent harm... not even Regal. A smile slowly crept across her face at the thought of whupping her ass, though.

Slamming the medicine cabinet shut, Royalty rocked against the counter.

"What am I doing?" she whispered before looking at her

reflection, but she didn't look like herself at all. Physically, she looked the same, but her eyes and her aura were unrecognizable. Squeezing the bridge of her nose, Royalty inhaled a deep breath.

She went back into her room and grabbed her phone. Powering it on, Royalty ignored all the missed calls and text messages while pulling up her father's contact information. She called him, and Marcus answered almost immediately.

"Baby girl. Are you okay?"

She squeezed the back of her neck. "Do you have pictures of her? Of my mother?"

Seconds passed, and Royalty held on to the silence.

"I... yes. I do."

"Did you know one day that I would find out?"

"I hoped you wouldn't, but in case you did, I kept a few things to give you that were hers."

Royalty smiled. "Seeing her, getting to know about her... I think that would help me out a lot right now."

She didn't want to tell him she felt she had no hope or reason to live. She didn't want to tell him she was grasping at straws, trying to find meaning in something. She didn't want to tell him that a part of her wanted to see her mother, so she'd be able to recognize her if she made it to heaven.

"Of course. I can bring everything to you if you'd like."

Royalty's head shook as she began to pace. Quite frankly, she was tired of having so many different energies and encounters in her space. Besides, the apartment was starting to feel suffocating, and she needed to get away.

"No. I can just grab it. You can put it at the front door, and I will pick it up."

"You can't even look at me?" he asked softly, and the pain in his voice squeezed her heart. As much as she didn't want to take his pain on and make it hers, Royalty still cared about her father.

"I just... I'm not in the right headspace, Daddy."

"That doesn't surprise me. I'm concerned about you. You're not talking to anyone and you're holding a lot in. If you don't want to talk to any of us or your friends, can you please speak with a therapist?"

Her head shook and eyes watered as she gritted her teeth. "That's not necessary. I need to feel connected to something. Someone." Royalty's voice broke when she said, "I just feel so alone."

"Baby girl, I'm so sorry."

Wiping her face, Royalty released a heavy breath. "It's fine." She sniffled.

"No, it's not fine. This is all my fault. I shouldn't have handled any of this the way I did. I failed you, Roy. Please let me help you and make this up to you."

"Besides giving me my mother's things, I genuinely don't think there's anything you can do."

"Can I ask you something without you getting offended?"

Tugging her bottom lip between her teeth, Royalty leaned against the dresser. "Yes."

"Are you safe with yourself right now?"

Squeezing her eyes shut, Royalty shook her head. "I don't think so," she confessed. "I'm trying to be. I-I *want* to be. I think if I had something of hers, something to feel connected to, maybe that would help."

"Okay, Royalty. I will handle this your way. If you want me to, I can grab the items out of storage. You can meet me there and get the box. We don't have to talk, but I would like to set eyes on you to make sure you're okay."

"All right, Daddy," Royalty agreed. "Just send me the address and time and I will meet you there."

"Okay. I love you."

A few seconds passed before Royalty replied with, "I love you too."

She disconnected the call, then headed to the bathroom to get herself together. As she showered, Royalty did something she hadn't done in a while. She prayed. Between the meditation within her heart and water trickling down her skin, Royalty felt calmer than she had in a while.

Once her shower was over, Royalty finished her hygiene and skin care routines, then dressed comfortably in a pair of distressed jeans and a loose-fitting graphic tee. In case it got cool, she reached for a hoodie, and her eyes bulged at the sight of one of Steven's. Pulling it out, Royalty pressed the hoodie into her face and inhaled its scent. She wasn't surprised that it smelled just like him. As soon as the first day of fall hit and Steven pulled out his hoodies, she snagged her favorite one.

Royalty headed for the living room, making her way to the fireplace. After tossing the hoodie inside, she lit the fireplace and watched it burn. For those fleeting moments, Royalty smiled genuinely. She couldn't deny how good it felt to receive some sort of vengeance. It might have been a small act, but it was one that made her feel powerful and in control. At that point, that control was almost euphoric.

For so long, it felt like the only thing Royalty had been feeling was pain. The happiness she felt as she stared into the flames was a welcomed change. Returning to her room, Royalty stepped into her shoes. She waited until the hoodie left nothing but ashes in the fireplace before heading out of her apartment to meet with her father. At the sight of Jennifer standing behind the door, Royalty rolled her eyes.

B. LOVE

"Go away," she grumbled, locking the door behind her. Royalty had no plans of speaking with her mother, or the woman that had raised her, and nothing Jennifer could say would change that.

Jennifer gasped, gripping the top of Royalty's arm to keep her from walking away. "You have lost your mind speaking to your mother like that."

Royalty chuckled, pulling her arm out of Jennifer's grip.

"You're not my mother. Daddy told me everything." Royalty paused, waiting to see how her words would affect Jennifer.

Jennifer's eyes widened and mouth parted as her head jerked back from the impact of Royalty's words. "How can you stand there and say that to me?"

"It's the truth, and honestly, it explains every damn thing. Daddy told me all of it. How he cheated and got another woman pregnant. How he planned to leave, but when my real mother died, you allowed him to come back." Royalty chuckled, crossing her arms over her chest. "You know what I don't understand though? Why would you agree to raise another woman's baby, knowing you couldn't handle seeing the face of your husband's betrayal?"

Jennifer inhaled a deep, shaky breath. The bark of laughter she released wasn't one of amusement. With her hands on her hips, she stared into Royalty's eyes as she nibbled her bottom lip.

"Now you don't have anything to say, Jennifer?"

"Your father was right, I'm not your mother... but he's not your father either. I'm not sure why he decided to finally come clean, but the least he could have done was tell you the whole truth."

"What do you mean the whole truth?" Royalty asked softly.

"You need to sit down for this."

"No, just..." Nostrils flaring, Royalty took a step back as her heart raced. "Just say what you have to say."

"Marcus *did* cheat on me, he even planned to leave me for her. The woman he cheated with didn't tell him she was fresh out of a relationship and not completely over her ex. For some reason, sharing her angered Marcus. I guess she hadn't planned to tell him, but when she found out she was pregnant, she realized she didn't have a choice. The baby... you... weren't his. At that point, she decided to make things work with your father, and that infuriated Marcus. He decided to get back at her for playing with his heart by taking you."

"And you just... let him get away with it? That's... He kidnapped me!"

"It wasn't my intention, and I didn't even know in the beginning. He'd given me the same lie he told you—that he cheated, and your mother died giving birth. I agreed to raising you, but yes, I did start to feel some kind of way as you aged. That was something that I probably should've spoken to a professional about, but I was ashamed. And yes, maybe I did treat Regal differently because she was my birth child, but neither of those are why there's been a disconnect between us. There's been a disconnect between us because I felt forced to stay with Marcus because of you."

"How can you blame that on me?"

"I wanted to tell your mother the truth about you when I found out. You were four years old. I had my suspicions because you looked nothing like your father, and I just felt in my gut that he was hiding something. He never wanted to go back to our old town, not even to see his family. It was like he wanted to build this world in Memphis that included just us. Marcus was always paranoid and looking over his shoulder... going from one job to the next. Something just always felt... off. Eventually, I decided to go look for answers myself. I went to see his mother and he all but ripped my head off when I came back home. That's when he finally came clean and told me he'd taken you from your real parents, and that your father is such a dangerous man that if he ever found out, he'd kill us both. I thought he was just being dramatic at first, but I looked into your parents, and he's right. Your father isn't just dangerous; he's powerful. His family is one of the founding families of our old town and the secret society that runs it. They'd placed all kinds of rewards up for information on you, and word had spread that the person responsible for taking you was a dead man walking. I... hated having you around because I felt trapped. That wasn't fair to you, but that's the whole truth."

Leaning against the door, Royalty slid down it. Accepting Jennifer not being her mother was a lot, but it made sense. Accepting Marcus not being her father... Royalty was having difficulty processing those words. Neither of them were her parents. All this time, she'd been raised to feel as if she was unworthy of true love, support, and acceptance from people that hadn't even created her. Marcus had taken her from her family just to put her in a house that stopped feeling like home as soon as Regal was born.

When the tears began to pour, Royalty didn't even have the strength to wipe them away. Jennifer tried to sit next to Royalty, but she lifted her hand to stop her.

"Please, I need some space."

"I know this is probably a lot to process, but you deserved to know the whole truth."

Royalty scoffed and shook her head. "You're only telling

me because Marcus told me about you. If he hadn't, you would have continued to treat me like an outcast, then gaslight me into believing it was all in my head."

"Roy…"

"I don't want to have anything to do with either of you."

Jennifer pulled her phone out and did something on it, then put it back in her purse. "If you change your mind, I'm here. If you don't, I understand. I really did love you as if you were my own, even if I didn't actively express that. I… sent you your mother and father's names. They are located in Rose Valley Hills. Like I said, your father's family was one of the founding families of Rose Valley, so with a quick Google search, information on them will be easy to find."

Jennifer leaned down and placed a kiss on Royalty's forehead, and it took everything inside of her not to wipe it away. Royalty didn't realize how long she'd sat there paralyzed until the sun set and tiny flying bugs began to swirl around her, pulling her out of her trance. Standing, she went back into her apartment and crashed on the couch, not even having the strength to make it to her bedroom. Just when she thought things couldn't get any worse, Jennifer showed up and further demolished her world.

seven

MARCUS

Marcus checked the time on his phone yet again. He'd been calling Royalty's phone and had yet to get an answer. It wasn't like her to not communicate. If she wasn't going to meet him at the storage unit, Royalty would have called to let him know. What had caused her to change her mind? Was she involved in an accident? Unable to let so many conflicting thoughts roam around in his mind, Marcus called yet again, and yet again, he got no answer.

Running his hand across the back of his head, Marcus sighed.

Had he overwhelmed Royalty by telling her a half truth?

She was already dealing with the fact that her sister had slept with her fiancé and had a baby on the way. Was now the time for her to find out Jennifer wasn't her mother too? That hadn't been the plan, but when Marcus saw the hurt in his daughter's eyes, he had to do *something*. All Jennifer had to do was apologize for not being as present and accepting of Royalty as she should have been, and the truth could have been avoided—but she was always... always so stubborn.

At the sound of tires on gravel, relief filled Marcus as he turned, but that relief quickly turned into confusion at the sight of Jennifer's car. Chuckling, Marcus crossed his arms over his chest with a shake of his head. His tongue rolled over his cheek as he watched Jennifer get out of her Infinity.

What was she up to?

Her ankles crossed over one another as she sashayed in his direction with a smug grin. Over twenty-years of faking the funk with Jennifer had aged him. When Royalty was first born, Marcus wanted to keep Jennifer around to make amends for cheating and show his gratitude for her agreeing to mother Royalty. Now, he wished he would have let her go and run away with Royalty. So many things would be different, better, if it would have been just him and his baby girl.

"What are you doing here? And where's Royalty?"

"She wanted me to let you know she won't be coming."

"Why not?" Marcus reached for his phone, prepared to call her again.

"I... wouldn't call her if I were you." Jennifer closed the space between them, gently pulling his phone out of his hand. "She's very upset about you kidnapping her, so I highly doubt she'll want to speak to you."

Marcus' jaw dropped, but he quickly composed himself. There was a chance Jennifer was lying, and he wouldn't dare allow her to think she'd gotten a rise out of him.

"What are you talking about?"

She laughed, circling him slowly with a disapproving shake of her head. "Even though you all try to portray me as this... neglectful monster, I genuinely care about Royalty, so I stopped by to check on her. Imagine my surprise when she told me the same lie you did when you brought her into our lives—that her mother was dead, and you were the greatest father ever by choosing to raise her with me. Did you *really* think I'd let you get away with that?"

Marcus' heart was beating so hard and loud, he heard it in his chest.

"You didn't..."

"Oh, but I did." Jennifer's pointer finger slid down the center of his chest. "See, you fucked up when you tried to put it all on me. If you were going to try to explain why I treated her differently, you should have told her it's because you took her from the woman you cheated on me with."

"Do you not realize you ruin everything?" Marcus almost whispered, trying to keep his calm. If he didn't, he'd explode. "All you had to do was apologize a week ago, and none of this would have happened. All you had to do was treat Royalty just as well as you treated Regal, and none of this would have happened. You always ruin every damn thing, Jen. I hate the day I even met you."

For seconds on end, they just stared at each other before Jennifer burst into a fit of laughter.

"You have got to be the most delusion bastard on earth." Her lips trembled as they snapped shut before she yelled, "You kidnapped her, Marcus!" Those four words, though truthful, sliced through his heart like a sharp machete. "You took her from her family and forced me to keep your secret just so I'd stay alive! And you expected me to do that lovingly?" Jennifer's voice cracked as her eyes watered. "I did the best I could," she whispered. Sniffling, she wiped her face and pulled in a shaky breath. "The truth is out now, though, and I don't care about the consequences. In fact, I hope you're punished severely for what you did to her, and if I get caught in the crossfire of that... I'll suffer just to make sure you finally get what you deserve."

After spitting on his feet, Jennifer turned and headed back to her car. "Stay the hell away from Royalty, Marcus. We've caused that girl enough pain. Leave her alone!"

With weak legs, Marcus staggered toward his car. Even with Jennifer's words, he refused to believe she'd told Royalty the truth. He waited until he was in the car to call Royalty again. This time, the call went straight to voicemail. Marcus punched the steering wheel three times with a roar before starting the engine and swerving out of the parking lot. He needed to see Royalty and explain why he'd done what he did, otherwise, there was no doubt in his mind that he would lose her forever.

♥♥♥

When Marcus made it to Royalty's apartment, he was surprised by the sight before him. Several men were clearing out her apartment, and two guarded the door. The only one he recognized was Danny, Simone's boyfriend. Marcus' brows wrinkled as he tried to look further into the apartment, and it wasn't lost on him that Danny's body shifted further in front of him.

"What's going on? Where's Roy?"

"I'm not allowed to say," Danny replied.

"What are y'all doing?"

"Fuck does it look like?"

The bite of Danny's words had Marcus jerking his head in the younger man's direction. "Who you think you talking to, son?"

Danny's grin was cocky as he chuckled, cupping his

hands in the center of him. "I ain't talking to *nobody*. Move around, we need to get these boxes outta here."

Marcus was no fool. No matter how angry he was or how disrespected he felt, he was outnumbered. He wasn't sure what all Royalty had shared with Simone and Danny, but it was enough to have Danny handling him differently. His best bet was to try to get as many answers as he could by maintaining his cool.

"Look, just tell me that my daughter is okay. I've been calling her repeatedly and getting no answer."

Danny's expression softened as his head tilted. "She's okay physically, but you know what you did, so I don't think she'll be okay emotionally and mentally for a while."

Squeezing the back of his neck, Marcus bobbed his head as his heart broke. "Can you please just give her a message for me? Tell her I'll leave her alone, but I really want to explain. If she doesn't want me to, I understand, but I need her to know that I love her."

Danny considered his words for a few seconds before agreeing with, "I'll let her know."

As much as he didn't want to leave, Marcus did. It was clear Royalty didn't want to have anything to do with him, and Marcus had no choice but to respect and accept that. What he'd done was unforgivable, but that wasn't going to stop him from trying to earn her forgiveness.

When he first hatched the plan to take Royalty, Marcus didn't have the purest intentions. He wanted to hurt her the way Cashmere had hurt him. She made him believe they had a future together, but Royalty's conception changed her mind. Cashmere took that as a sign to make her relationship with Ace work. Marcus wanted to take Cashmere's heart and future, just like she'd done with him. The moment he took Royalty out of the hospital that night, his desires changed. He didn't care about hurting Cashmere; he just wanted to give Royalty the world. In the beginning, that seemed possible, but when Jennifer had Regal, the dynamic changed.

In a matter of seconds, Marcus grew to love Royalty more than he realized was possible and committed himself to protecting and loving her for the rest of her life. Unfortunately, he was the one responsible for filling her with more pain than any person should ever feel. Regal's betrayal was now a blip on the radar. Cursing under his breath, Marcus made it to his car and fought the urge to try to find Royalty. He'd give her space... for now.

eight

Royalty

TWO WEEKS Later

"Wow," Royalty muttered, looking at the huge mansion in front of her. Mansion didn't seem like the proper word. This was a true estate. From first glance, Royalty saw an area by the garage that looked like a car wash, a detached smaller home, and a glass room that was off to the back side that looked like an athletic area. Her awe turned into frustration at the thought of Marcus taking her from this lifestyle of opulence.

From the research she'd done on her parents, their wealth wasn't new. Ace Lew was born into his riches, and technically, Royalty was too. As anxious as she'd been to meet them, Royalty had to force herself not to drive out of the circular driveway. It felt like she was in a completely different world.

It also felt like second nature to call Destiny or Simone, but this was something Royalty would need to handle on her own. Three days passed after finding out she was kidnapped before Royalty was looking up the names Jennifer had given her—Ace Lew and Cashmere Fifer.

Apparently, Ace ran a secret society along with four other men that was talked about by everyone, but only those involved knew the true inner workings. Outside of that, Ace also had several businesses in the medium-sized town of Rose Valley Hills. Cashmere was just as influential. Her family was responsible for all utilities and internet, and Cashmere was the town hall president, where both companies operated.

"What am I doing here?" she asked, staring at the front door. "They've lived twenty-six years without me. Am I really going to be able to fit into their lives here?"

At that point, leaving was her only option. Royalty had her entire apartment in Memphis packed up. Even if she didn't stay in Rose Valley Hills, which was three hours outside of Memphis, she would have to go *somewhere*. She'd left her job, friends, and the family she'd known all her life behind. Was Rose Valley Hills really the place where she'd have her new start?

As she was about to pull out of the driveway, the iron

doors opened, and an older version of herself stepped out onto the porch. It wouldn't have surprised her if the men at the security gate told her she was about to have a guest, since they'd asked her who she was there to see. Cutting off her car, Royalty cursed under her breath.

There was no turning back now.

After saying a quick, quiet prayer, Royalty got out of her car. Her hands trembled so much, she pulled them behind her back. They made their way to each other, stopping in the center of the driveway with just a few feet between them. Already, Cashmere had tears pouring from her eyes, and it forced Royalty to look away. Though she wasn't responsible for Marcus taking her, a part of Royalty felt responsible for the pain that had been consuming Cashmere for years.

"Your dad is on his way. There was an emergency that demanded his attention. Otherwise, he'd already be here."

With a nod, Royalty looked at her. Cashmere had nutmeg brown skin, slanted eyes, and heart-shaped lips... all features Royalty saw each time she looked in the mirror.

"You look... just like me," Cashmere continued, head shaking in disbelief. "I always wondered if you would look like me or your father." Her sob caused Royalty's tears to fall. "You look just like me."

"I never saw myself in their looks or attitudes, but you..." Royalty covered her mouth, briefly losing herself in how similar their features were. "I see me all in you."

Cashmere chuckled, closing the space between them. "I'm sorry, but I have to hug you." Royalty nodded adamantly, and as soon as her mother's arms wrapped around her, Royalty melted. They cried harder, somehow finding strength in the other's weakness. Royalty didn't realize how long they'd been standing there hugging and crying, and honestly, she didn't care. The only thing that forced her to pull away was the sound of tires screeching and a door slamming before large, strong arms were pulling her away from Cashmere.

Before she could even look into her father's eyes, he was lifting her into the air and holding her as if she was a baby. Hearing loud sobs permeate from such a large man sent a shiver down her spine. Royalty held him close, wishing she could soothe him the way she ached to be soothed each time she cried as a child because she felt she didn't belong. Now... she knew why. Now... there was no doubt in her mind that Rose Valley Hills would be exactly where she belonged.

♥♥♥

Hours later, Royalty was sitting in the first floor sitting room looking at photo albums. She'd taken a tour of the estate and talked to her parents on and off, but more than anything, Royalty just wanted to sit in their presence.

"Are you staying here?" Ace asked, standing next to her. "I have to make a run, but I want you here when I get back."

Royalty nodded softly, agreeing with a smile. "I can stay. I didn't really make any hotel arrangements because I wasn't sure how long I'd be here, if I even stayed at all."

"There's absolutely no reason for you to stay at a hotel. There are nine empty bedrooms here, and if you want more privacy, you can stay in the smaller house outside."

"Plus, Cade will be back home tomorrow morning and he wants to see you," Ace added.

"Is he my younger or older brother?"

Cashmere took Royalty's hand into hers. "Older. We had Cade while we were still married, so he has your father's last name. You came right after our divorce, that's why you have mine." Cashmere smiled softly, eyes lifting toward Ace. "You were the reason we got back together again. I was trying to force myself not to go back to your father because we'd just gotten divorced, and I admittedly used Hamilton as a distraction. When I found out I was pregnant, that seemed like confirmation that Ace and I were supposed to fix our issues instead of running away."

Hamilton—that was Marcus' real name. He and Jennifer had changed their names and even gone as far as to get fake social security numbers and licenses to conceal their identities.

"He goes by Marcus now."

Ace's jaw clenched and fists balled before he excused himself.

"I didn't think he'd change his name and identity to hide," Cashmere admitted. "We looked for you. I don't ever want you to think we stopped. Hamilton... Marcus... just fell off the face of the earth. We had the resources to consistently check for use of his credit cards, social security number for jobs or applications, even mortgage loans, but nothing ever came up. And to know that you were three hours away in Memphis all this time..."

"I'm sorry for what he did to you. You didn't deserve that. None of us did."

Swallowing hard, Cashmere nodded her agreement. "You're right. And all that matters is that you're here now. We have a lot of time to make up for, and I hope you're ready for what Ace and I have in store for you. There isn't anything we're not going to give or do for you."

There wasn't a time Marcus and Jennifer had ever denied Royalty of financial security, but there was so much more that was lacking in their relationship. As she hugged

Cashmere, she prayed she would finally receive all of those things from her biological parents. In the back of her mind, Royalty hoped her relationship with Cade would be better than her relationship with Regal too.

"What did you name me?" Royalty asked as Cashmere held her hand and led her outside.

"Lei Armani Fifer. My best friend's name was Layyah, and she was there with me every step of the way throughout my divorce, pregnancy, and reconciliation of my relationship with Ace. Unfortunately, she died in a car accident three days before you were born, so I named you after her." Cashmere's smile didn't reach her eyes as she swallowed hard. "Losing both of you almost took me out, but I knew I had to live for Cade."

Royalty understood that feeling all too well. Unable to resist, she pulled her mother into her arms. In that moment, Royalty didn't know if she'd change her name back or not. There was no rush for that. Though... a new name and start in Rose Valley Hills could potentially help Royalty figure out her true purpose and identity. It felt as if she'd been given the chance to reinvent herself and start life anew, and Royalty was determined to make the most of that.

ten years later

nine

LEI ARMANI FIFER
Formerly known as Royalty
January

As she always did, Lei waited for her father, Ace, to open the door of his Corvette so she could get out. Its low seating caused her to shift both legs and place her feet on the ground simultaneously before she stood. Ace extended his arm, and Lei wrapped her arm around it with a small smile. Dressed in black silk, Ace was the picture of class and elegance when he picked her up for their weekly daddy-daughter date that evening, and Lei had effortlessly matched his fly in a floor-length black silk dress. The crisp January air forced her to use her light-colored ankle-length mink fur coat to keep warm.

Saying her life had changed drastically over the last ten years would be an understatement, but the transition from Royalty in Memphis to Lei in Rose Valley Hills hadn't been easy.

Not even a month after Lei left Memphis, Marcus was gunned down outside of a bar, drunk. Karma seemed to have come quick. It started with Jennifer filing for divorce before Marcus lost his life. It didn't matter how angry Lei was with Marcus for taking her from her parents, his death rocked her to her core. She grieved him for years before finding a sense of normalcy with the pain. Like a circle in a box, it still remained. Some days, the circle was so small, it didn't bother her at all; others... it was so big, it took up space in the entire box. A part of Lei believed she grieved Marcus as hard as she did because they never got a chance to speak about him kidnapping her.

When she decided to stay in Rose Valley Hills, she changed her number and didn't bother telling anyone other than Destiny and Simone where she was. The only reason she knew about Marcus' death was because Bridgette sent her a message on Facebook. Lei had just decided to press charges against Marcus and Jennifer right before he died. While she wanted them to pay, she couldn't stomach the idea of sending them to prison in the beginning. When Marcus died, it didn't seem fair for Jennifer to carry the burden of that punishment alone, so she dropped the charges against both. Besides... life punished Jennifer for Lei.

Six months after Marcus' funeral, Jennifer's health began to decline. She battled breast cancer on and off for three years straight, unable to work and losing her job in the process, before things started to finally look up for her. Jennifer moved in with Regal... along with her daughter and Steven... and allowed depression to send her into an alcoholic slump. The next two or three years of her life were spent drinking her days away. It wasn't until Regal threatened to put her out that Jennifer finally started to get her act together. Apparently, it took three stints in rehab before Jennifer felt confident and strong enough to find solid ground on her own two feet. She was back working again and living alone, and Lei was glad Jennifer had gotten herself together.

It was crazy how the truth somehow made them closer. Though they hadn't seen each other since the funeral, Jennifer reached out after rehab to fix what she'd broken in Lei. While Lei appreciated the gesture, it wasn't necessary. One of the first things she did once she got settled in Rose Valley Hills was seek a therapist. Lei had, however, allowed Jennifer to call and text her a couple of times out of the week. With the truth out, the way Jennifer handled Lei was more sincere. The pressure of a mother-daughter relationship was removed, and Lei could honestly say she considered Jennifer a friend. A friend from her past, but a friend, nonetheless.

While Lei had no desire to ever be in Jennifer's presence, she appreciated the fact that they were able to speak cordially with one another and there not be any hate in her heart. Regal was a slightly different story. Though becoming a mother at twenty-one had matured Regal and forced her to care about someone more than herself, giving birth to who should have been Lei's niece did nothing to fix their broken bond. Regal apologized, and for Lei's peace she accepted, but the two hadn't spoken since.

She knew through Jennifer that Regal and Steven got married after living together for the first three years of their daughter's life, and Lei didn't feel any kind of way about it. As far as she was concerned, the kind of man whose character would allow him to sleep with his fiancée's sister was not the man Lei wanted to spend the rest of her life with, and Regal had done her a favor.

As they stepped inside the foyer of Lei's home, Ace pulled the thick golden envelope he'd stuffed inside his coat pocket out and handed it to Lei. She didn't have to look inside to know what it was. Every week, he gave her anywhere from ten to a hundred thousand dollars just because. Her brother had her spoiled too, because he paid every one of her bills and gave her cash to use however she saw fit. There had been no reason for Lei to fear transitioning into her birth family; Ace, Cashmere, and Cade treated her as if she'd been in their lives from day one.

While her father and brother had filled every space in her broken heart, her relationship with Cashmere was a bit more complicated. Though the two were close, a part of Lei still had a guard up. After what she experienced with Jennifer and Regal, Lei didn't want to allow another woman to break her heart. Steven was wrong, but his betrayal didn't hurt as deep as Regal's did. For that reason, Lei handled Cashmere as carefully as she could. They talked often and spent time together, but there were certain parts of Lei that she kept to herself, and there were also things she didn't expect from Cashmere... though she desperately wished she could.

Those parts of her that sought validation, acceptance, and nurturing still yearned for those things, despite Lei's fear that Cashmere would not be able to deliver. There were times Cashmere would try to provide them, but Lei's guards would cause her to shut down. While she prayed one day she'd be able to pull herself out of that trauma and allow her mother to soothe the five-year-old girl filled with longing, Lei wasn't sure that day would actually come. She loved her mother, though, and was grateful for the relationship they did have—no matter how delicate it was.

"Thanks, Daddy."

Stepping out of her heels, Lei placed the envelope on the wall table and slipped inside of her house shoes that were underneath it. Only socks and house shoes were allowed on her marble floors.

"You're welcome. I hope you enjoyed yourself tonight."

Lei's smile spread as she nodded and hung her coat on the rack. "I always enjoy myself with you. Plus, you took me to my favorite sushi restaurant, so that's always a win."

Ace chuckled as he shook his head. If she could, Lei would eat sushi for every meal. "Are you going to work tomorrow?"

With a sigh, Lei rested against the wall table and curled her aching toes. The red bottom heels were gorgeous but painful every time she had them on. She made the mental note to have her masseuse come by a few days early as she thought over her father's question.

"I'm not sure. It'll depend on if any of my clients made a last-minute appointment. If they didn't, I'll probably work from home. This case with Cade is going to drain me, I can feel it already. I need no distractions while I pile through all of this discovery and prepare."

Ace's expression turned serious. Though her parents were millionaires and had quickly made her one too, Lei still worked to keep herself busy. She loved being a defense attorney, fighting for people and giving them a voice. Now that she'd found hers, Lei refused to *ever* be silenced. The only thing she didn't like about her job was the cases that forced her to go against Cade. He was a no-nonsense prosecutor who had a 96 percent success rate. Every case she'd had against him so far was either a mistrial or she lost, but Lei was determined to win this time around.

"I never want your job to come between you and your brother. Enough time has passed with you not being in each other's lives. Don't ever let a case take more of that away from you."

"I won't, Daddy. Cade and I agreed to never let what happens in the courtroom come between us personally. I'll excuse myself from a case before I let that happen."

"Good." Ace placed a kiss on her forehead before heading for the front door. "Get some rest, Princess."

"Yes, sir. Let me know when you make it home."

"I will. I love you always."

"I love you too."

Lei pushed herself off the wall table to lock the door behind him. Even after a decade of being in Rose Valley Hills, there were still times she couldn't believe how different her life was. How filled with love it had become. With all the love her true family and new friends showered her with, Lei still hadn't worked up the courage to open herself up to romantic love again. Steven's betrayal, though buried by the truth of her biological parents coming out, still scarred her and made Lei never want to give a man her heart again. No part of her desired love and marriage anymore, but she did want a baby.

No one knew, but having a baby was on the top of Lei's to-do list. She wanted to find a sperm donor by her thirty-fifth birthday last year. A high-profile case halted any personal plans she had. Defending a well-known gang member hadn't been in Lei's plans, but when her father asked her to as a personal favor, she agreed. One of the perks of being one of the founding families of Rose Valley Hills and its secret society was having just about anyone at their disposal. With that perk came favors and responsibilities to people Ace otherwise wouldn't deal with. There was such a high threat level throughout the trial that Ace insisted Leigh have personal security twenty-four seven. In that moment, the last thing she wanted to do was carry a child and worry about their life and her own.

This year, Lei was determined to return her priority to her personal life. For years, she'd excelled in her career and prioritized making memories with her family. Now, it was about what she wanted, and Lei wanted to be pregnant by the end of the year.

After locking up behind her father, Lei grabbed her phone out of her clutch and headed toward the stairway. As she walked, her steps were halted by the sight of Jennifer's missed call and text message. Normally, she communicated with one or the other, so it alarmed Lei to see that she'd done both. Quickly making her way up the stairs and into the bedroom she'd converted into a closet, Lei emptied her clutch and placed it back on its shelf on the wall. She went into her bedroom as she returned Jennifer's call, and she answered after the third ring.

"Hey, thanks for calling back tonight."

"It's fine. Are you okay?"

"Yes, I'm good. I didn't mean to alarm you. I was just hoping we could talk tonight because I need to get the invitations sent out tomorrow morning."

"Invitations?" Lei repeated, sitting on the cream couch in front of her king-sized bed.

"Yeah. I'm... getting married. I need your address to give to the planner. She's sending the invitations out in the morning."

"Oh. Okay. Um... congratulations."

"Thank you. I was also wondering if you'd like to be in my bridal party. I know that's a big ask, but I just... wanted to include you somehow if possible. It would be naïve of me to think us talking throughout the years means things are one hundred percent good between us, but I at least had to try."

"I appreciate the invitation, but I would have to think about that, Jennifer. We talk, but we haven't seen each other in ten years, and I... I kind of like it that way. I'm not sure how I would feel seeing you after..."

"Yeah, no." Jennifer chuckled, a bad habit she'd been doing for as long as Lei could remember when she was nervous or frustrated. "Of course. I get it. If you don't want to come, I understand. And if you want to come and not be involved, I understand that too. Whatever you're comfortable with."

With a sigh, Lei looked up and focused on the crystal chandelier that hung above her bed. Conversing with Jennifer because of their history was one thing, but returning to Memphis and facing her was a whole other beast. Had she been too lenient with Jennifer? Did she handle her with too much grace? What could have possibly made Jennifer think Lei would be involved in her wedding, as if she hadn't mistreated her out of resentment after allowing Marcus to bring a kidnapped child into their home? True, Lei saw firsthand the power her family had on both sides, but still. She couldn't understand how much fear Jennifer had to have in her heart to go along with something like that.

"Can I get back to you on this, Jennifer?"

"Yes, and I promise I'll understand no matter what you decide."

With a nod, Lei stood. "Okay, well, I guess I'll talk to you later."

"All right. Have a good night."

Lei disconnected the call and tossed her phone onto the bed before sliding out of her dress and starting her night-time routine. The whole time she did, she considered calling Cashmere and getting her advice. Though Cashmere didn't agree with Lei keeping Jennifer in her life, she accepted it. Whether Jennifer was the most loving and affectionate mother or not, she was the mother Lei had for the first twenty-six years of her life. It seemed the worst Jennifer treated Lei the more she wanted a relationship with her. No matter the horrible thing Jennifer went along with, Lei's love and attachment to her wouldn't allow her to just... not talk to her anymore.

Deciding against calling Cashmere so late to discuss a woman whose name alone could change her energy, Lei decided to pray and sleep on it before making her decision in the morning. Just as long as that old need to earn Jennifer's love and approval didn't rear its ugly head, Lei was sure she would say no. If it did, Cashmere wouldn't hesitate to remind her she owed Jennifer nothing more than her hate.

ten

Lei

"LOOK, I know she was your mother for a long time, but there's nothing she can ever say or do to make what she participated in okay. I know you can't turn your love for her off, and I don't want you to feel like you can't come to me regarding her, but I'll *never* steer you down a path that leads to you seeing that lady or being more involved in her life than you already are. It's bad enough that you talk to her regularly. *Now* she expects you to be in her wedding?" Cashmere scoffed. "So she just wants to forget the fact that she helped a crazy ass man hide you from your family, then made you suffer for it?"

"Ma." Lei's voice was strained as she pulled the white chocolate-covered fruit that had been chilling in the refrigerator out. "I didn't call to get you worked up."

"Anytime it involves that lady, I'm going to get worked up. I hate that you made me promise not to make her pay for what she did to us."

"It's not like she's the one that took me."

"No, she isn't, but she is a mother herself. Even if she had her baby after he took you, she should have held her baby in her arms and immediately been filled with guilt over keeping you."

"Well, she wasn't, and you really need to let it go, Ma. Jennifer has been punished enough. I'm back with you, and we're good. Please stop holding onto that. You're only upsetting and stressing yourself out."

"I don't see how you can stomach even talking to her. Even if you didn't want to hold her keeping Hamilton's secret against her, she didn't treat you right, Lei. How are you okay with that?"

Chuckling, Lei hung her head as she gripped the edge of the counter. It wasn't her plan to discuss this with her mother before the girls arrived, but Cashmere didn't answer when she called her earlier, and she'd just now returned the call.

"The Jennifer that didn't give me what I needed no longer exists. I wouldn't allow her in my life. This version of Jennifer is more caring and kinder. Our friendship is authentic because there aren't any pressures or secrets between us. I know it doesn't make sense to you, Ma, and I don't expect it to." Lei paused and nibbled her bottom lip. "I apologize for even coming to you."

Cashmere sighed into the receiver, allowing several seconds to pass before she replied.

"You have nothing to apologize for, Princess. I'm sorry for coming down on you so hard. You're being a good person and I shouldn't make you feel bad for that. I don't know if Jennifer genuinely wants to stay in your life or if it's her guilt over how she treated you, but whatever the case, it's your choice. If you believe she's a changed woman and want to be in her life, I accept that. If that extends to you being in her wedding, I'll have to respect that, too."

Lei heard her mother's words, but she could tell by her tone that Cashmere wasn't as okay with this as she tried to appear to be. Whether she went and participated in the wedding or not, Lei made up in her mind not to discuss Jennifer with Cashmere going forward. She hadn't taken into consideration how triggering conversations like this were for her mother. For whatever reason, Lei believed if she had been able to forgive Jennifer when she was the one taken, Cashmere should too.

"All right, Ma. I have to get ready for Yandi and the girls, so I'll talk to you later."

"You're letting all of them women come to your house?"

Now that got a genuine smile out of Lei. She hated being in large groups and the introvert preferred one-on-one connections and conversation. Throughout her time in Rose Valley Hills, Lei had met and connected with a lot of men and women over the years. Infinity and Yandi were her closest friends, and they had some of the same friends that Lei acquainted herself with. While she wouldn't call them friends, she did enjoy when they got together in small groups.

"I'd rather they come here than go to a public place and be around even more people."

"Yeah... but are you going to be okay with them lingering in your home, Lei?"

Lei shrugged. "I'll probably want them gone in an hour or so, so I already have a plan to get them out. I'm only bringing out a few bottles of champagne and wine. Once those run out, they'll be running out too."

Cashmere laughed. "All right, Princess. Try to enjoy yourself. I love you."

"I love you too. Bye."

After she disconnected the call, the latest Labrinth album that she was playing before Cashmere called permeated the speakers all throughout her two story six-bedroom home. Lei was careful about the energies she allowed into her home. It was a gift from her parents when she decided to stay in Rose Valley Hills. Mostly all the leaders of the secret society lived in the same neighborhood, and their families lived only blocks behind. Lei's home was in the subdivision behind her parents and only three streets away.

Yandi, Lei's best friend, asked if they could have girls' night at her home. They took turns hosting the event every few days, and this was the only way Yandi knew Lei would participate. The women of Rose Valley Hills were a completely different breed compared to what Lei was used to in Memphis, in good ways... and bad.

Outside of the wealth they possessed, their characters and attitudes were different. The feminine women were overly feminine and soft while the women in the streets were just as gutta and gritty as the men they led and stood beside. It had been difficult finding her tribe, but Lei was confident she'd done so with Infinity and Yandi... and the friends that were attached to them to a certain extent.

"Okay. Let's get this together," Lei mumbled to herself, looking over the spread on her island and counters of charcuterie, fruit, and champagne and wine. She considered having the items prepared professionally, but decided to use the creative outlet to unwind instead.

It took her about forty-five minutes to get everything plated and on trays, then Lei took it to her spa area, where they would be communing. She'd asked her masseuse, nail tech, and esthetician to come over in case anyone wanted to receive treatments while they were there. Just as she'd begun to roll the cart of wine and champagne out, her doorbell rang.

Lei headed toward the front door, humming under her breath. It didn't surprise her that Infinity was the first to arrive. The two embraced, complimenting each other on their attire for the day.

"What do you need me to do?" Infinity asked after taking her shoes off, following Lei down the hall back to her spa.

"If you could set the wine and champagne up while I get the glasses, that would be great."

"I got you. Now you know they are going to be bringing their own bottles, right?"

"I know, but I don't drink that heavy liquor some of them are on, so I wanted to make sure I had other offerings."

Not long after, Yandi was arriving, along with Lei's staff. She'd specifically retired the women from having to service other clients to ensure they would always be available when she needed them. Because her brother paid all of her bills, Lei was able to use the hefty salary she made as a defense attorney on literally whatever she wanted—and keeping a staff for her maintenance was always at the top of her priority list.

"Thank you for agreeing to letting everyone come over, Lei," Yandi said before popping a grape into her mouth.

"Of course. I appreciate you always trying to include me in what you all do."

"Honestly, I'm going to always go hard for you. You accepted me and didn't judge me in a way that not too many people do. You're my sister for life."

Lei didn't miss Infinity's roll of her eyes. "Lei doesn't judge you because she doesn't know you as well as the rest of us do."

With a sigh, Lei grabbed a glass of wine. While Yandi and Infinity may have been Lei's best friends, they definitely weren't close. They rolled in the same circle and tolerated each other, but the two women could barely stand each other. The only time they tried to get along was when they hung out with Lei. Otherwise, they wouldn't talk to each other at all.

"Please, ladies, don't start," Lei requested.

"That's her. She always has something slick to say," Yandi replied.

"It's not slick; it's the truth. You can play this innocent role with Lei, but I know you for who you *truly* are, and I'm *never* going to pretend as if I like you."

"Okay." Lei lifted her hands to silence them. This was one of the main reasons she preferred one-on-one engagement. Outside of being overwhelmed by multiple personalities and energies at once, women were too gossipy and catty for Lei's liking. She'd had enough drama in her life to last a lifetime. Now, Lei demanded peace. "That's enough. I know you two don't really care for each other. If you have to avoid talking to each other to keep the peace, do that."

Quite frankly, Lei hated their friends' group was so tied that they had to be around each other at all. Along with Yandi and Infinity, there was sisters Mercedes and Lexus, and Jaqueline, but everyone called her Jack. Mercedes and Lexus were the daughters of another secret society family, so Lei often saw them at events, and that's how she ended up getting to know them. When Yandi found out they were acquainted, she brought the group together as one.

Though she didn't talk to Jack often because of her dealings in the streets, Jack was one of the most beautiful, chill, sweet women Lei knew. Mixed with all of Jack's sweetness was a spice that came from being one of Memphis' highest earning female drug dealers. She looked like a model, and that was a part of what allowed her to move the way she did. No one would expect the beautiful brown bombshell to be riding around the city with a draco just in case some shit popped off.

Jack often spent her time in Memphis, so Lei wasn't expecting her to be in attendance.

Lei made her way out of the spa room while Yandi pulled a long case from her purse that held her pre-rolled blunts. Infinity followed behind, taking Lei by the hand.

"I'm sorry, Lei. I'm not trying to bring bad vibes into your home. I know how important peace is to you."

That was Infinity—never allowing ill feelings to linger longer than they had to. That was probably what Lei loved about her most. Infinity was kind and authentic. There weren't too many people who had her heart. She was relatable and empathetic in a way that allowed her to connect with almost anyone... even when she didn't want to. Just as loving and accepting as she was, Infinity was just as raw, too. She didn't play with anyone and wouldn't allow anyone to disrespect or play with her, either.

"It's cool. I know how you feel about her. I hate that you and Mercedes are so close, because I doubt if you'd deal with Yandi otherwise."

Infinity chuckled as she released Lei's hand. "You're right, I honestly wouldn't. I stay close to protect y'all because that girl makes my spirit scream every time she's around. She's been in survival mode since she was a child and nothing she's ever done has been out of love or care for others. I can admit that she's been a good friend to you and out of trouble, so maybe you're the good influence she needs, but I'll never let my guards down with her."

Before Lei could respond, the sound of the doorbell stopped her, and she was glad about it. It didn't matter how many people tried to tell her about Yandi's bad ways in the past, that wasn't the version of her Lei dealt with, so she didn't want to hear about it. One thing that had changed about Lei over the years was that she didn't overplay her role in anyone's life or try to make them out to be something they weren't. She accepted everyone she encountered for who they presented themselves to be.

From the first day she met Yandi, she had presented herself as a woman out for herself who wanted to have a good time. While she might not share secrets with Yandi or have the spiritual and emotional connection she had with Infinity, Yandi served her purpose in Lei's life and made sure she always had a great time.

A pep was in Lei's step as she neared the door. She smiled genuinely as she opened it, ushering Mercedes and Lexus in with a wave of her hand. The sisters were close, but they had their sibling rivalry too. All Lei could do was pray today was a good day for them, because if it wasn't, it would turn into a bad day for everyone else.

"I'm just saying, Lex, it's different depending on the

man. You've dealt with bum ass street niggas all your life, so of course you wouldn't see the benefit in it."

Mercedes hugged Lei as she addressed her sister.

"What are y'all talking about?" Lei asked, hugging Lexus next.

"Girl..." Lexus animatedly rolled her eyes, causing Lei to chuckle. "That pen pal program. They added a dating option, as if a woman to mooch off is the last thing those niggas need."

Lei smiled as she locked the door, curious about where this conversation would go. Her father had started Pen Pal Partners, a pen pal program that allowed inmates to talk to the outside world for free. Back when it first started, it was limited to written letters sent by mail. With the elevation of technology, inmates were now able to receive letters from anyone in the world online. Each inmate who qualified was set up with an online portal. If a person wanted to see their record and reason for arrest, they had to pay extra. Otherwise, just the basics were shown.

"A dating option? So people are really starting relationships with inmates online?" Lei confirmed.

"Hell yeah, and I think it's a great idea," Mercedes replied as they headed down the hall.

"Why don't you agree, Lex?" Lei asked.

"Because they obviously did something bad to be arrested. Is it really wise to hook them up with someone outside those bars? I just think a lot of women are setting themselves up to be used and possibly physically hurt and abused if they deal with these men when they get out of prison."

Infinity asked, "Y'all talking about the pen pal dating option?" as they entered the spa.

"Your dad started that, didn't he?" Yandi confirmed, looking at Lei.

"He did. Apparently, one of his friends was severely depressed while doing a life sentence years ago and committed suicide because he was so lonely. Daddy felt moved by it and decided to start the program so those that were doing their time and missing that human connection could have people to talk to."

While Mercedes set top shelf brands of tequila on the rectangular table, Lexus pulled out a bottle of Hennessy.

"That's sweet in theory, but I just don't think it's safe," Lexus said, maintaining her stance.

"Listen, I've been burned by more men in church and the corporate world than men in the streets," Mercedes shared, and even if she didn't want to, Lei had to agree.

Their conversation flowed effortlessly as they began to fix their plates and drinks. The spa was all white and gold, like the rest of the main rooms in her home. She had cream furniture in some spaces, but in the spa, the chairs were gold and bronze. Her master and guest bedrooms were black and silver. Lei's chill room, game room, and movie theater were less uniform in design with pieces of furniture and games that she'd collected over the years whether they matched what else was in the room or not.

Once they were all comfortable with their plates and drinks, Lei said, "I admire what my dad is doing. Not all men and women that are locked up are guilty, and even some that are guilty of the crimes they committed have changed. I think it's noble to give them a chance to have love and companionship if they genuinely deserve it."

"So you'd sign up and date one of them?" Yandi asked with a playful smile.

"I mean..." Lei shrugged, smirking herself. "The last

corporate man I fell in love with cheated on me with my sister and got her pregnant. No bad boy I dated ever did anything as bad as that."

"Damn," Lexus mumbled before taking her shot of Hennessy and making them laugh.

"I'm just saying... we shouldn't judge them just because they're in prison. If their hearts are pure and they have integrity and good character, they deserve love and companionship, just like Lei said," Mercedes agreed.

"I love how for this y'all are, but would either of you really sign up and see this through?" Infinity checked.

"Let's make this interesting," Lexus said, sitting up in her seat. "Mercedes and Lei should sign up and talk to a few men to see what will pop off. If either of you can find a good friend or great love, I'll pay for your wedding or give you six figures for a Christmas present."

"What if they lose?" Yandi asked.

"Then they have to give me six figures."

"Sheesh." Lei's head shook as she sat back in her seat. "I remember me and my girls used to bet twenty dollars."

Though they laughed, Lei was serious. She could more than afford the bet, but something about them so casually agreeing to bet such a large amount of money for fun was still something she had to get used to.

"You down or not?" Infinity asked.

"I'm down," Mercedes agreed with no hesitation. "You down, sis?"

"I mean... I'm cool for looking for a true friend, but marriage isn't in the cards for me."

"Don't say that, Lei," Infinity said softly. "You never know what God has in store for you."

Not bothering to have that conversation, Lei merely nodded. While she'd accepted that what happened ten years ago needed to happen for the truth to be revealed, she still had no desire to open her heart to men again. For one, she loved to be so careless with her heart... that left her with little room for a repeat.

It didn't matter how much she told herself all men weren't like Steven, he and Regal had taught her a valuable lesson—when faced with doing what's best for self or others, most people will do what's best for self—and Lei had valued romantic love less from that day forward. Her heart was much too valuable to risk for something as fickle and fleeting as love. Though she could honestly say she wished she had a man that was hers and hers alone, Lei could also say she'd be at peace with the successes in the other areas of her life if she never received that.

"Okay. I'll do it."

"Yassss this is going to be good!" Yandi cheered, lifting her glass of champagne. "I'ma join too and talk to whoever y'all choose, just to make sure they do right by y'all. We have to have a way of making sure they are on the same page as y'all."

Infinity rolled her eyes, and Lei chuckled. She knew her friend had something to say, but she held it in, releasing a shaky breath instead. Giving Infinity's hand a squeeze, Lei mouthed, "Thank you," silently.

Just as quickly as they'd started talking about it, their conversation shifted again. Before Lei knew it, three hours had passed, and she, surprisingly, wasn't ready for any of them to leave.

eleven

Lei

"YOU GIVE THE BEST HUGS."

At the sound of Cade's compliment, Lei grinned. He held her tighter, rocking her from one side to the other. With a giggle, Lei tightened her arms around him. She'd always wanted a big brother, and Cade had quickly become a sibling she couldn't live without. One whom she loved with her whole heart. There wasn't anything about that man that she would change. Even his flaws were correct.

"Thank you, brother. I love you."

Cade cupped her cheeks and placed a kiss to the center of her forehead. "I love you too. How are you?"

He held her hand and led her into the dining room, where her parents were already seated and waiting for their kitchen staff to serve them dinner.

"I'm good. Crazy thing happened when I linked with the girls yesterday, actually. I wanted to talk to Daddy about it and see how he feels."

"See how I feel about what?" Ace asked, standing to give her a hug.

Lei went around the long gold and white table to embrace her mother before sitting across from Cade.

"A conversation was started yesterday about your pen pal program. While some women think it's unsafe and a bad idea, others think it's a good idea."

"Which one are you?"

"I think it's a good idea… which is why I agreed to a bet."

Cashmere's brows wrinkled as she asked, "What kind of bet?"

Chuckling, Lei nodded and thanked Whitney as she poured her a glass of both water and wine. "Well, some of them think you can't find love or friendship with someone in prison, and I disagree. Mercedes and I have until Christmas to find a good friend or true love."

"What do you get if you win?" Ace asked while Cade shook his head.

"If either of us win, Lexus will pay for the wedding or give us six figures for Christmas. If we lose, we have to do the same for her."

"Are you sure about this, sis? I don't want you getting hurt."

"Oh, I'm not worried about that. I'm not looking for love, just the opportunity to offer someone companionship. If I get a good friend out of it, I'm okay with that."

"Still, be careful," Ace advised. "Do not let any of them convince you to be their sponsor, and don't connect them with anyone else, no matter how much they ask you to reach out to someone on their behalf. Don't tell them what you do for a living, because they can either prey on you and try to use you as their attorney or punish you because they're locked up. Use the P.O. Box you're going to receive when you sign up always, and never give them your real address or phone number." Ace sighed. "I don't even want you to put your picture on there."

Lei giggled. "Daddy, if I don't put a picture, only the creeps are going to try to talk to me. No man of substance is going to give a faceless profile a second look. You're asking for me to become a target."

"I hate to agree but she's right," Cade said.

"Fine, but don't let them know Cade is your brother or who your parents are. I trust this program works, but we sometimes have people in the program that shouldn't be, and I don't want anyone to take advantage of you or hurt you in any way."

"Yes, sir. I'll be careful, I promise."

With a nod, Ace lifted his glass of brown liquor to his lips. Though her parents could be a bit overprotective, Lei appreciated it. There was a time she wished her parents made a fuss over her, and now, she had parents who did.

♥♥♥

Because the bet required Lei to sign up for a dating profile and the regular pen pal program, she was required to submit her health records through a sealed portal for the website moderators to look over before her account was approved. That took about a week, and after that, they made both of her profiles live.

She and Yandi met up at her favorite cocktail bar to go through the profiles. Admittedly, some men were worthy of #jailbae hashtags on social media, but none of them made her want to reconsider her vow to never open her heart for romantic love again. Lei did, however, find five men to start her search with. The process was for them to view each other's profiles, based on compatibility, and then select the option to match. If both parties wanted to be matched, that's when they would be able to send each other virtual letters and handwritten ones if they desired.

"So, how are you feeling about your matches?" Yandi asked.

"I feel okay. Two were very attractive but only one was really my type. I mean, if I was looking for a relationship, he'd be my type, but I'm not on that so…"

Yandi chuckled and rolled her eyes. "Yeah, okay. If you say so. Listen, that Gabriel brother that's locked up… I *gots* to have him. The connections I could get being associated with this family alone would make this worth it for me."

"Gabriel? What was his first name?"

"Noah. The dark-skinned cutie that favors Trevante Rhodes."

"Oh yeah, now he was fine as hell. He looked a little bit too rough for me though."

"That's just my type! Hopefully, we can get some conjugal visits without being married. He looks like he got that heavy dick. Just thinking about it is making my mouth water. Mm!"

Lei doubled over in her seat as she laughed heartily,

because she knew Yandi was telling the truth. If there was a way for her to sneak inside the jail for some sex, Yandi would do it with no hesitation. Lei admired how liberated Yandi was sexually, because she had always been a bit more reserved. While Lei had no problem becoming intimate with a man she deemed worthy, it was never as casual as it was with Yandi. Even with her not being in a serious relationship for years, she still took her time getting to know men and trying to build some kind of secure bond before giving herself to them.

"Girl, if you don't stop. Them people are not going to let you have a conjugal visit if y'all aren't married."

"You never know until you try, and if we match, I'm definitely going to try."

"I believe you," Lei said before chuckling and taking a sip of her cocktail. She hated to admit it, but Londen Graham had her feeling the same way. As soon as his profile picture popped up, Lei squeezed her thighs together and bit down on her bottom lip. The physical reaction she had to him made her want to skip his profile, but her fingers had a mind of their own. They moved her mouse until it hovered over *Match* and clicked it. "I'm going to see if Mercedes has matched with anyone yet. Hopefully, we don't pick the same guys."

"I know, right? That could get messy."

"I don't think so. Mercedes is actively dating but I'm not. If she wants someone that I match with, I don't mind unmatching him."

Yandi sucked her teeth. "Fuck that. It's every woman for themselves. You got six figures on the line, just like she does. Don't make it any easier for Lexus to get that money off you."

Lei didn't bother to reply. She wasn't hard pressed

financially, so this bet wouldn't change her at her core. If she didn't have the money to blow, she wouldn't have agreed. No man or amount of money would cause her to treat Mercedes or anyone else poorly for that matter. This was one of the times Yandi showed just how out for self being in survival made her. While Lei would always respect the honesty of it, that was a character trait that made her look at her friend a little differently.

twelve

Londen

EACH TIME he lifted the weights and felt them hover over his chest, Londen coached himself to go harder. For some reason, he allowed Noah to talk him into adding an extra fifty pounds to bench press, but Noah refused to be defeated. Even if it felt like his arms were about to break, he'd finish his set.

"Let's go, brotha. It ain't on you, it's in you. Show these niggas why you the beast."

Noah slapped the beast tattoo that was on Londen's neck, causing him to release a growl and push his way through the rest of the reps in the set. As soon as he lifted the last one, Londen stood, hopping on the tips of his toes as he beat his chest.

"That's my nigga." Noah grinned as they shook hands and embraced.

"You got next?" Londen checked, and even though Noah replied, their attention shifted to a guard as he called Londen's name. "Yeah?"

"Warden wants you."

Londen had never been one to wear his thoughts and emotions on his face—that was one of the rules his OGs had taught him young. With one bob of his head, Londen followed the guard, lips lifting upward at the sound of Noah telling the guard not to try no funny shit. Even without the warning, Londen wasn't concerned about that. Though he was locked up, he wasn't imprisoned by *anything*. Both he and Noah ran the institution with their money, power, and respect. There wasn't anything Londen couldn't do besides walk out of those doors toward freedom.

The walk from the outside workout area to the warden's office seemed to take forever. As soon as Londen stepped inside, his eyes scanned the small square space—tan walls with a few degrees on them, a dark brown, chipped desk set right in the middle of the room, short metal storage containers were on the far-right wall, and there was a gray fan with dust buildup blowing right in front of the warden's desk.

"You can wait outside," Bloom instructed, dismissing the guard with a wave of his hand.

"What's this about?" Londen questioned, cupping his hands in the center of himself.

Bloom waited until the guard closed the door behind him to hand Londen his cell phone. Londen looked down at it before accepting it, and the sight of Lew on the screen made his heart drop. If Ace Lew was calling to speak to him, something wasn't right. They'd agreed when Londen started his sentence almost ten years ago that it was best if they removed all forms of communication and connection. The only thing Londen cared about was receiving that payment from Ace January first of every year. As long as that happened, Londen was good.

"Yeah?" Londen spoke, turning his back to Bloom.

"My daughter has joined the pen pal program. Get ears in place to make sure I can get intel on who these men are that she connects with. I don't want her dealing with anyone that ain't damn near Jesus in that motherfucker."

As amused as Londen was by Ace's tone and words, he was stuck on the fact that he said his daughter. Last Londen knew, through rumors alone, Ace's daughter had been kidnapped at birth. Did this mean she returned?

"Daughter?" Londen repeated. "She's older than nine, right?"

Ace chuckled. "Yeah, she's thirty-five. It's Lei. My baby girl... She's been back with us for ten years now."

Londen remained silent, doing the math. He'd always been intuitive and a quick thinker. The last job Londen executed was for Ace... in Memphis. All Ace told Londen was that a man had taken something of value to him and he needed a permanent punishment. That was all Londen needed to hear. He went to Memphis and killed the man without losing a second of sleep over it.

Two months later, Londen was arrested in Memphis and charged with a murder he didn't commit. Londen had so many bodies under his belt it seemed like Poetic Justice for him to be tried and convicted for the one he didn't do. Between the prosecutor having a list of victims that she promised to spend her career tying him to and his attorney assuring Londen that his best bet was to take a plea deal to avoid life in prison, Londen settled for the twenty-five-year sentence with the promise of parole after year ten. In exchange, he would have to admit guilt and the prosecutor would admit to not having enough evidence to successfully try and win a case against him.

Londen hadn't expected Ace to do anything for him while he was incarcerated, but finding out the man he was being charged with murdering was a body Ace collected made it all make sense. Apparently, the gun used was the same one Ace had given Londen to handle his Memphis problem with, and that's why Ace wanted the case closed as quickly as possible. If that gun was tied to Hamilton's murder or anyone else's, there was a great chance Ace would eventually become a suspect.

It didn't make sense to Londen for Ace to be handling those types of problems on his own. That was literally what he paid people like Londen for. If Ace *did* kill the man, it had to be warranted.

"Was she the reason?"

Ace didn't reply right away, and Londen didn't feel the need to provide more details. Ace knew *exactly* what he was referring to.

"Yeah, she was." Londen's head bobbed once. He didn't mind catching that body even more now. Hamilton was the one that had taken Ace's baby girl and brought his entire family a lot of pain. He deserved what he'd gotten... and then some.

"Is she using her real name?"

"She's using Royalty. I told her to limit as many personal details as possible. I think her profile will say she's an author, which is true. She writes legal guides, but no one can know who she is and that she's connected to me and my son."

"I got you."

"Thank you. I'll reach out through Bloom in a few days."

"Aight, bet."

Londen disconnected the call and handed the phone back to Bloom. Until now, Londen had no desire to sign up for the pen pal program, but he would to keep Ace in the loop. It would be easy to weed out who was talking to who. As much as men liked to clown women for gossiping, they could gossip to. And when a person was locked up twenty-three hours out of the day, sometimes all they had to do was talk.

Lei

Tussi,

We matched. I'm a little unsure why, and I hope you don't take offense to that. I knew we were options but I didn't think you'd actually click Match if that makes sense. Based on what you said you were looking for in a friend and lover, I thought you'd skip right past me. It's nice to meet you. Can you tell me what made you want to connect?

Lei rubbed her fingers together before sending the letter to Tussi. She had two more men that she had to message. Unlike other apps, since she matched them first, she would have to message them first as well. The task of initiating a conversation with men was foreign to Lei, and she was honestly glad she'd soon be meeting Infinity for lunch so they could talk. Now that the process had started, Lei was tempted to change her mind. The desire to prove Lexus wrong had gotten her into a situation that she wouldn't otherwise place herself in.

While Lei stood behind what she'd said and what she believed, she didn't need any new friends, and she wasn't in the market for male companionship. She'd convinced herself that she was just trying to save face, but now that she had to put herself out there, Lei was dreading connecting with men just for the friendships to turn sour.

Trauma was a motherfucker.

Healing felt like a scheme.

No matter how healthy she felt emotionally and mentally, the most random times and things could remind her of the pain of her past.

Being lied to by the people she thought were her parents for over twenty years, combined with her supposed sister sleeping with her fiancé, had seemingly scarred Lei in a place she was unable to reach. If people you loved could harm you in such a way, Lei feared what a stranger was capable of doing.

"Just do it," she grumbled, clicking the *Compose* button to send a message to Andre.

Andre,

Hi. It's nice to meet you. Your profile is interesting in an elusive kind of way. You gave just enough to pique my interest and make me want to know more. Is there more to you as your profile suggests?

. . .

SCRATCHING the center of her forehead, Lei released a huff. She checked the time on her phone, noticing she had seven minutes left before she'd need to leave if she was going to be on time for lunch with Infinity.

At the sight of Cade's text, she opened their thread to respond.

> Brother: Where you at?
>
> Home now. I'll be heading out soon.
>
> Brother: Where you going?
>
> The View for lunch.

He didn't reply, and Lei wasn't surprised. When Cade got the information he needed, he was done. Deciding to send her last message now instead of putting it off, she pulled up Londen's profile and looked it over again briefly.

Londen,

At this point, I've hit the limit on my social meter. I'm not even sure why I'm doing this anymore. I don't know what to say. Maybe I should send you this message another day.

. . .

WITH A GROAN, Lei deleted the message and started over.

London,

Hi.

QUICKLY PUSHING SEND, Lei stood and scurried upstairs to grab her shoes and purse. At that point, she didn't care if one or all men responded. There wasn't a chance she'd truly connect with any of these men. If she did, they'd have to truly work for it.

♥♥♥

When Lei pulled into the parking lot of The View and saw Cade getting out of a black town car, she smiled. He headed over to her car, holding a bouquet of white roses. As tattered as her heart was because of Steven, her brother and father had been doing all they could over the years to restore her faith in men. That was easier said than done, though. Lei was convinced they weren't making men like them anymore.

"Cade!" Lei squealed, accepting the flowers. "These are beautiful, brother. Thank you!"

"You're welcome, Princess," he replied, accepting the hug she offered.

"Did you take the day off?"

"Yeah. I was going to take you and Ma to lunch, but I decided to just stop and see you for a sec' since you already had plans."

At the sound of a door closing, both sets of eyes looked in that direction. Lei grinned as Infinity approached them.

"Apologies, love."

"For what reason exactly?" Infinity asked, closing the space between them.

"If I would have known you'd be with my sister, I would have gotten you some flowers too."

Infinity's head lowered bashfully for just a second before she almost cooed, "That isn't necessary, Cade, but thank you."

He licked his lips and eyed her frame before returning his attention to his sister. "I'll let you get to your friend. Have a good day, ladies."

"You too," they agreed simultaneously before heading across the parking lot.

The View was one of Lei's favorite restaurants. It was located right on the beach. Its entrance was by the parking lot, and the back of the restaurant had the perfect ocean views. Lei loved that she could sit as close to the beach as she wanted without getting sand on her feet. It was the place she often came to after a long day of work. With the restaurant being divided into two levels, she often opted to sit upstairs, where there was a full bar, several fire pits, and the ocean view.

Once the hostess showed them to their table and they

made themselves comfortable, Infinity asked, "Why are you looking like you worked a three-day shift in two hours?"

Lei chuckled. "Girl, because that's how I feel. Sending messages to those men stressed me the hell out. I can't remember the last time I approached a man for conversation first, if ever."

"Are you regretting your decision to do the bet?"

"A little. Not because I changed my mind about men deserving love and companionship... I just don't think it will actually come from me."

Infinity's expression softened and shoulders slouched. "Why not, Lei?"

Their waitress arriving kept Lei from answering right away. They both ordered Mai Tais before Lei responded.

"I guess I'm just not as open as I thought I would be."

"Is this because of your ex-fiancé?"

Lei nodded, mouth twisting to the side as her eyes watered. "God. I feel so stupid even being affected by that now. That was ten years ago. I shouldn't even remember his damn name."

"Now that is not true. What you went through was horrible. It's totally understandable for you to be traumatized."

"I just..." Lei sucked her teeth as her head shook. "Want to be completely healed. Like... how much of my mind and time do I have to give these people? I want to get to a place where I never think about them at all."

"Do you honestly think that's possible if you continue to talk to Jennifer?" Lei didn't reply right away, so Infinity continued. "And... I know you don't want to hear this, but you giving up on love doesn't help either. Love heals. How do you think you're going to release the power that situation has over you if you never try to love again? You're basically letting them and the pain win. I know it's to protect yourself, but some wounds can only be healed through love."

With a sigh, Lei ran her fingers through her extra small knotless braids.

"Maybe you're right but I'm scared. I can admit that. All I can think about is being hurt even worse. Those were my people. If they could do me like that, what's stopping the next man from doing worse?"

"His character. His fear of God. His integrity. His mama." They shared a soft laugh. "There are good men out there, sis."

"I know, I know. The logic of that does nothing for the pain in my heart, but I know you're right."

"Can you at least promise me you'll be open to love? Even if you don't go looking for it, can you promise to accept it if it finds you?"

Lei thought over Infinity's request before she agreed, and as she figured it would, talking to Infinity helped her feel lighter. Their waitress returned with their drinks, and they ordered seafood dip as their appetizer. While Infinity opted for a ramen bowl, Lei got fried lobster and jalapeño sushi instead. She loved the seafood-Japanese fusion of the restaurant's menu. Though almost everything on the menu was good, Lei often gravitated toward a sushi roll or salmon tacos.

Their conversation shifted effortlessly as their lunch progressed, and by the time their entrées arrived, Cade was walking over to their table with a bouquet of red roses in hand for Infinity. She lifted them to her nose and inhaled them before standing and giving him a hug. Lei's mouth dropped when Infinity placed a kiss to the corner of Cade's mouth. Biting down on his bottom lip, he put a step of space between them and watched as she sat back down.

"You are such a gentleman," Lei said before bursting into a fit of giggles.

If Infinity's cocoa brown skin could redden, Lei was sure it would have in that moment.

All Cade did was shoot her a wink and squeeze her shoulder before he walked away.

For a while, Lei stared at her best friend with a goofy grin.

"What!" Infinity yelled quietly before smiling so hard she covered her mouth to hide it.

"I'm just trying to figure out why you won't give my brother any play."

Infinity's eyes rolled playfully as she shook her head and set the roses on the table.

"You know I can't go there with Cade. I love bad boys too much."

"My brother ain't no square."

"No, he's not. I know Cade can take it there when he needs to. But... I love roughnecks. Tatted up, grills, baggy jeans... that type."

Infinity was proof that opposites did, in fact, attract. She screamed good girl from her job and appearance to the way she carried herself. Lei couldn't blame her though. There was something about the excitement of bad boys that appealed to her... and it was even better when the bad boys could make a woman feel good.

thirteen

Lei

THAT WEEKEND

While Lei waited for Destiny and Simone to join her for their monthly Zoom call, she decided to finally check her pen portal for new messages. Unfortunately, when she left Memphis, she didn't just leave her family's betrayal behind —she left her best friends behind too. Simone and Destiny were true friends who gave her the grace to navigate her life as she saw fit. Because she hadn't stepped foot in Memphis for years, they came to Rose Valley Hills to spend Thanksgiving with her every year. Other than that, they caught up via Zoom once a month.

Simone and Danny were now married, and Destiny had recently gotten engaged to her high school sweetheart Pierre.

She smiled at the sight of three new messages. While she was curious about what all three men had said, Lei gravitated toward Londen. All she'd said to him was hi, so Lei couldn't help but wonder what he had to say.

Royalty,

I appreciate you sending a message first, since that is what the program requires. I appreciate, even more, being able to initiate our first conversation. While I'm not sure if that was your intention or not with the short message, I intend to take full advantage of it. The desire to know what led a beautiful woman like you to a program like this is the first thing that enters my mind. I refuse to believe you're so lonely that you have to seek companionship through this program. Perhaps you're living a life that is unauthentic and you desire a connection that will allow you to be yourself. Because what amount of judgment could an imprisoned man give you, right? Or maybe it's a bet or research. Whatever your reasoning, I'm glad to make your acquaintance. How much would you like to share about yourself? And how much about me would you like to receive? Looking forward to your response.

. . .

"Hmm," Lei hummed under her breath. While Lei wasn't sure what she expected Londen to say, that wasn't it. She found herself looking at the bottom of the screen to see if he was online for a live chat. Since he wasn't, she decided to quickly draft a reply.

Londen,

Honestly, your message caught me off guard. Because I'd only said hi, I wasn't expecting you to respond. I did want you to, but by the time I'd written your message, my social battery was empty. Truth—it was for a bet. My friends and I were talking and the bottom line was that men in prison, when they are pure and authentic, deserve love and companionship. We discussed how rehabilitated men that were still locked up deserve love from the outside world. I truly believe that and bet my friends that I could find a true friend or love by December. Honestly, I'm not looking for love here or anywhere, now or forever, but I was open to the idea of friendship.

I'm not sure how much of myself I want to give. I think it would be a safe space to share myself with someone I'd never see in person. You can share as much as you'd like to give. I don't really know how we would do this. Our profiles give the basic facts like our names, age, and my profession. I haven't paid the upcharge to see what you did and how long you have in there. If you want to share that with me, you can, if not, that's okay too.

. . .

LEI WAS SO content with the message she'd gotten from Londen that she didn't bother opening Tussi and Andre's messages. Last she heard from Yandi, she'd matched with Tussi and Londen too. Mercedes had shifted all of her attention to one man—Noah. Lei wasn't sure how she felt about Yandi talking to Londen and Tussi. Even with her reasoning, it didn't sit well with her. The idea of Yandi supposedly talking to these men for intel, running the risk of falling for them herself, was also a reason Lei was hesitant to converse with the men. Londen, however, already had her interested enough to be worth the risk.

Royalty,

You wanna know what made me connect? You fine as fuck I can't even lie. You got the kind of face that make a nigga wanna make love to you missionary so he can look into your eyes. I hope you don't take offense to that. You're really pretty, that's what I'm trying to say. As a man, I'm stimulated most by what I see, and your looks captivated me. Do you really want to be my friend? If so, I would love that. I wanna know all there is to know about you. I wish we could talk on the phone, but I know you probably ain't tryna do that no time soon. Either way I can talk to you, I wanna talk to you. I'm usually in the library every day at three, so if you want to do the live chat option, we can do it then.

LEI DIDN'T REALIZE how hard she was smiling from Tussi's letter until a call from Jennifer came through and her smile fell. For a few seconds, Lei just stared at her phone as it rang. She hadn't talked to Jennifer since she asked her to be a part of her wedding party. After talking to Infinity, Lei started to wonder if she was holding up the last part of her healing by remaining in contact with Jennifer. Every time they talked, she was taken back to their past together. Even though pain wasn't always attached to the memory, Lei was tired of having the memories.

After clearing her throat, Lei answered with, "Hello?"

"Hey. I was calling to see if you'd given anymore thought to what we talked about."

"Yes, I have actually. I... don't think that's a good idea, Jennifer."

"Oh." She paused. "Okay, I understand."

"Also..." Lei sighed and closed her eyes. After breathing deeply, she said, "I think we should stop talking. I think I've talked to you as long as I have to prove to myself that I was okay, but I'm never going to get over what you and Marcus did or what Regal and Steven did as long as I'm talking to you. Our friendship is a constant reminder."

"I... I'm sorry. I didn't realize you felt that way."

"Yeah, well, I didn't either. I talked to a friend who made me realize that. If I want to truly heal and release any memory of that time in my life, I can't talk to you anymore."

"But do you... do you not want to remember anything at all? Was it so bad that you just... want to completely forget us, Royalty?"

Gritting her teeth, Lei swallowed hard. "It's Lei, and no, it wasn't always bad, but a lot of it was. Besides, no matter how good it was, you guys lied to me. I didn't belong there with you. No amount of good times can change that."

"Well, I certainly don't want to make your life worse. When I told Marcus that I told you the truth, that day was a day of clarity and release for me. After all the years of hardening my heart because of that situation, that day, I finally felt free. I wanted to be better and treat you better and I don't know... these conversations... they make me feel like I wasn't the horrible person I know I had been in the past.

That's not your burden to bear, though. It's not your responsibility to make me feel better about the way we treated you. I appreciate you talking to me for as long as you have and giving me a chance to show you I could be as good and loving to you as I was before things changed. My number will never change, and I'm always here if you ever want to talk."

Lei nodded rapidly as her eyes watered. With flaring nostrils, she fought to compose herself. She didn't think it would be this hard to say goodbye. Was it attachment or real love? Either way, no matter how hard it was, Lei was sure she was making the right decision.

"Thank you for understanding, Jennifer. I wish you nothing but the best, and I hope this new marriage is one that allows you to love and be loved in a healthy and prosperous way."

"Thank you, Ro—Lei. I love you."

A few beats of silence passed before Lei said, "I... love you too," and quickly disconnected the call.

She wiped her face and released a hard breath before running her fingers through her braids.

"This is for the best," she reminded herself, looking around her room. "No matter how it feels right now, this is for the best."

Deciding not to message Tussi back, she made the mental note to live chat with him the next day. In that moment, all Lei wanted was to do was go to her parents' home so their love could confirm she was doing the right thing.

fourteen

Londen

LONDEN HAD no patience to wait for a computer to be freed up. Honestly, he didn't have to. As soon as he entered the library, his eyes scanned the twelve computers. Tussi and Noah were seated on opposite sides, across from each other. The differences in both men were like night and day. In simplest terms, Noah was who Tussi aspired to be.

Walking toward where Noah was seated, Londen pulled in a deep breath. He couldn't focus on his meditative hour wondering if Royalty... Lei... had messaged him back. He'd gotten a few messages from other women, beautiful women, but Lei was the one that intrigued him most. A part of Londen wondered if he could break the walls she had up and get her to be honest about who she was with him. Ace would hate it, but for some reason, Londen felt like he'd love it.

"Move," he commanded, not bothering to raise his voice, and the man seated next to Noah quickly vacated his seat.

Tussi shook his head, grumbling, "Pussy ass nigga," under his breath.

Noah and Londen locked eyes, chuckling under their breath.

"What you doin' in here?" Noah asked, checking the time on the computer.

"Royalty," was all Londen asked.

"Not lil shorty with the braids?" Tussi confirmed. "I'm talking to her too."

It took Londen a few seconds to process Tussi's words. It wasn't lost on him that Lei would have been talking to other men but hearing that she was talking to Tussi had him thinking differently of her. Maybe they were fresh enough in their conversation to where Lei hadn't been able to realize how much of a fraud Tussi was. The illusory state he lived in could manipulate those that didn't have the ability to see a person's true core, and Londen hoped that wasn't the case with Lei.

"Fuck you telling me that for?" Londen asked.

Tussi's hands lifted in surrender. "I'm just making conversation, big brotha." The right side of his mouth lifted into a smirk. "Wanted to see if we are talking to the same female."

"Nah." Londen chuckled, squeezing the bridge of his nose. "Trust me, we're not."

Londen was convinced—Tussi may have been talking to Royalty, but he was going to get Lei.

"What's up with you and One?" Londen asked Noah, referring to Mercedes.

Noah wasn't as secure and detached as Londen. He was far more possessive. If anyone suggested they were talking to Mercedes, he'd break their fingers to ensure they couldn't do it anymore.

"Man..." Noah's head shook as he sat back in his seat. "I like her. She's unique. Feisty and fiery, but soft and sweet."

"You gon' let her come see you?"

"I'on know about that. If there's a chance for me to get out soon, I'd rather the first time she see me be as a free man, you feel me?"

Londen understood completely. He was on the same wave with Lei. His parole hearing was coming up, and even though the prosecutor made it seem as if his release would be guaranteed at the ten-year mark, Londen wouldn't place any bets on his freedom until he actually had it.

"I feel you. Them two weeks can't fly by fast enough for me."

Their conversation fizzled out, allowing Londen to shift his attention to his portal. He quickly replied to the messages he had, saving Yandi and Lei for last. Yandi was beautiful, that Londen couldn't deny. There was something about her that told him to stay away. Even if he wasn't invested in getting to know Lei, he didn't see himself talking to Yandi consistently. From the conversations they'd had so far, she seemed more concerned about who he was, who he was attached to, and the power and status they had more than anything else.

Seeing that Lei was currently online, Londen's eyes shifted toward Tussi.

> Londen: Whoever you talking to, tell them you have to go.

Lei's dots popped up for seconds on end, but all she said was…

> Royalty: Okay. Hold on.

Londen watched as Tussi's face covered with confusion as he read Lei's message. Sucking his teeth, he nodded and rubbed his palms together, and Londen could barely contain his amusement. Clearing his throat to hide his chuckle, Londen returned his attention to the computer screen.

> Londen: Thank you for proving you can be a good girl.
>
> Royalty: What's my reward for letting you have me all to yourself?
>
> Londen: Send me a physical address so I can send you something. You don't have to trust me enough to send me yours.
>
> Royalty: 40110 Sanders Lane

Unable to resist, Londen pulled up a new window and searched the address. He could tell by its appearance that it wasn't her home, but he appreciated the fact that she sent something for him to work with.

> Londen: Give me a couple of minutes to set this up.

> Royalty: Okay… but can I have a hint about what it is?

> Londen: No.

The series of crying emoji she sent made him laugh. Standing, Londen told Noah, "Don't let nobody get on my shit. I'm not done."

"Got you, brotha."

Londen left the library and made his way back to his cell. He grabbed a hundred-dollar bill from under his Bible and handed it to the guard, who gave him an iPhone in return. Londen sent a text to Walter, one of his personal assistants, letting him know he was about to call.

"You good?" Walter answered.

"Yeah. I'm about to send you an address. I need you to go to Aoki's warehouse and have her to make twelve dozen bouquets of red roses. Pay her whatever she needs to make that happen today. While you wait, go to Elite or Smoke, whoever has it available, and get a necklace or bracelet that has a diamond crown. Have it all delivered to the address I'm about to send you, along with champagne and a charcuterie tray from Cree's restaurant."

"Got you."

Londen waited a few seconds for Walter to confirm he had the address, and when he did, he thanked him and disconnected the call.

Making his way back to the library, Londen intentionally walked the long way around. His eyes scanned Tussi's screen, and at the sight of Yandi's profile picture, Londen shook his head. It seemed these women were for everyone.

> Londen: Apologies for the delay. You'll be getting a delivery there today.

> Royalty: Thank you Londen. You're really sweet.
>
> Londen: I'm actually not.
>
> Royalty: What do you think that was then?
>
> Londen: An exchange. I value your time and attention so I rewarded you for it.
>
> Royalty: Oh, so you're that type?
>
> Londen: What type?
>
> Royalty: The type who can't be sweet and kind. Are you that much of a gangster Londen?

Londen chuckled, considering his words carefully. This was why he liked her.

> Londen: I'm a gangsta and a gentleman, but honoring your time, to me, isn't sweet. Saying it's sweet suggests I did that as a pleasantry. Any nigga can do that. I did it because I honor you making me a priority. That sweet shit comes and goes, but my honor and value are what will always remain.

Almost a minute passed before Lei replied.

> Royalty: I like you.

Licking his lips to hide his smile, Londen mumbled under his breath, "I like you too."

fifteen

Lei

"OH MY GOD."

Lei's eyes watered at the sight before her. Lei hadn't allowed herself to have assumptions or expectations about what Londen was going to do because if they weren't fulfilled that would lead to disappointment. Even if she had allowed herself to consider options, none of them would have matched what London had actually done.

"A dozen, dozen roses." She gasped, covering her mouth. Giggling, Lei stepped further into the room. Her eyes widened at the sight of the diamond necklace. Lifting it, she ran her fingers across the sparkling crown. "Wow, this is beautiful."

"All I need to know is who sent this and does he have a brother."

With a laugh, Lei turned to face Normani, her receptionist.

"Honestly, I don't know if he has a brother or not. There's still so much I don't know about him." Lei paused, taking in the charcuterie tray from her favorite grazing restaurant. "If I would have known he was doing all this, I wouldn't have given him your address. I'm so sorry about all this traffic."

"It's totally fine, Lei. I'm just glad you're finally letting a man spoil you."

Lei chuckled. "You act like I don't date."

Normani sucked her teeth. "Maybe once a year, if that."

Lei couldn't argue with that. If she entertained a man, it was just long enough to trust him with her body, and she never let the same man dip into her fountain once his time that year was up. The less consistent things were, the fewer chances she had to get attached. Since the year had just started, Lei hadn't selected her friend with benefits for the year. Londen would have been a damn good contender if he was free. Quite frankly, from behind bars, he'd done more than a lot of men she'd allowed in her presence.

After deciding to let Normani keep a bouquet of the flowers for her trouble, Lei started the process of packing everything into her Maybach SUV, which was a lot more difficult than she expected it to be. By the time she was done stuffing every free space, Lei was getting behind the wheel and releasing a tired sigh. The sound of her phone vibrating caused her to hurriedly shift the contents of her purse around until she found it. Though her father made it clear, it was best that she not talk on the phone with any of the men she made her pen pal, Londen quickly became the exception to that rule.

At the sight of the FaceTime request, confusion covered Lei's face. When he told her to be expecting his call, she wasn't expecting it to be like this. Still, she answered, holding her breath until she saw his face. As soon as their eyes locked, she grinned.

"Hey," he greeted, mirroring her smile.

Unable to reply, Lei stared at him.

He was *definitely* her type.

A coily, short afro connected to a thick beard. His skin was the same shade of her favorite dark chocolate. Lazy dark eyes stared into hers until she lowered them to look at his skin colored, juicy lips.

"Damn, you're beautiful," she complimented with a disbelieving shake of her head. His profile picture hadn't done him justice—at all.

"Royalty."

Writing that as her name was one thing, but hearing someone call her that always triggered Lei.

"Oh that's... not my name. Not anymore."

His head bobbed once. "Are we dissecting that or moving on?"

With the pockets of conversation they'd had so far, Lei loved his speech and how intentional he was with his words.

"Moving on."

"Cool, but... I need something to call you. Unless you want me to call you Baby."

"Baby works," Lei agreed with a soft smile.

"Okay. I'll accept that for now."

Chuckling quietly, Lei nodded her agreement. Maybe one day she'd reveal who she truly was, but there was no rush for that now.

"Thank you. I didn't know what you were going to send, but I certainly wasn't expecting all of this."

"I wanted to make a good first expression."

"You did. This is the kind of gesture that a woman never forgets, though I really don't think it was a gesture."

"Then what do you think it was?"

"A glimpse into the kind of man you are."

At the sound of a blaring alarm, Londen barely flinched as he looked down one side of the hall and then another. He released an irritated exhale.

"I gotta go, but I'll call you later, aight?"

Lei felt the pout creeping up and preparing to disfigure her mouth, but she wouldn't allow it.

"Okay, be safe."

Londen gave her one last fleeting look at his engaging smile before telling her, "I will, Baby," and disconnecting the call.

Instead of immediately driving away, Lei allowed herself to memorialize his gruff voice and handsome face. A slow smile spread her lips as she started her SUV. Now that she'd seen Londen and heard his voice, there was no doubt in her mind that things were about to progress like a whirlwind.

sixteen

London

WHEN LONDEN and Lei progressed to handwritten letters, they agreed to finally start sharing the facts about each other. Hearing her admit Royalty wasn't her real name meant a lot to Londen, because it proved even with her desire to protect herself, she still wanted to be open and honest with him. He'd been anxious to receive her letter, and as soon as he got it, he left the card table and returned to his cell to read it alone.

Londen,

I can admit, I'm a little hesitant to write this. I know you said you have a certain amount of power that allows you more freedom than most men in your position, and that no one will read the contents of this letter before it's given to you, and I appreciate that. That's not the only reason I'm unsure about sharing the facts about myself with you. While I don't think you have impure intentions toward me, I have enough experience from my past to know thinking that does nothing for me. I want to be honest with you about who I am, because I believe we can have a true friendship, but that's a hell of a lot easier said than done.

Even with me expressing my fears, I'm going to try.

You said you wanted me to start from the beginning of my life. I can, but it'll probably seem like you're talking to two different women by the time I get done.

I was born on May 7th in Rose Valley Hills, but I was raised in Memphis. When I was five, my parents had my baby sister. I had... a fairly normal childhood, I suppose. Financially, I was taken care of. I did well in school. My relationship with my parents and sister was strained, and it only got worse with time. It felt like my sister and I were always

111

pitted against each other, and I was never good enough.

My mother stopped being as loving, nurturing, and affectionate as she used to be. My father tried to give what I lacked, but they argued a lot because of it and eventually he started treating me like she did. For years, I thought it was because they just loved my sister more than me. Turns out, my mother treated me differently because she resented me. I wasn't her child. I wasn't my father's child either. He had kidnapped me from my real parents in Rose Valley Hills.

I found out the truth days after my wedding was canceled because my fiancé slept with my sister and got her pregnant. So... yeah. My name used to be Royalty, but after going through all of that, I wanted nothing to do with that part of my life anymore. As soon as I got settled here in Rose Valley, I changed it to what my mother named me. I've been here with my real family for ten years now, and the life I have here is... like a reward for the bullshit I went through in Memphis. I feel like I'm finally where I belong, and I'm so grateful for that.

One day I'll tell you my name and who I come from, but I fear if you know, that will *end this between us and honestly... I don't want it to end. This was a lot, so I need a break. I can't wait to hear from you.*

. . .

L̲o̲n̲d̲e̲n̲ s̲t̲a̲r̲e̲d̲ at the letter for a while before setting it on the bed beside him. He wanted to tell Lei he knew who she was, but did he really? He knew her name and that she was Ace's daughter. He knew she had been kidnapped because Ace paid him to murder the man that had done it. But did he really know her? Londen couldn't say, but he could say he hoped he had the chance to experience her in all ways.

seventeen

Lei ♥

Baby,

First, thank you for sharing that part of your past with me. I can admit I'm the kind of man that can find out anything I want to know. The connections and resources I have make very little unavailable to me. With that being said, I prefer to know what you want me to know and have what you want me to have, in the same way you've patiently waited for me to tell you why I'm in here instead of paying to get my records yourself.

I imagine going through something like that would make anyone have an identity crisis, so I'm not surprised you changed your name. I apologize for what your first set of parental figures did to you and your sister and fiancé. No one deserves to experience anything like that. I am happy that you made your way back to Rose Valley for more selfish reasons though. If you would have stayed in Memphis, even though that's where I'm passing this time, I don't think we would have met.

I like to think all things happen as they should within God's reason, so if all that comes out of that fucked up situation is you being exactly where you are right now living the life you are, I pray it's a good enough life for you to think it was worth it.

We agreed our next three letters would cover our past, present, and future, but after hearing your origin story... mine sounds boring as hell. Out of fairness, I'll tell you, anyway.

I was born on October 29th in Rose Valley Hills, like you. My parents are still alive and married. I have one sister and one brother who's serving a life sentence in Mississippi. As fucked up as that sounds for both of us to be in prison, it didn't come as a surprise to anyone that this would happen. Even with all the money, power, and freedom we gained, the seeds that were sown in our younger days were bound to yield this kind of harvest.

Before I got locked down, I was given the chance to go legit, but I didn't appreciate it, so it was taken from me. I can honestly say that passing this time for the last ten years has opened my eyes to what's most important in life, though, and when I do get out, I intend to take full advantage of my second chance.

But anyway... my parents. They were a normal couple, I suppose. Both were raised in the ghetto and wanted better for their children. By the time my siblings and I were old enough to realize we were poor, my father had started trying to find ways to make us rich. Naturally, selling drugs was the easiest way to get to the riches in that environment. Pops ended up having an accident on the job at the workhouse he slaved at for twelve hours a day, six days a week. Instead of using that money to get us out of the ghetto, he used it to invest in a few corner boys in exchange for 50 percent of their profit.

Quickly, he went from making a few hundred a week to a few thousand. Then tens of thousands. Then hundreds of thousands. He ended up opening his own importing and exporting warehouse, where he moved both legal and illegal products. Eventually, my parents stopped working and my brother and I took over. While I handled the illegal side, Matthew ran the legal dealings. Fast forward years later, people wanted in on our business because it became a safe hub for suppliers to export their drugs to dealers without risk and consequence.

We were used to people trying to muscle their way into our business, but my brother handled things differently from me. While I was the logical, cool headed brother who weighed all possibilities and handled my business privately, Matthew was the reckless wild card who would shoot a nigga in broad daylight. He did that in the wrong place, at the wrong time, and he left me to handle the business alone. I ran things for a couple of years before ending up in a cell just like him, but with a shorter sentence.

I was charged with murder like him, but instead of life, I was given twenty-five years. If it makes you feel safer conversing with me, I didn't commit the murder I'm serving time for. Ironically, I'd done a lot of dirt and gotten away with it. I suppose me being here was karma's way of balancing the scale, and I've made peace with that. I don't think we have too much in common as far as our pasts and childhoods are concerned, but I can say that you've intrigued me from the moment I saw your profile. While I can't say exactly what it is about you that has me enamored, I can only hope the more you learn about me doesn't make you want to reveal yourself less.

eighteen

Londen

Londen,

First, I feel led to make clear... nothing you said in your letter changes how I'm starting to feel about you, nor does it make me want to talk to you less. You aren't the first drug dealer I've talked to, but you are the first man that I've talked to that has taken another life. I'm not sure how I feel about that, but I have no room to judge. Given the right set of circumstances, I think anyone can take a life. The version of you I'm speaking to doesn't fill me with fear, and right now, that's enough for me.

So we're on to the present. Okay, this is where things get tricky. My dad wanted me to keep everything about myself a secret when I told him I was doing this pen pal program but I don't know. It's something about you that makes me feel safe with you. I trust that whatever I tell you stays between us and that you won't try to use it against me or my family. If you do, they'll fuck you up.

My real name is Lei. Lei Armani Fifer. I took my mother's maiden name when I came to Rose Valley because that's what it was when I was born. My parents were married when they had my brother, then they divorced, then had me. They say I was what brought them back together again so for me to have been taken, I can't imagine how devastating that was.

My father is Ace Lew, and my brother is Cade Lew. It would surprise me more if you didn't know who they were than if you did. I'm a defense attorney. I do some work for the secret society but I'm not an actual member of it. No kids, never been married, and I don't even have any pets. I want that to change really soon though.

Are we really friends, or are we just using that word fraudulently? If we're friends, I should be able to tell you that with me turning thirty-six this year, I really want to have a baby. Not a marriage or even a man, but a baby. My best friend teases me about using a sperm donor, but that's the safest option for me at this point.

I can admit that because of my past, I don't trust people as openly as I should, which is why it's so surprising to me that I'm as open as I am with you. Maybe it's because you're locked up and I don't have to worry about being with you and you doing something to hurt me. I don't know. Either way, I want to be pregnant by the end of the year. Being hurt by literally everyone that was closest to me may have made it hard for me to trust people and commit to relationships, but I can't let that stop me from having my own family.

I don't know what else there is to talk about in my present, so I guess I'll end my *letter here. If I haven't scared you away, I can't wait to hear from you soon.*

. . .

SCRATCHING the corner of his mouth, Londen stood and began to pace his cell. So many things about her words were rattling around in his mind. If Lei was so open because he was locked up, how would she feel if he told her he'd be getting out soon? Would it matter? Her father had asked him to keep her from the wrong men, not to pursue her himself. Even if Ace didn't care about them dating, how would Lei feel about him being the man who murdered the man she thought was her father for years?

Londen couldn't think about that right now. If all they had was a few letters and days until he was released, Londen would take full advantage of that.

nineteen

Lei ♡

Baby,

Is it okay if I still call you that? Thank you for being completely honest with me. I am familiar with your family because I'm familiar with the secret society. Who isn't? They are like the checks and balances system of the south. Political plotting, policing and protection, the removal and giving of power... not to mention how they technically run the government in Rose Valley Hills. Yeah, I'm very familiar with it... and your father. Neither he nor you being a lawyer make me want to stop what we're doing, but I can understand why he would think it would. I know a few bums in here who would try to misuse and abuse you because of both.

I know this is supposed to be the letters where we talk about our future plans, and I'm hesitant to share mine with you. You might think it's because I dread spending another fifteen years in here, but that's actually not the case. I'm up for parole soon, and there's a really, really good chance I'll be getting out.

If I do, I figured I'd spend my days chilling and spending the money I have saved on myself and the people I love. Even with my wealth, I still plan to be productive and active to avoid trouble. I've only had two dreams in my life—to be a chef and have my own restaurants and seasoning line or to be a profiler for the FBI. With the route I took, I could never become a profiler, so I'll be focusing on the first dream with my free days.

Maybe this is a bit forward of me, but I'd love to cook for you one day. I know they say food is the way to a man's heart, but back in the day, I made many women swoon with one taste of my spoon. Ha-ha. For real, though, I would love to experience you outside these bars... I can feel the fact that me being behind these bars provides the security you need to be open with me, so if I never get to see that pretty face of yours in person I understand.

With this being the last of our past, present, and future letters... I intend to give you a call and hear your voice to learn more about you. If you're okay with that, I'll talk to you soon.

. . .

WITH A SMILE, Lei set the letter down. It wasn't her intention to release a content sigh but she did, and all eyes were suddenly on her. They were at Mercedes' home and Lei was in such a rush that she grabbed the letter from Normani's mailbox and couldn't wait until she got home to read it. What Londen said was true—not being around him physically was making it easier for her to talk to him, and Lei didn't know if him being a free man would change that.

"What?" Lei's tone was playful as she checked the time.

"What are you reading that has you smiling so hard?" Mercedes asked.

That day, it was just her, Yandi, and Lei. They agreed to

meet up to see how their pen pal connections were going. Lei would have preferred to talk to Mercedes alone about it since they were the two who were in on the bet with Lexus, but Yandi insisted on being included.

"A letter from Londen. I really like him."

"Oh, so y'all are done with the portal now?" Mercedes confirmed. "I'm thinking about letting Noah write me letters but I'm not sure."

Yandi rolled her eyes and sucked her teeth. "Girl, do you know who Noah is? Trust me, that man ain't got no reason to be on some foul shit with you."

Though Lei didn't care for the way Yandi packaged her words, the meaning behind them was true. Noah Gabriel, and the Gabriel family, were nothing to fuck with. He wasn't the kind of man Mercedes needed protection from; he was the kind of man she could be protected by.

The Gabriels were on the opposite side of the law and the streets compared to Lei's family and the secret society. While the secret society made rules and executed law and order, the Gabriels often broke the law and took justice into their own hands. The secret society was run out of Rose Valley Hills but the Gabriels had a criminal organization that was run out of Memphis. A lot of Noah's family and business partners were in Rose Valley Hills. They operated under the radar to avoid pressure from the community to be pushed out by the secret society.

Rose Valley Hills was one of the safest and supposedly drug free places in the south, and members of the community planned to keep it that way. Seeing as their tax dollars and donations fueled the secret society, Ace and the rest of the men who ran it made sure the town could trust their efforts. Though, from Lei's understanding, they had an agreement—as long as the Gabriels and their men kept the secret society safe, they were free to do whatever they pleased in the town.

"Regardless, I want to take this slow. I don't want to become a target because of my connection to him. Plus, if my parents knew I was dealing with him, they would give me a hard time about it."

Yandi's eyes rolled again, and she chuckled as she shook her head. "That's what I don't understand about y'all. Both of y'all are grown ass women, yet y'all are so afraid of what your parents think about the men y'all deal with."

"First of all, it's not fear; it's respect," Lei clarified.

"And second," Mercedes added. "This shit is deeper than your simple-minded ass can understand. We have a lot to take into consideration dealing with these men. Both of our families are in the secret society, and she's a lawyer. We have an image to uphold in this town. If people found out I was dealing with Noah, that wouldn't be the best light for the secret society. People don't know we deal with the underworld the way we do, and it's best if it stays that way for the time being."

"I guess," Yandi said with a shrug. "Either way, Lei needs to decide who she wants to complete her bet with between Londen and Tussi. You can only choose one. It's clear she's going to use Noah."

"I mean... I don't know," Lei admitted. Though her mind told her to go with Tussi because he was the safer bet, her heart was all in for Londen. "I am going to see them both next week and make up my mind."

Mercedes gasped and clutched her chest. "You're going back to Memphis?"

"Unfortunately." Though Lei smiled, her heart began to palpitate just at the thought. "I didn't plan to ever step foot in that city again, but I do want to see my girls and Londen.

I'm really leaning toward him. Tussi is cool and what we have is light. He's the safer option for friendship, but I don't know. It's just something about Londen. I genuinely love talking to him."

"Tell me about it," Yandi agreed. "They're both fine but Londen got that BDE. Tussi's cool as hell, though, so whichever one you don't pick I'll be satisfied with."

Lei's brows bunched as she looked from Yandi to Mercedes, who was looking just as confused as she was.

"What do you mean, whichever one I don't pick you'll be satisfied with? You were only supposed to be talking to them to see if they would get serious with another woman while talking to us."

"Well, yes, but I like the both of them too. Why not have a little fun?"

"Nah." Mercedes head shook as she stood. "I don't like that."

Lei put the letter in her purse as Mercedes refilled her glass of wine.

"Why not? At least I'm telling her I'm going to talk to one of them. It's not like I'm hiding anything."

"That's not the point. Your intentions aren't pure right now, and God ain't gon' bless that shit. Whatever you think you gon' get out of this is going to blow up in your face."

With a groan, Yandi stood. Her eyes lifted toward the ceiling. "You are always so damn dramatic. It's not like I'm fucking the niggas, and I'm being nice by letting her choose which one she wants first. If she wasn't my girl, I would've been took Londen."

Lei chuckled, and covering her mouth didn't reel it back in. "The fact that you think that is even a possibility is hilarious."

Standing, Lei walked over to the rose gold drink cart to

set her glass down. At that point, she was ready to get home to her solitude. She was grateful Infinity wasn't there, because things would have taken an even crazier turn if she was. Mercedes called Yandi out on her shit, but she'd never been the kind of woman to go back and forth.

"You tryna say you look better than me?"

Lei scanned Yandi's frame. Yandi was drop dead gorgeous, but her attitude at times could make her ugly. She had walnut brown skin, hazel eyes, and bowtie shaped lips that many men and even some women lusted over. Her features were delicate... modelesque. Lei was confident in who she was and what she had to offer and knew no woman was better than her, just different. Anytime Yandi, or anyone else for that matter, insinuated they were worthy of comparison or competition, it always tickled Lei.

"The fact that you think your looks would make Londen choose you over me, let's me know you don't really know him at all."

"And you do? Y'all have been talking for what, a couple of weeks?"

"Yes, and that's more than enough time for me to know that man values more than a pretty face, especially while he's behind bars. Beyond your looks, what have you offered him?"

"This pussy." As much as Lei didn't want to, she laughed.

"I'm done with you. Goodbye, crazy."

"Bye! Let us know when you get home."

Lei gave Mercedes a quick hug before doing the same with Yandi and heading out. Very rarely did she take her friends' words seriously. Did Lei trust Yandi enough to think she wouldn't try her luck with Londen? No. Did she care enough to be intimidated by her efforts? Not in a million years. For some reason, there was something about Londen that she felt possessive of, and Lei had never felt that way before. She couldn't allow herself to think there was a chance he could be free. It would hurt too much if his parole was denied.

Maybe it was best if he stayed away. If he was free, he'd expect things from Lei that she hadn't given a man since Steven, and the last thing she needed was to be back in that headspace again. she'd been doing just fine without a serious relationship, and she refused to lose six figures and even more pieces of her heart because of Londen Graham.

twenty

Lei

LEI HAD NEVER BEEN the type to purposely ingratiate herself with others, but there was something about Londen that had her thinking of ways she could be more pleasing to him. Ways she could make him smile throughout the day. Ways she could show him she appreciated having him, just as much as he appreciated having her.

Perhaps the biggest show of her appreciation was Lei making that three-hour drive to Memphis. It was the first time she'd done so in almost a decade. There wasn't anything Lei believed could ever make her return to her old home... then came Londen. Londen was a being Lei had to experience. So, as difficult as it was, she pushed all ill feelings about her past to the back of her mind and took that drive, though she wasn't sure why.

After doing research, she learned Memphis wasn't like Rose Valley Hills when it came down to visiting people in jail or prison. Memphis visits were done virtually. Even if a person went down to the jail, they still spoke to their friends and loved ones virtually. Still, Londen requested her presence, so Lei agreed. If it made him feel closer to her knowing she was actually there, she would give him that.

Out of fairness to herself, she set up visitation with Tussi as well. Andre had long since been out of the running. It wasn't anything specific he'd said or done. Lei hadn't juggled several men in what felt like forever, and she simply didn't feel connected enough to make time for him. As she sat in her car in the lot across from the large tan building, Lei looked her face over in preparation for her video call with Tussi. He was cool, but their connection was surface level. There wasn't anything about talking to Tussi that made Lei feel better or replay their conversations.

Her alarm sounded, letting Lei know it was time to log in for the visit. She closed her eyes and pulled in a deep breath before logging in. As soon as Tussi's face appeared on the screen, Lei smiled. He was attractive in his own right. Her favorite part of him was his long locs. They appeared to come down past his armpits, but she couldn't see just how long they were. And he had the most seductive, light, almond-shaped eyes.

"Damn, it's good to see your pretty ass face."

"Thank you, Tussi. How are you?"

"I'm good as hell now. Why you make me wait so long to see you?"

Lei grinned, relaxing in her seat. Talking to Tussi had always been a relaxing experience. There was never pressure of what she said and shared. If Lei was to be honest with herself, she could see a casual friendship blooming between them. Not one that would force them to talk daily, hang out, and have deep life altering conversations... but Tussi was the kind of man she'd love to talk to every once in a while just for some lighthearted fun.

"Well... I was nervous, I suppose." The innocence that laced her tone caught Lei off guard. "I know we're grown, but I don't do this often."

"Do... what often? Talk to men?"

"Outside of family and work-related topics, yes."

Tussi's expression softened. His smile was warm and voice light when he said, "Well, thank you for switching it up for me. I'ma take it slow and make sure you feel comfortable, aight?"

She wasn't expecting it to, but his words made her pussy pulse. Maybe it was because she wasn't expecting such a gentle response from him. Regardless, that was exactly what he'd done. Their thirty-minute visit flew by, and Lei was actually sad when it was over. Before that disappointment could settle within her, she was getting a call from the number Londen often called her from, and that immediately lifted her spirits.

"Hi," she answered, biting down on her bottom lip.

"Are you sure you want to do this, Baby?"

"I am. You change your mind about wanting to see me?"

"I'll never do that."

Blushing, Lei looked down at the cream trousers she had on. "Well, I'm ready to log in to see you."

"Nah. I need to know exactly where you are. I'm about to send someone to come get you."

Sitting up, Lei looked around the parking lot, suddenly feeling exposed. "What? I thought visits were only being done virtually?"

Londen released an airy laugh. "That rule doesn't apply to me."

"Oh. Well... I'm in the parking lot right across from 201."

"What kind of car?"

"Maybach SUV."

"Okay. I'm going to send two. One to bring you to me and one to stay with your car to make sure no one tries to break in it. Next time, I'll send a town car, so you won't have to drive that down here."

"Okay," she agreed softly, fighting back her smile. "I'm really about to see you?"

"You are. Give them about ten minutes, aight?"

Nodding, Lei released a shaky breath. "Okay."

He disconnected the call without saying goodbye, as always, and Lei had to keep herself from releasing a squeal. When he asked her to come down, Lei wasn't expecting this, but she should have known he was up to something. Londen was aware of her past. If he asked her to step foot in Memphis—it would be for a good reason.

The minutes rolled by slowly, but eventually, two police officers made their way toward her. While one told her he was staying with her car, the other told her he'd escort her to Londen. The walk seemed to be just as long. Her heart beat sporadically against her rib cage. By the time they made it to a room with a closed door and guard in front of it, her palms were clammy. Resisting the urge to rub them against her trousers, she opened and closed her palms and reminded herself this was no big deal—except it was. It was a very, very big deal.

The guard in front of the door gave her a nod before turning and opening it. With an ushered hand, he guided her inside. Her eyes made a quick scan of the small room, bare except for the black square table in the center. At the sound of the door closing, Lei jumped and looked back. When her eyes returned forward, they landed on Londen.

He looked damn good in an all-black sweatsuit that complimented his brown skin beautifully. Slowly, she made her way over to him, eyes watering as they remained locked on his. Lei hadn't expected to be in his presence, but this was a beautiful surprise.

"Londen," she whispered, clutching her throat.

twenty-one

Londen

"LONDEN," she whispered, clutching her throat.

For a while, Londen was too stunned by her beauty and presence to speak. Sure, her pictures and their FaceTime talk showed her beauty, but seeing her in person magnified it. He was six feet even, and with her heels, the top of her head came to his chin. She had nutmeg brown skin and slanted coffee brown eyes. It was taking everything in Londen not to kiss her small, pointy nose... and her medium-sized, heart-shaped lips. When he couldn't resist the urge anymore, Londen lowered his lips to hers. Londen moved his mouth over hers, devouring its softness. Her demanding lips caressed his, returning his passion tenfold.

"Mm," she moaned into his mouth as he took two handfuls of her ass—it was thick... just how he liked. Rubbing it, Londen groaned when she sucked his bottom lip into her mouth. After he smacked and squeezed it, she hissed and moaned again, and the reaction had his dick throbbing so hard Londen forced himself to pull away.

Wiping his mouth, Londen took a step back. His breathing was ragged as he stared at her. Shaking hands slipped down her perfectly neat braids as she looked back.

"I'm trying to earn you and that pussy, but if you kiss me like that again, I'm going to sit you down on my dick."

Lei smiled softly and wiped her mouth. The pleasurable assault from his lips had smeared her lip gloss and gotten quite a bit of it on his own mouth. She removed her cashmere coat and tossed it against the table. The cream silk shirt she had on showcased her hardened nipples. All he could think about was her breasts being concealed by such a thin, lacey bra that it was unable to hide the protruding buds.

She was hippy. Small breasts... juicy ass.

"Damn." His head shook as he stared at her.

Her eyes rolled playfully as she closed the space between them. "You're only reacting to me like this because it's been ten years since you've been this close to a woman who doesn't work here."

"Nah." Londen chuckled with a shake of his head. Sitting down, he pulled Lei down onto his lap. "I'm not going to let you downplay your power like that. I'm reacting to you like this because it's *you*."

She didn't need to know he'd had visits throughout the years, but no woman had gotten this reaction out of him.

"You are absolutely stunning, Lei. I'm honored you came to see me."

"Who are you?"

Though Londen was aware of the meaning behind her question, his head tilted, and he remained silent as he considered how he wanted to answer. If he wanted to answer at all. He was sure Lei was used to dealing with a certain caliber of man, but there was no doubt in his mind that she'd never experienced his breed before.

"Londen Graham."

Her cheeks heightened as she chuckled and looked toward the ceiling. "Londen, you know that's not what I mean. Who are you?"

"Do you really want to spend the little time we have together talking about that?"

"Seeing as it's the reason we're even able to be face to face right now... yes. I do."

"Okay. I'll give you that. First, I want to know how you're feeling. It's been a long time since you've been in my city. How are you?"

Her body softened against him as she loosened her grip around his neck. "I'm... okay. I haven't been in the city, and I think not seeing a place or thing that brought back memories helped. I got off the interstate and was here in a matter of minutes, which I'm grateful for. If I can avoid places that bring back memories, I believe I'll be good. Now, if I were to see them, it would be a different story. Every time thoughts of them crept in, I reminded myself I was coming here for you."

"For the bet," Londen corrected.

Her head shook as she smiled sweetly. "No. I came here

for you. I have to make my decision tomorrow, but I wanted to see you."

"Do you have an idea of what you're going to do? Who you're going to pick?"

Even though Londen was a confident man, he never overplayed his position in a person's life. Lei made it clear she wasn't looking for love, and there was no doubt he could make her feel that very thing. He wouldn't be surprised if she picked Tussi because he was an easy way for her to win the bet. With Londen, it wouldn't be just six figures on the line—her heart would be too.

"My heart wants me to pick you naturally, and that's exactly why I don't want to."

Londen hadn't been the smiling, goofy type. Even in his childhood, he was the serious sibling. Lei, however, had a way of pulling smiles out of him effortlessly.

"You're willing to deny your heart because the last nigga you gave it to hurt you?"

"I haven't given him as much power as your question suggests."

"Are you sure? Because that's what it sounds like."

Their eyes remained locked for seconds on end before she huffed and looked away. "It's not about him. It's my way of protecting me."

"From love?"

"From pain," she replied quickly. "The less people I love and let in, the less chances I have to be hurt."

"True, but that's also less chances to experience authentic love. You deserve that."

"I get it from my family and friends, so I'm good."

"Nah, Baby." Londen chuckled as he squeezed her thigh. She was avoiding his eyes and the sight was cute. Licking the corner of his mouth, Londen turned her face in his direction by her chin. "I'm not talking about familial or platonic love. I'm talking about the love that completes you and makes you feel safe, secure, and warm in a cold world. The kind of love that makes you feel invincible. Like you're never alone. The kind of love that gives more than it takes. Unconditional. Fulfilling. Yours and yours alone." When her head lowered, he lifted it again. "One you don't have to share with anyone else. Can you honestly tell me you don't want that? A love, a man, that's yours and yours alone?"

Nibbling her cheek, Lei looked into his eyes as hers watered. "He was supposed to be mine and mine alone, but he cheated, so..."

"He wasn't meant to be yours then. I can guarantee you that the man who is will be so satisfied with himself that he won't need to seek fulfillment in a woman that isn't you. Niggas ain't breaking up happy homes because of anything their woman lacks. It's always because of something that's fucked up within themselves. Something they don't have the courage to fix, so they break their woman's heart in an attempt to cover their own holes."

"And I'm to believe you're satisfied enough with yourself to be faithful to me?"

"Yeah," he answered simply. "I can show you that with time, though, if you'll allow me to. I'm confident my character can speak for itself. All I need is a chance."

"Why do you want one? I mean... we know a bit about each other, but not enough for you to want to take on the burden of loving a woman like me."

"I know enough."

She paused, waiting eyes staring into his for more. "That's all you're going to say?"

Londen released a hearty chuckle. "Yeah, Baby. You'll learn, I show more than I ever tell. I want you to experience me for yourself and learn to trust what I'm willing to offer you."

Lei rested her forehead on his for a brief moment before lifting it and kissing his.

"I'm even more curious about who you are now."

Londen considered telling her the full truth. If he did, he'd have to tell her he came into the fold of the secret society through her father for killing the man who kidnapped her. That was a truth he'd tell her one day, but only when he was sure she was willing to give them a chance and he talked to Ace about it first.

"I told you I was in the streets."

"Right, but a lot of men in prison are. What makes you different?"

"My wealth, reputation, and connections." Londen paused, rubbing his hand across his beard. "I bounced from Memphis to Rose Valley Hills. Before I was arrested, I started doing more work for the secret society. Hits and protection mostly. That protection extended to some very powerful people here in Memphis. As thanks, I live a more... favored lifestyle while I'm here." He shrugged, as if what he was alluding to was normal.

"So when you said you know my father; does that mean you know him personally? Did you work for him?"

"You know I can't give you information on my clients or what I do for them. That's a part of the oath."

"Well, can you at least tell me what side of the law you intend to abide by if you are released early? Are you going back to the streets, or will you continue with the secret society?"

"I can't think that far in the future. I have to actually get paroled first. If so, that decision will be determined by a lot of things... including you."

"How so?"

"If we're together, I'd want to stay out of the streets. That's not a guarantee that I'll be in the secret society though. That lifestyle will demand a lot of my time and energy. After doing a decade in here, I want to live my life for me."

"I understand. I was the same way when I first made it to Rose Valley. Every decision I made had to benefit me most. It took about two years before I even wanted to start working again."

Maybe they had more in common than Londen thought.

"I'm glad you understand."

Londen did have a lot to consider though. If he went back to Rose Valley Hills, temptation to get back in the streets would be on every side. His family and friends were there, anxiously awaiting his arrival. Memphis would probably be his best bet, but would Lei want to follow him there? Did he deserve for her to? She had a complete life setup there. Was it fair for him to bombard his way inside and demand change?

Those thoughts and decisions would have to wait. In that moment, all Londen wanted to do was enjoy having Lei in his presence.

twenty-two

Londen

IT WAS Londen's intent to cancel his pen pal membership when he and Lei started talking, but when they started with their handwritten letters, he completely forgot about it. When he did sign in to cancel his profile, he saw a message from Yandi asking to visit him. He started to tell her no, however, the knowledge of her being Lei's friend caused him to say yes. A week later, she had a visitor profile setup for their virtual visit, but Londen decided to see her face to face instead.

When she walked into the room, her aura immediately took up space. Londen watched as she removed her shades, tossing them into her large, luxury handbag. Yandi released a tired huff, as if it was an inconvenience for her to have to walk for herself. With a chuckle, Londen ran his hand down the back of his neck as she walked over to the table where he was seated. He desperately wanted to get inside her mind and see if she had any qualities like Lei at all. How did these two women end up as friends?

Yandi sat across from him and licked her lips, staring at him with a confident smile.

"You wanted to talk?" Londen confirmed.

"Yes." She cleared her throat and cupped her hands on top of the table. "I wanted to warn you. Lei is my best friend, but I like you and wanted to make sure you knew the truth."

Quite frankly, Londen hadn't shared enough of himself with Yandi for her to like him. From his first conversation with Lei, he decided she was the woman he'd place his effort with. Before they had their first FaceTime conversation, he did chat casually with Yandi, but after seeing that she was talking to Tussi as well, Londen lost interest.

"What version of the truth would you like to share, Yandi?"

Her smile dropped before it widened again. "Lei is only talking to you for the purpose of a bet. She's talking to another man in here too. I wanted you to be aware that you're being used."

Londen chuckled softly, sitting back in his seat. He stared at her for a few seconds before sighing and looking toward the ceiling. Londen had no idea what Yandi wanted to say, but he certainly wasn't expecting it to be this.

"What's the reason for you sharing this with me?" Londen asked, though he already knew the answer.

Yandi shrugged, but she was confident when she said, "It's the right thing to do."

"For who? You? Because you're not doing this for Lei."

She laughed nervously. "What do you mean?"

"I mean, if that's your friend, you should be more loyal to her than me. That's your friend, right?" Yandi's bottom lip poked out and brows wrinkled as she considered his question. She nodded. "Then you're not being more loyal to me than her, you're being more loyal to yourself. You came here to tell me that, hoping it would make me cut her off and fuck with you."

Her hands lifted as she shrugged again. "So what if I did? This should, at least, prove to you I'll always be honest with you."

"Nah. This doesn't show me you're honest; it's shows me you're willing to sacrifice anyone if it means elevating yourself. It also shows me you aren't to be trusted." Londen stood. "I'd *never* fuck with a woman like you." Placing his palms on top of the table, he hovered over it and told her, "I'm not going to let anyone hurt or disrespect Lei, especially someone she trusts. You'd be wise to not think I can't protect her because I'm locked down. For the sake of Lei's heart, I'm not going to tell her about this betrayal, but if she gives me any indication that she doesn't trust you, I won't hesitate to let her know about this visit."

"Londen…"

"Get the fuck outta here."

Londen was so disgusted by the display he didn't

bother waiting for the guard to escort her out. This was one time he was actually glad to return to his cell.

♥♥♥

"Nigga... I know you didn't."

At the sight of Chase walking past them with a white bandage wrapped around both hands, Londen chuckled.

"Didn't what?" Noah asked, tossing a card onto the table.

"Break that man's fingers because he was talking to Mercedes."

Noah's tongue slipped across his teeth. "I told him he can either unmatch her or get them fingers broke so he couldn't message her. He thought I was playing, I guess."

"And you don't see anything wrong with that?"

"Not at all."

"Bruh, you can't just force every man in here that she matches with to not talk to her."

"I can actually, and the quicker they accept that, the better off we'll all be."

Londen knew there was no point in trying to talk some sense into Noah. When he committed himself to the pursuit of a woman, he didn't let anything or anyone stand in his way. His fierceness and passion when it came to love had always been something Londen admired. All it took for him was one heartbreak, and he decided he'd stick to casual arrangements. Lei had him wanting more though, and he hoped she felt the same way.

"Yo..." Tussi almost sang, squeezing the shoulders of one of the old heads they were playing cards with. "Y'all know the Royalty chick I been talking to?"

Setting his cards face down on the table, Londen

scratched his nostril and gave Tussi his full attention. Lei was supposed to tell her girls she was choosing him when she made it back to Rose Valley Hills that evening, and Londen wondered if that was what Tussi wanted to gossip about.

"What about 'er?" Noah replied.

"So apparently I been talking to her friend too. Lil shorty hipped me to who Royalty's family is. Royalty ain't even her name. Anyway, I'ma have to get her in here and dick her down so I can make some shake with her Pops. From what I heard, that nigga got *big* pull. I'm tryna be out this ho ASAP."

"Yandi told you that?" Londen checked, trying to keep calm.

He wasn't upset with Tussi... yet. All he was, was a nigga looking for a come up. Yandi obviously hadn't taken his threat seriously if the first thing she did was take a call from Tussi and tell him Lei's business.

At that point, Londen wasn't sure what her end game was. Telling him about the bet was one thing, but telling Tussi who Lei really was put things on a different level. Nothing about that would make Londen stop talking to her, unless she believed Tussi was capable of taking Lei from him if he put forth more effort. This seemed... personal... and Londen had no idea what Yandi would gain from blowing up her best friend's spot.

"Yeah. You talking to her too?"

"Nah, not anymore. She tell you anything else about Lei?"

Tussi's head shook. "Just that she was a lawyer, and her folks are in the secret society."

"Regardless of what she told you, Lei is off limits."

It felt as if the air around them thickened. Eyes that

weren't on them before were on them now. That changed quickly when Noah stood and told everyone, "Mind your fucking business."

"Let me have this seat for a minute, OG," Tussi requested, to which the older man temporarily evacuated his seat.

As he walked away, he chuckled, as if Tussi had just set himself up for failure and hadn't even realized it.

"Really ain't shit for us to discuss," Londen clarified, turning slightly in Tussi's direction. Though he didn't believe Tussi had gained his respect, he'd give it to him for the time being, anyway.

"I'm just tryna get an understanding of why you feel you have any say in what I do and who I talk to."

"When it concerns Lei, it concerns me."

"Unless you married the bitch without my knowing, ain't shit you can do to stop me from talking to her or whatever the fuck else I want to do."

Noah released a long, animated sigh. He stood and grumbled, "Mm, mm, mm," under his breath. "You gon' regret that shit, young nigga."

"I'ma give you one chance to correct yourself and apologize," Londen warned.

Tussi's face distorted before he laughed. "Fuck you, Londen. These other pussy ass niggas might fear you, but it ain't an ounce of bitch in my bloo—"

Before Tussi could get the word out fully, Londen's grip on his neck was sending his face into the table. Blood immediately began to pour from his nose.

"You said it ain't no bitch in your blood?" Londen taunted. "Let me see."

By the third time Londen had smashed his face into the

table, Tussi's eyes were rolling into the back of his head as he lost consciousness.

"Aight, that's enough," Noah decided, gripping Londen's hand.

Londen was so calm, he immediately released his hold. Looking down at himself, Londen sucked his teeth at the sight of splattered blood on his arms and shirt.

"Nigga wetter than some pussy in this bitch. Got my shit soaked."

As Londen pulled the shirt over his head and used it to wipe his arms, three guards jogged over to tend to Tussi.

"Put that mane in solitary when he wakes up. He needs time to think about what the fuck I said," Londen ordered, leaving the common area to head to his cell.

As calm as he was trying to remain, his frustration with Yandi was starting to brew. He said he wouldn't mention what she'd done until Lei expressed a lack of trust in her. Perhaps Yandi wasn't expecting Tussi to tell the whole quad about their conversation. Whatever the case, it was taking everything inside of Londen to not make a call to have Yandi permanently removed from Lei's life. She'd experienced enough heartache from people she loved and trusted, and Londen meant it when he said he wouldn't let anyone hurt her in that way again.

twenty-three

Lei

"I WISH you were here so I could thank you properly," Lei admitted.

A few days ago, she gave Londen her real address in preparation for a surprise he had for her. After she messaged Tussi and told him she could no longer talk to him, Londen had been even more present. Since she hadn't heard from Tussi, Lei could only hope he didn't take the news too bad. Maybe he didn't care enough about her to give a response. Either way, with the attention Londen had been showering her with, Lei didn't care at all.

Even if she tried to deny it, what was brewing between her and Londen went beyond friendship. Fear had embedded itself deep within her heart when it came to love, and Londen was slowly digging every drop of it out.

That evening, he had a night planned that she would forever remember. That was often the case when it came to Londen though. The effort he was exerting beyond bars showed her not just that he was a man of action as he'd said before, but that the right man would come in and remind her of how good being loved on could feel. Lei may not have been ready to commit just yet, but Londen was definitely breaking down her walls.

He'd had one of his favorite private chefs come and prepare a five course meal for Lei. Before she ate, a personal stylist was there to let her choose her outfit, shoes, and accessories for the evening. Londen joined her via FaceTime, and it was hard to dwell on the fact that he wasn't there physically because of how much she enjoyed herself.

"Just seeing that pretty smile is more than enough for me."

"Do you need anything else from us, Boss?" Walter asked.

"Nah, that's it."

"Then we'll conclude our stay for the evening." Walter turned in Lei's direction. "I left all of our numbers on a pad in the kitchen. We are at your disposal, twenty-four-seven. Call any time."

"I will. Thank you, and you all enjoy the rest of your evening." Lei walked behind the crew of people and locked the door behind them before telling Londen, "Okay, so did the staff come because you're locked up, or have you always lived such a life of luxury?"

London smiled, and Lei had to admit, she loved the sight of it. The sight of those pretty, white, straight teeth against his smooth dark chocolate skin... always made her smile.

"I hired a staff as soon as I was able to afford to. Not just for the luxury of it, but for security back then too. With drivers, I was never pulled over and arrested for anything as a passenger, you feel me? Fewer trips to stores because I had personal stylists. Less potential of being used and lied on because I had assistants to handle business for me. Having people I could trust around me just made life easier."

"I feel you. That was my definition of luxury, even before I moved to Rose Valley. I've never been really materialistic, though the men in my life love to spoil me. The things that provide me with ease and comfort are truly luxurious for me."

"I'm glad you mentioned that. I know your folks do a lot for you, but there are things I'd like to start doing as your man."

Lei giggled before she could hold it back, stopping dead in her tracks. "My man?"

"Yeah." Londen's tone was softer than she'd ever heard it before. "Your man."

Her smile widened as she continued toward the kitchen, pleased when she saw it spotless. Thanks to his staff, all she'd have to do was undress and climb into bed.

"I'm sorry, I didn't know you were my man."

"You didn't?" Between his gasp and the offended expression that covered his face, Lei couldn't help but burst into a fit of laughter.

"No!" she yelled playfully. "I didn't."

"My apologies, Baby. I need to rectify that."

"I'd say so."

Tugging her bottom lip between her teeth, Lei grabbed the opened bottle of 1882 Graham Port 'Ne Oublie' Tawny Port and prepared to head to her room. In mentioning during one conversation that she loved sweet wine, London had begun to have a bottle delivered to her several times a week. That week, the seven-thousand-dollar bottle had been one that she'd been dying to get her hands on since she had it a few years ago at a tasting. Ideally, she'd like to stock up since they were limited in quantity, but every wholesaler she'd found over the years only had one in stock.

Londen waited until she was in bed to say, "We still have a lot to learn about each other. Honestly, I enjoyed writing you letters and would love to continue to do so. What I do know, is that I want you to be mine. I want to spoil you and give you the love and life you deserve. If you're more comfortable waiting until I'm free to commit, I'm cool with that. I know it might feel like a long-distance relationship, and I'm not sure how you'd get along with that."

"I've never been in a long-distance relationship. What I can say, is that I feel closer to you in a just under a month than I felt to anyone else in the last decade. I feel connected and secure with you, but I would like for us to take things slow. Would you be content with knowing I'm only being courted by you, and I don't want to be with anyone else but you?"

"For now, but when I get out, you're going to be mine, Lei."

"I would love that. Do you have an idea of when that will be?"

"I do, but I don't want to tell you until it's 100 percent certain. Is that okay with you?"

"Yes. I appreciate you sparing me from potential disappointment. I have high hopes that you'll be out soon, though."

"Me too, gorgeous. Me too."

twenty-four

London

Babe,

Today has been the longest dragging day. I've taken on a new case and it's consuming so much of my day. Times like this make me question why I'm working when I don't have to. Between my father and my brother plus what I make doing keynote speaking and writing law guides, I really don't have to work. Well, I know why I'm working. I'm working because I love giving a voice to the voiceless and defending those on the wrong side of justice.

Mercedes told me about what you and Noah are doing next month. I think it's pretty cool that you all give backpacks and supplies to children every semester and do food drives every other month. Why haven't you mentioned that before? If there's anything I can do, I'd love to help. Even if it's just pack plates and baskets and hand them out. I know that would technically connect me to you and Noah, but I'm okay with that. If we're going to be together eventually, I have to prepare for how that would look. Don't get me wrong, I don't care about the optics personally... but I do care about how that would affect my career and my cases.

We said we were going to use the next couple of letters to talk about our hobbies and interests and whatnot, and I'm looking forward to seeing if we have anything in common. It's crazy that we haven't discussed this already. I like that, though, because it shows our connection is based on a damn good vibe.

Okay! So, my hobbies and interests. Yoga, crocheting, and volunteering are probably my top hobbies. It probably sounds weird to consider volunteering as a hobby, but I love it that much. With this second wing of my life, God has blessed me with so much that I have no choice but to give back. When my caseload isn't heavy, I like to volunteer weekly. If I can't, at least twice a month.

I do love riding motorcycles and going to Betty's cigar and cognac lounge every Friday as well. I said if I didn't have my baby by next year, I'd buy a motorcycle. Should that be something we discuss as well? Before things got more serious between us, I told you I wanted to be pregnant by the end of the year. Do you want children? If so, how many and when do you want to start your family? If not... should we end things here? Because I doubt if you'd be comfortable with me going on with my plans, anyway.

My favorite movies are Matilda and Smokey and the Bandit. I watch 80s and 90s shows for comfort. My favorite color is rose gold. I love to swim. The instruments I can play are piano/keyboard, drums, and flute. A strange fact is that I don't care to travel. My home is my favorite place in the world, so I don't like to leave it unless I absolutely have to. Plus, I have a thing about germs and I'm very particular about the spaces I dwell in, even if temporarily. When I do travel, I love going to beaches and islands or places where I can shop till I drop.

I think my favorite place to go in the US is Sausalito. When I go there, I literally get a houseboat and spend days there, sitting on the water. I know it's not the prettiest or clearest water, but there is where I always feel most connected to God.

What else can I tell you? I don't want to be cliché and tell you what I want or need in a man. I would prefer to see if you are those things naturally and tell you when they arise. I don't think you would try to finesse me into thinking you're someone you aren't, but that's the safest way for me to know you are sincere.

I guess I'll end the letter here, hoping I get to speak with you tonight.

twenty-five

Lei

Baby,

The first thing I want to address is the kids topic. I do want them, at least two. So much of my life has been spent doing things I

B. LOVE

was sure would take it away from me. Even now, passing this time behind bars, I wasn't completely sure I'd make it out of here alive. Having power and connections mean nothing to a nigga that has hate in his heart with nothing to lose. The greatest of men tend to be taken away by the weakest of sorts. So I'm surprised that I've not only made it to thirty-seven, but that I've almost completed my time without someone in here trying to take my life. I've never been fearful, but I've always been a realist. Every man has a price, and for the right price, a nigga could have easily tried to slit my throat and risked his own life. I said all of that to say, when I get out of here, I intend to live... fully... and that includes starting my family soon.

I would like a period to get established and remind myself how to live freely while also traveling and enjoying myself, but God willing, a family won't be too close behind.

It's cool that you play several instruments. I play piano and drums as well. I'm self-taught and I never learned to read music, but I can play anything after listening to it once. Maybe we can create our own music together. You being an advocate for volunteer work means a lot to me, because I love giving back and helping anyone I can. I don't do it for the recognition, which is why I hadn't mentioned it to you. If you truly wanted to help, I'd love for you to join us.

The traveling thing caught me by surprise. I figured you'd be the kind of woman who loves to travel. Your reason for not wanting to makes sense though. To me, traveling is an experience... one that I get great pleasure out of. Hopefully, I can take you places that make you comfortable enough to enjoy yourself, because I'd love for you to experience the world with me.

I've already shared with you my love for cooking. I wouldn't say that's a hobby; it's more like a passion. My sister has always been a supporter of me using my cooking to get out of the streets. She already has a million ideas of things I could do to keep myself busy enough to not go back to my old ways when I'm released. We don't have the closest bond anymore, and I'm at peace with that.

Megan left Tennessee as soon as she became legal, and I thank God for that. I never wanted her to get caught up in our bullshit. She works for TSA now and lives a normal, healthy life. Because of her work hours, we don't talk often, but that's my heart and I'll do anything to protect her. Just knowing she's safe and loved gives me peace.

I admire how close you are with your family now. At one point, I used to have the same kind of bond with mine. I'm not sure how things will be when I get out. All my life, I lived to appease my parents, specifically my father. If I'm not bending to his will, I don't know how he will respond to me. The average son would have his father's approval no matter what, especially if he was trying to live right, but I can't say that will be the case with Simpson Graham.

Hobbies... Your environment determines how you spend your time. My hobbies today aren't the same as they were ten years ago, and I don't know what they'll be when I get out. I will always love reading and music... playing my instruments. Hanging with the guys. In here, I've started watching TV and movies more, and that used to be something I never did. Before I got locked down, I was a firm advocate in having several different kinds of rest and hobbies. I'm looking forward to learning you while I relearn myself.

twenty-six

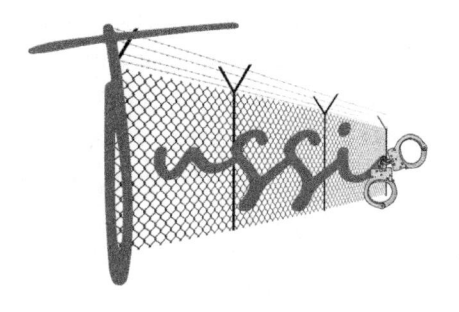

Tussi

THIS WAS the third time Tussi had called Yandi and gotten no answer. He needed her to have a virtual visit with him ASAP. A lot of things could be forgotten, but disrespecting him, especially in public, was not on that list. Londen had to pay, and he was going to use Lei to do it.

Tussi felt like a kid on Christmas when Yandi told him

who Royalty really was. In seconds, he had a plan in mind. She was going to help him get an early release, then he'd work with the secret society under her father. Granted, Tussi was already looking at less time than most believed. His sixty-year sentence had been dropped to twenty-five because he'd given names of several dealers and locations of their trap houses along with evidence to tie murderers to victims. That information wasn't on his file, so he never had to worry about an inmate getting a correctional officer to look up his record and see the drastic decline in his sentence.

Twenty-five years was still too long. Too much of his life to spend behind bars. There was no doubt in Tussi's mind that Ace could help get him out, and he was determined to convince Lei to get him to do it. What Tussi wasn't prepared for was for Londen to be attached to Lei. Niggas like him felt like they ran this shit, and to a certain extent... they did. That was the level Tussi aspired to be on, but his money wasn't long enough, and he hadn't put in enough work before he was locked down to make that happen.

If Londen had set a claim to Lei, no one else would have the balls to talk to her in the pen pal program. Unfortunately, there weren't too many women of her caliber who signed up, and the ones who did always had weird fetishes and reasons for wanting to connect to a man behind bars. About a year ago, Tussi started messaging a millionaire who wanted him to break out just to kill her husband. He considered it, but with the deal he had set up, Tussi wasn't willing to risk it.

Deciding to call Yandi once more, Tussi looked behind him to see if anyone was waiting for the phone... not that it mattered. He wasn't getting off until he was done. After putting in his ID number, Tussi dialed Yandi's line again. This time, she answered.

"Hello?"

"Set up a visit for Wednesday at two."

"Okay. You good?"

"Yeah."

After disconnecting the call, Tussi's eyes scanned the crowd of men that were huddled up by the phones. His eyes settled on Montrell—the nineteen-year-old who was serving a life sentence because his friends convinced him he was tougher than he was. With all the dirt Tussi had done in his life, seeing young boys come in so early always broke his heart. They didn't allow themselves time to live and enjoy pussy before they were giving up their freedom for street or gang shit.

"Aye," Tussi called. When their eyes connected, he bobbed his head to the right. "Let me holla at ya."

Montrell's eyes went from Tussi to the older man that had taken him under his wing. It was the same one that had given up his seat for Tussi days ago. He'd spent time in the infirmary then solitary after Londen's attack, and Tussi was determined to get even. The OG whispered something in Montrell's ear that caused him to bob his head before Montrell slowly walked in Tussi's direction.

"Wassup, big brotha?" Montrell greeted, accepting the handshake Tussi offered.

"Who you got outside?"

Montrell shrugged as they slowly began to walk. "Nobody. My mama can't afford to be doing shit for me 'cause she gotta take care of my lil' brothers and sisters."

"I can keep your commissary stocked and time on your card but you gotta work for that shit."

Montrell's feet stopped moving. "Doing what?"

"Getting me information on what Londen and Noah are up to. Whenever you see them two together, I need you nearby listening in on their conversation. If they mention getting out of here or the name Lei, tell me."

Sucking his teeth, Montrell shook his head and crossed his arms over his chest. "Hell nah. They would kill me if they thought I was listening in on their conversations."

"Well, I'ma kill you if you don't." Tussi paused, jaw clenched as he closed the space between them. "Now you can get something out of this shit, or you can do it for free. Either way, you gon' do it." Montrell's head tilted as he released a long breath. His eyes shifted over to his OG, but Tussi told him, "It ain't shit he can do for you. So what you wanna do?"

Montrell's head hung briefly before he agreed with, "Aight, I'll do it."

Tussi chuckled. "As if you had a choice."

twenty-seven

Yandi

AFTER TAKING a sip of her green juice, Yandi sat on the bar stool and cut on her laptop. While she waited for the Apple device to power up, she scrolled her Instagram feed and checked to see how many likes the morning selfie she'd posted had gotten. Yandi lived for the validation she received from strangers on the internet. There was something about having hundreds of women envying her and men lusting after her that gave her the confidence to tackle anything throughout her day.

According to who was asked, they'd give a different version of Yandi that they encountered. Most men would say she was a woman who knew exactly what she wanted, and if they didn't provide that, she didn't waste her time with them. Most women would say she wasn't a good person or friend because of her selfish ways, while others would say she was the best woman they'd ever encountered because of her genuineness.

Growing up with a mother who finessed and hustled for everything she had instilled that same drive in Yandi. Her relationships were often transactions, and Yandi would make sure she got all that she could out of a person in case their relationship ended. Yandi had never known true peace. Glimmers of it came with a rich man or giving friend, but true peace hadn't made its home in Yandi since she was a child. Being in survival mode, constantly looking for ways to take left little room for rest.

As tormented as Yandi was mentally and emotionally, she gave no hints physically. Between her rigorous workout routine, consistent plastic surgery maintenance, and clean eating and drinking throughout the week, Yandi was almost a picture of perfection. On weekends, she allowed herself to have cheat days, but even those were done in moderation. Her face and body got her far with men, and Yandi wasn't going to let *anything* ruin that. Unlike Lei and Mercedes, Yandi didn't have guaranteed wealth because of her family.

Her father was a married preacher who disowned them publicly yet came to drop his load inside her mother in exchange for money every few weeks, and her mother hadn't worked a steady job for more than six weeks in all of

Yandi's life. Everything she had, Yandi worked for, and her pride wouldn't allow her to let anyone make her feel bad for it.

"Let me see what this nigga want," she grumbled, opening the Chrome browser.

For Tussi to be asking to see her face, it must have been important. Most of their conversations were done over the phone at that point. Unfortunately for her, Tussi didn't have the power and pull she wanted him to have. He was just a regular man in prison—nothing like Londen and Noah—who had their noses up her best friends' asses. Yandi was much too nice allowing them first dibs because of the bet. She should have taken one or both from the jump. If she would have, not only would she have access to their money, but she'd have more power and connections because of those attached to them in the outside world.

Now, she was stuck with Tussi... a man who was great to look at but didn't have much else to offer.

As soon as Yandi saw Tussi, she gasped and covered her mouth. His eyes were purple and slightly swollen and his nose was distorted. There was a cut down the middle of his top lip, as if it had been cut by his teeth.

"What the hell happened to you?"

"You is what happened to me." He sat up in his seat. "I was talking about the news you gave me on Lei and Londen did this to me."

Yandi huffed and rolled her eyes. "Why were you talking to them about it? I told you that in confidence. If he tells her I told you, she's going to kill me."

"Fuck all that." Tussi sucked his teeth. "I need to know how close you are to her. She needs to get me up outta here, and I need to make that nigga pay."

"Are you... Do you think this is something we should be talking about on here? Don't they monitor these chats?"

Tussi's head shook. "Nah. Once they approve of your location, we're good. It is recorded, but I got somebody that can handle that."

"Mhm," was all Yandi offered. Of course, he'd have a connection to someone on the inside. "So what exactly does this have to do with me, Tussi? I can't make Lei fuck with you if she wants to be with Londen."

"Look, all I need you to do is put in the good word for me. I need her number so we can connect."

"I'm not comfortable giving you her number. Plus, if she knows I'm talking to you, she's not going to want to. You might just have to take this loss, Tussi."

"Nah, ain't no L's. She's way too beneficial to me for me to just let Londen have her. Plus, he fucked up when he snuck me. His ass gots ta pay."

"I understand, but... I just don't know how you think you're going to make that happen."

Yandi didn't want to say what she was thinking—that Lei would be out her damn mind to entertain him while she had Londen—because that would further piss Tussi off. Between his tone and the frown on his bruised face, he looked like he had no room for jokes or unwanted truths.

"You tryna say I can't take 'er?"

"No. I'm just saying you need a damn good plan to do so. Look..." She paused, considering how honest she wanted to be with Tussi. Anything they could have had romantically was over now that she knew how little power and money he had. Tussi wasn't broke, but he had no source of income in or out of his cell. There weren't any men working on his behalf to keep his cash flowing while he was sat down. What money he had would have to be stretched to keep him comfortable during his sentence. On the bright side, he never asked her for anything, but for a woman like Yandi, his independence wasn't enough. "I can't lie, I would love to be with Londen, but I know that's not going to happen as long as he's stuck on Lei. Trust me, you need more than a conversation to make her leave him alone."

"If I come up with a good plan, can I trust you to help me execute it?"

"If the plan ends not just with you getting Lei but me getting Londen... yes. But it has to be good, Tussi. I'm not shining in the most favorable light with Londen right now because I told him about the bet."

"I got you. I'll call you when I got something in mind."

After Yandi ended the call, she called her girls on a group FaceTime to see if they wanted to get into anything that evening. Until she secured her next sponsor, Yandi had nothing but time on her hands.

twenty-eight

Lei

ONE MONTH Later
February

IN THAT MOMENT, all Lei wanted was Londen. Times like this, she hated not being able to see him whenever she wanted. Even with the privilege Londen was granted, Lei hesitated to take full advantage. If she had it her way, she'd demand to see him, but she knew it was wisest to wait until their scheduled visit tomorrow. With the way she was feeling, Lei wanted to get a hotel suite and head to Memphis tonight.

"Lei," Cade called, voice low and stern.

She ignored him, as she'd been doing since they left out of the courthouse. This wasn't the first time she and Cade were on opposite sides of the judge, but this was the first time she'd ever been so disgusted by her brother's tactics. The low blows he landed during his opening statement were an indication of just how low Cade intended to go, and Lei wasn't looking forward to this war at all.

"Lei."

Cade jogged forward and grabbed her arm. Yanking away from him, Lei turned to face him.

"What, Cade?"

"Are you upset with me?"

"Obviously so."

"Why?"

"Because you painted Garrett out to be a monster when you *know* that's not true." Cade's shoulders caved and he exhaled a hard breath as he looked toward the sky. "You know that man did not kill his wife and children. You're looking for someone to blame, I get it, but hasn't he lost *enough*? You're going to punish a grieving man just because the police were too lazy to look for the real killer?"

"Look." Gritting his teeth, Cade rubbed his palms together and closed the space between them. He lowered his voice when he said, "We agreed we'd never take what happens in the courtroom personally."

"I'm not. You were wrong."

"That's your opinion."

"Can you honestly look me in my eyes and tell me you believe Garrett isn't innocent?"

Cade chuckled. He squeezed the back of his neck and shook his head. "It's not my job to convince you he's innocent, sis. That's your job. It's my job to convince that jury that he's guilty, and that's what I intend to do."

He started to walk away, but that didn't stop Lei from saying, "You don't care about Garrett's guilt. You just want someone to pay. Even at the expense of sending an innocent man to prison?"

Cade's back was still turned as he said, "We're never going to agree on this, Lei, so let's just drop it. We promised not to let our cases come between us. Don't switch up on me now."

Lei's eyes watered as she watched him walk away. It would have frustrated her if it was anyone, but for it to be her own brother, it hit Lei in a deeper place. Outside of the courthouse, Cade was a completely different person. One who was kind, compassionate, and understanding. The moment he stepped in front of the judge, he became a judgmental, cutthroat beast. While those traits made him an awesome prosecutor, it made him a horrible person in Lei's eyes.

She kept trying to tell herself not to let the case affect her so much, but in that moment, all she wanted to do was crawl into London's arms and cry.

🩶🩶🩶

Lei was stretched out in the middle of the bed, grinning from ear to ear. She'd come to Memphis a few hours after court, just to feel closer to London. After telling him about what happened, he had his assistant book her a suite at the

Peabody hotel. He'd added a package that came with champagne and chocolate-covered strawberries. Lei took a long, hot bath, then indulged in the treats. Just the act of him caring for her in that way lightened Lei's mood, but she felt even better when he called her again to check on her.

"I feel good, babe. Just... feeling closer to you has a smile on my face. I can't wait to see you tomorrow."

"Glad I could help. I never want to hear so much sadness lacing your tone."

"Trust me, I didn't want to be crying on the phone, but I was glad you called. I really needed to talk to you."

"You can always express your feelings with me. I want to be that safe space for you."

The soft taps on the door had Lei sitting up in bed. "Um... did you have Walter to order room service or something?"

"Open the door and see."

Hopping off the bed, Lei slipped her silk robe over her gown and almost toppled over, trying to put on her house shoes. Up until that point, she was sure her love language was words of affirmation, but the more Londen spoiled her, the more she reconsidered that. Lei opened the door, and at the sight of Londen and a guard standing behind him, she gasped and dropped her phone. She took a step back weakly before hopping into his embrace.

Londen's laugh was soft and light as he stepped inside, tightening his grip around her. The door closed and locked behind him as Lei cupped his cheeks with tears in her eyes.

"Are you real? Is this really happening?"

Londen covered her lips with his and gave her a kiss that had her body weakening against him.

"Does it feel real?" His lips were more persuasive than Lei cared to admit.

"I have to be dreaming. There's no way you're standing in front of me."

Londen scoffed as he carried her to the bedroom. "I'm Londen Graham. I can be anywhere you need me to be."

"But, babe..." Her mouth hung open and head shook in disbelief. "How are you here?"

"A lion is still a lion, even in a cage."

It was in that moment that Lei realized just how powerful Londen was. Even with his hesitance to share everything about who he was and what he did, Lei now wondered if it was wise for her to know. All she cared about was his presence. She'd ask questions later. Right now, she just wanted to enjoy her favorite being.

"Londen," she almost whispered against his lips before connecting them with hers again. "I don't think I have the words to describe how grateful I am to have you here. Whatever you had to do to make this happen, I hope I can do something so that you know it was worth it by the time you leave."

"You don't have to do anything, Baby. I came here because I was worried about you. As long as you're happy by the time I leave, that's more than enough for me."

"How much time do we have?"

"Four hours," Londen answered, placing her on the edge of the bed.

She crawled up it, telling him, "You need to take off your clothes."

He gave her a sexy chuckle and obliged. With nothing but his boxers and socks on, Londen climbed into bed and made his way between her legs.

"I can't believe you're really here."

"There isn't anything I wouldn't make happen for you, Lei. I hope you can trust that now."

Biting down on her bottom lip as her eyes watered again, Lei nodded. "I do," she muttered, before sniffling. "I really do."

They both laid down and wrapped their arms around each other.

"You smell good as hell," Londen complimented, running his fingers up and down her arm. "It's going to be hard keeping my hands off you."

"You don't have to."

His head shook. "Nah. I want our first time to be special."

"Londen... You left prison because I cried on the phone. Baby, you can have every drop of cum in my pussy."

The sound of Londen's laughter was like music to her ears. He licked his lips as he gripped her thigh, and the warmth of his skin on hers had Lei's lips parting.

"I can have every drop?"

Lei made sure to enunciate each word as she told him, "Every drop."

Those words activated a more primal side of Londen. His lips and hands were on her—everywhere. Quiet moans poured from her mouth as he took his time fondling her neck, breasts, and thighs through her gown. When his hand slipped under, the sharp contrast between the cool softness of the silk and warm roughness of his hand had Lei in sensory overload.

Londen's hand wrapped around her neck and pushed her further down the bed... gently, slowly. The act had her back arching and lips parting at the same pace of her legs. He made quick work of removing her robe and gown. Lei's heart seemed to rush to each spot on her body that his lips and hands touched. From her nipples to her thighs, Londen made sure to show every inch of her the same amount of love.

The second his warm mouth wrapped around her clit, Lei's body softened like jelly against the bed. Each lick, slurp, and nibble was more intense than the other. He gripped her thighs and kept her legs wide as he pleasured her to the brink of convulsion. Her clit pulsed as he placed his focus there. When he moaned against her, Lei's legs began to tremble as she came.

"I want to make you cum again. Can I?"

The answer was a rapid thud of her swollen bud. "Mhm," she moaned, biting down on her bottom lip.

And so he did—twice more—before entering her with two fingers. It took him almost no time to find her spot, placing pressure on its ridges as they expanded against him. She felt the warmth at her core. The puddling of her desire.

"I'm about to squirt," she warned, pushing at his head.

He only lifted slightly, looking at the mess she created in awe.

"I love watching this clit bloom. These walls pulse. This cum leak. Mmm..."

His words only intensified her orgasm. Lei's legs locked around him, but he pushed her legs back and pressed them into the bed, giving himself a clear view of her pussy.

"Come here," she begged, and Londen obliged.

He made his way up her body before removing himself from his boxers. Looking between them, Lei licked her lips at the sight of his long, curved shaft. She was now convinced he wasn't just the shade of her favorite dark chocolate but that he'd taste as good too. Savoring him would have to wait. In that moment, they *both* wanted him inside.

Londen stretched her near virgin-tight walls, giving himself to her inch by inch. By the time he made it to the heated core of her body, Londen's dick was throbbing inside of her. Watching his cum ooze out of her like white icing on a honey bun had Lei releasing a guttural groan. His body jerked as he moaned her name, and that was enough to have her eyes rolling into the back of her head as she came.

His strokes were long and slow as he began to pleasure her. Skin to skin, lips to lips, they moved as one... soaring higher until the peak of delight was reached. Her orgasm crested like an ocean wave, drowning him and letting him even deeper inside. Lei cried out his name as her nails dug into his back. This wasn't just sex. Just a moment of physical desire. They were tying their souls together and tearing them apart. And when Londen lifted himself and looked into her eyes, Lei was convinced she wouldn't want to have it any other way.

twenty-nine

Lei

LATER THAT EVENING

Somehow, showering together led to Londen deep stroking Lei from behind as she held on to the wall for support. Each time she felt his cum seep out of her, it seemed to intensify her arousal even more. She lowered herself to her knees and took him into her mouth, sucking until he came again, then she stood, and they finally washed and cleaned their bodies.

Once they were clean and moisturized, they ordered room service. While they ate, they remained silent, looking at each other every once in a while with goofy grins and soft laughs.

"I never do this," Londen confessed, covering his now empty plate.

"Do what?"

"Smile and laugh. Not this often."

"Well... I'm glad I can provide that for you."

Lei's arms wrapped around his neck, and she loved how much of a height difference they had without her heels. There was something about looking up and into her man's eyes that always made Lei want to submit to his lead. Londen pushed her braids off her shoulders so he could look her face over intently.

"You are so fucking beautiful, Baby. Ain't no flaw in you."

Burying her face in his chest as she smiled, Lei released a content sigh. "They're there. You just... accept and like me so much you don't care to see them. That'll change when you get out and we're spending more time with each other."

"Maybe, but it won't change how I feel about you. I'm falling in love with you unconditionally because that's what you're giving me."

"If you keep talking like that, I'm not going to want you to leave."

"Very soon, you won't be able to get rid of me."

"Come talk to me," she requested, taking his hand and leading him back to the bed. "We don't have much time left."

"What do you want to know?"

"Tell me one thing you want, need, and something that induces your happiness."

Londen didn't answer her right away. Instead, he made himself comfortable in bed and pulled her back down to his chest. She rested her ear in the center of his chest, eyes closing as she relaxed from the soothing sound of his heartbeat.

"I want stability. I need respect. Quality time makes me happy. What about you?"

"I want companionship. I need someone I can trust and feel safe with. This might sound weird, but being prioritized makes me happy. That's why what you did for me today means so much."

"It makes sense, considering your childhood. I can imagine how important it is for you to feel chosen. Good enough." Londen tilted her head up to look into her eyes. "You know I'll never use that against you, right?"

All it took was a few seconds of thought for her to truthfully admit, "Right."

"Good." He placed a kiss to her forehead. "How do you feel loved?"

Their conversation went on for another hour or so before Londen announced it was time for him to leave. Lei slowly walked behind him, holding his hand tightly, as if that would allow her to keep him to herself.

"I don't want you to go, but I'm so happy I got to see you, babe. Thank you for this."

"You don't have to thank me for taking care of you. That's what I'm here for."

Lifting herself to the tips of her toes, Lei connected their lips, enjoying inhaling his exhales like every time she'd done so in the past. Taking her hand, Londen guided it to himself, allowing her to feel how quickly her kisses made him hard. With rapid urgency, clothes were removed, and her back was being pressed into the wall with a heavy thud. Lei didn't give a damn about the guard outside the door or anyone else hearing the sounds of their lovemaking. Her being craved the intricacy of connecting with this man, and there was nothing she could do to stop that.

Londen ate her moans, driving himself into her with hard, swift strokes. She was so close, so desperately close to release. It was like her pussy knew this was the end. Holding her orgasm hostage, her walls refused to pulse and give Londen the cum he'd earned.

He moved to the dresser, spreading her legs and entering her slower yet just as deep.

"This pussy mad I'm about to leave? I know she wants to cum."

"Londen," she whimpered, pushing at his hard abs. "I can't."

"Yes, you can. Trust me. I'll be back soon."

Her eyes fluttered until they closed. She relaxed against the mirror, panting and chest heaving as he fucked her into oblivion. Londen took his time with her—as if there was nowhere else he needed to be. He lengthened his strokes, allowing his hands to intensify her pleasure. While one hand thumbed her clit, the other teased her nipples.

"This visual is going to taunt me when we're apart. Replaying you unraveling against my dick is going to be the end of me."

"That's it... I'm about to cum."

"That's a good girl. And I'll give you mine as your reward." They came together, and her hand wrapped around his shaft as it emptied inside of her. "Fuck, Lei." He grunted, pulling her hair and tilting her head back so he could kiss her deeply.

As she trembled against him, Lei whimpered into his mouth. She wanted every kiss he had to offer, but she was so spent, she could barely kiss him back. Londen rested his forehead against hers as they regulated their breathing. Before she could stop them, tears were forming in her eyes.

"I really don't want you to go," Lei confessed, wrapping her arms and legs around him.

"I don't either, but I promise I'll call you as soon as I'm back in. We can talk until you fall asleep."

Sniffling, Lei unwrapped her body from his. Londen avoided her eyes, and she figured it was best that way, because hers were seconds away from leaking.

thirty

Londen

AS MUCH AS Londen didn't want to, he ended his FaceTime session with Lei once her brother arrived. They had to talk, and Londen understood how important it was for her to fix things with him. The moment he sat next to Noah and prepared to speak, Montrell casually walked toward them. Instead of sitting right next to them, he made his way to the table directly behind them.

"Does he think we're stupid?" Noah asked, causing Londen to chuckle and shake his head.

"I don't know, but we can find out." Turning slightly, Londen said, "Aye, com'ere." Montrell looked around, and it took everything inside of Londen not to laugh. "You, nigga. Bring your ass over here."

Montrell walked over, chin jutted out a lot higher than it should have been. "Wassup?"

"Who got you runnin' up behind us?" Noah asked.

"Watchu mean?"

"You know what the fuck I mean, and I'm not going to repeat myself."

Montrell's head tilted as he casually looked around. "I don't know what you talking about, big brotha."

"You willing to die for whoever setting you up? They mean that much to you?" Londen confirmed.

Montrell's eyes widened, and he shook his head adamantly. "It's Tussi," he grumbled. "He told me he'd keep my commissary stacked if I listened in on y'all conversations."

"What is he looking for?" Noah asked.

"Details on y'all getting out of here or some' about Lei."

With one bob of his head, Londen stood. He stepped so close to Montrell their toes touched. "If you value your life, you're going to forget about whatever he offered you."

"I would but he said he'd kill me if I didn't do it, so I'm fucked either way."

"Nah. I'll handle him. You just stay in your fucking lane and walk in the opposite direction when you see either of us," Londen said, pointing down at Noah.

Montrell nodded and ran his hand down his chest before taking a few steps back and jogging away.

"Your parole was approved," Noah said as he stood.

"You'll be out of here in two weeks. Either let me handle it, or let it ride."

"You know I can't do that."

Before Londen could step forward, Noah was placing his hand in Londen's chest. "I need you to practice the discipline I know you have. Regardless of what he's trying to do with Lei, he has no power. And from what you've told me about your connection with her, she ain't giving that nigga no play." Noah stepped directly in front of him and said, "Let me handle it if you want it handled, otherwise, let it ride."

"I don't put shit past no man at this point. Find out what he's up to and let me know."

"I got you," Noah agreed before walking away.

The last thing Londen wanted to do was have an issue with Tussi or anyone else for that matter so close to his release, but something was telling him Tussi would be a problem. Londen waited until Noah was out of sight to walk over to Tussi and sit next to him. Without acknowledging him, Tussi lifted his feet and placed them in the chair that was across from him.

"I can make your life in here far more miserable than you think it is," Londen declared. Tussi looked over at him. "You think your records are sealed, but they aren't. I know what your snitching ass said and did to get your time reduced." Tussi's eyes ballooned before he quickly played it off. "If you fuck with me or my girl, I'm going to make sure everybody in here knows what type of time you on, *especially* Devin." Londen stood. "You snitched on his brother and got him locked up, just for him to be murdered in three days, right?" Londen smiled. "How do you think Devin's going to take that news?"

Clearing his throat, Tussi stood. "I don't know who told you that, but it's a lie."

"Yeah, okay. Just remember what the fuck I said."

"Really, bruh?" Noah pushed Londen back gently before wrapping his arm around his shoulders and leading him in the opposite direction. "You just couldn't resist, could you?"

"I kept it gentleman. But he shouldn't try me going forward. If he does, I'm blowing up his spot with no hesitation."

"Do I want to know what you got up your sleeve?"

Londen chuckled. "Nah, but when I put it into play, everybody in this ho gon' know."

thirty-one

Lei

"WHAT'S UP WITH YOU?" Mercedes asked, softly shoving Yandi in her arm. "You've been acting weird all night. I could have stayed at home for this."

Lei wanted to agree with Mercedes, but she remained silent instead. It was Yandi's idea that they go out that evening, but she'd had an attitude since they arrived. Usually, when something was bothering Yandi, she couldn't wait to discuss it. Whatever the issue was, she was keeping it under wraps.

"I agree," Infinity said, and as soon as the two words left her mouth, Yandi was laughing.

"Of course your co-signing ass agrees. You take every opportunity you can to talk shit about me."

"Can y'all please not?" Lei requested before she could stop herself.

"Wow." Yandi laughed as she stood from the round table. "Now when these bitches talking shit about me, you're silent, but the moment I say something to Infinity, you got something to say."

"I didn't say anything because Mercedes is right; you *do* seem off, and you have for a while."

"Regardless, you're supposed to have my back, just like you had Infinity's back."

"What does having your back have to do with anything?" Mercedes asked. "All Lei said was, can y'all please not? You act like she cursed you and your firstborn for saying something to Infinity."

"Might as well," Yandi mumbled. "Lei don't really fuck with me like she claims to."

"Okay, woah." Lei lifted her hands. The chuckle she released wasn't from amusement. "I don't know what's going on with you, but I'm not about to let you take it out on me."

"Seriously. You're more upset with her than me and Mercedes, and we're the ones that called you out on your shit," Infinity said.

Ignoring Infinity's statement, Yandi grabbed a hundred-dollar bill from her wallet and tossed it onto the table before storming away.

"What the fuck was that?" Mercedes released a hard breath before chuckling.

"I have no idea," Lei replied, pulling her wallet out as well. As far as she was concerned, their evening together was over. The last thing she wanted to do was to be out involved in drama. She did enough arguing and going back and forth every time she was in a courtroom. "I'm going to head out too, though. Y'all be safe."

Absently, Lei hugged both women before leaving. When she made it outside and saw Yandi in her car, animatedly talking on the phone, Lei rolled her eyes and chuckled as she walked to her car. She had no idea what was going on with her friend, but she hoped Yandi got it together—soon.

🖤🖤🖤

It seemed Londen could feel when Lei was having a bad day. That evening, he had flowers, cash, and jewelry delivered with a note that said he'd be calling her at eight. Lei had never been more anxious for the sun to start to set. She hated to talk about the petty happenings within her friend group, but Lei had to get her mind off Yandi before she could truly focus on Londen. By the time she was done telling him about how distant and unlike herself Yandi had been acting and how she'd almost bit her head off earlier, Londen was sighing heavily into the receiver.

"I didn't want to tell you this, but I need you to be aware of the energy and intentions that's around you."

Lei's heart skipped a beat. She clutched the teddy bear Londen had gotten her tighter, sitting up in her bed.

"What is it?"

"Right after your first visit here, Yandi came to see me."

Lei's brows bunched as she tossed her feet over the side of the bed. "What? Why?"

As she paced, she listened to Londen intently. "She said she was trying to look out for me. She told me about the bet and you talking to Tussi, assuming I didn't know. Her intention was for me to stop talking to you and pursue her. I made it clear to her that wasn't going to happen and her disrespecting or hurting you wouldn't be tolerated." He paused, and Lei held on to the silence. "After that, she told Tussi who you really were and about the debt. I handled him, but he's like a dog with a bone. He thinks Ace can help him get out and go legit, so if he's been writing you more, it's because he's trying to use you to get to your father because of Yandi."

"Wow. I... don't even know what to say."

"Yes, you do. You just don't *want* to say it."

Plopping down on the edge of her bed, Lei squeezed her eyes shut as they watered. "Did you plan to share this with me had I not mentioned her?"

"No. I didn't want to plant seeds in your mind and heart, but I did tell her if you expressed the smallest amount of doubt in her, that I would tell you."

"I guess that's why she's been acting different toward me lately, but that still doesn't explain why she's been snapping on anyone else."

"If she has a plan in play that isn't going how she wants, it could explain her frustration."

"True, but what could that plan be?" Lei chuckled as she stood and began to pace again. "I hate to say this, but all Yandi cares about is her next sponsor. Unless she's trying to get you or Noah, I don't see what she could be so frustrated about."

"Well, that's not going to happen, and I can say the

same for Noah. Mercedes has my brother smitten. I haven't seen him like this in years."

Lei chuckled. "Yeah, she mentioned something about him breaking a guy's fingers so he wouldn't talk to her?"

"That was all it took for these niggas to see how serious he was about her."

"It's crazy because that's why Yandi was supposed to be setting up her account, anyway. To make sure the guys we chose for the bet weren't playing us and trying to talk to other women. Somehow, that turned into her own pursuit."

"I know that's your friend, but you need to watch her, Lei." Lei. That was the first time Londen had ever called her by her real name. "When a person is used to getting what they want and that stops, they become desperate to do whatever it takes to win. You don't have to worry about me entertaining her. I haven't spoken to her since that day, but watch her, and be steadfast in keeping yourself safe—physically, mentally, and emotionally."

Londen had given Lei a lot to think about. Some answers were given, but now, she had even more questions...

thirty-two

Lei

"BEHAVIOR IS COMMUNICATION, Princess. You might not like what her actions are saying, but you need to listen to them, anyway."

That was Cashmere, and she was saying everything Lei needed but didn't want to hear. It wasn't her intention to talk to her mother about Yandi when she made it to her parents' home, but she was so disturbed by the fact that

Yandi hadn't been answering any of her calls that she talked about it to herself and Cashmere chimed in.

She was supposed to be going to grab sushi with her father, but her appetite was getting smaller and smaller.

"You're right. Her ignoring my calls is all I need to hear from her right now. I don't know... A part of me wanted to give Yandi the benefit of the doubt. I do trust Londen, but I was hoping, because she's my friend, that there would have been more to the story."

"Based on what you know about Yandi, if this situation was happening with someone else, what do you think she would say to you about it?"

Lei couldn't accept the fact that Yandi would do this to her. The more she talked to her mother, the more Lei realized that was the problem. She'd broken her rule of never overplaying her position in someone's life. Whether they were best friends or not, Lei had a great understanding of Yandi's character and the kind of person she was. If she wanted Londen, them being friends wouldn't stop her from going after what she wanted.

"She would say that she's more loyal to herself than anyone else. And that she's going to do whatever it takes to secure what she wants."

"Okay," Cashmere said softly, covering Lei's hand with hers. "So if her actions and behavior have said that in the past, are you confident enough in your knowing of her to trust that that's exactly how she feels about you now?"

"I can't even say those words, Ma. Yandi was the first woman I connected with here. What is it about me that makes women treat me this way?"

"Oh, baby, it's not you." Cashmere pulled Lei into her arms. "It's not you at all."

"It has to be, because why else would this keep happening?"

"Do you trust Infinity?"

"Yes."

"Do you think she would do something like this to you?"

"Never."

"That proves you can pick good women to have in your life. You didn't choose to grow up with Regal. Some people are just... too selfish or too evil to care more about anyone than themselves. Your responsibility is not to avoid them, because we honestly never know. Your responsibility is to remove them from your life when they show you who they really are. Not all people with ill intentions are so open about it like Yandi. Because she is, you have the ability to protect yourself from anything she might try to do to you. Cut that girl off, right now, Lei."

Nodding, Lei wiped a quick tear before it could fall.

"You're right. Thanks, Ma."

When Lei sat upright, their conversation continued to shift. They talked about Cade and the trial, and how Lei couldn't wait for it to be over. Cade had come over after her time with Londen, and she was clear headed enough to talk things through. Though Lei still didn't like how Cade was portraying her client, she could admit that it was her responsibility to paint a better picture in order to prove Garrett's innocence.

Somehow, they started talking about Londen, though Lei didn't mention him by name. She was very careful about the details she shared about him, since her parents weren't too excited about her doing the bet.

"You know I wasn't looking for love in all of this, but in him, it has found me."

Cashmere mirrored Lei's smile. "How does it feel? To connect so closely with someone after so long."

"It's... an adjustment." Lei giggled and covered her face. "Just talking about him makes it hard for me not to smile and giggle, and I've never been that kind of woman."

"Well, real love has that effect on you... regardless of how you find it."

"I'm so scared to love him. I want to be loved by him, but the act of loving him back?" Lei released a quiet whistle as her head shook. "That scares the shit out of me, Ma."

"Why, Princess?"

"Because I know loving him is what opens the door for hurt. He's not the kind of man that would intentionally hurt me, though, I have faith in that. I just... keep telling myself he's not Steven and it's okay for me to trust and love him."

"And he's okay with that?"

"Yes. He's comfortable with us taking things slow." Her smile widened as her mind took her back to the last time they were in each other's presence. "The last time I saw him, he told me he was falling in love with me, and I just... couldn't say it back."

"Are you showing him with your actions?"

"I... don't know. He does so much for me, I don't know what to do for him in return. He says I make him smile and laugh, but that doesn't seem like enough."

"Trust me, that's more than enough. That means you increase his happiness, and for a man in his position, that's the kind of medicine he needs. And it doesn't hurt to ask him how you can return his energy and make him feel just as loved as he makes you feel."

"We actually talked about that the last time we were together. He told me his love language and what he wants and needs from a woman. I think I just want to do more because of how amazing I feel with him."

"Feel with who?" Ace asked, making his way deeper into the living room.

"No one," Lei replied, standing to give him a hug. "You ready to go?"

Ace chuckled. "You know I can find out who you're talking to with one phone call, right?"

"Yes, but I also know you wouldn't invade my privacy like that. You're going to be a healthy father with boundaries and respect my desire to wait a little longer before I tell you myself."

With a huff, Ace looked down at Cashmere, who shrugged and looked away.

"Come on, so we can go."

Lei chuckled as he walked out, and it turned into a full laugh when he looked back at them and stuck his tongue out.

"Would you like to join us?"

Cashmere's laugh died down instantly. "Really?"

"Yeah. I mean... if you don't have anything else to do."

"Oh, no." Cashmere stood, smiling widely. "I would love to. Thank you for including me, Princess."

"Of course. I don't have to include you, Ma. Whenever you want to do something, just let me know."

"I try to give you your space. I know your relationship with Jennifer was strained and it effects our relationship too."

"That's true, but I think you've been a little bit too lenient and understanding."

Though Lei chuckled, she was slightly irritated by that truth. She wasn't upset with her mother; she was upset with herself for not speaking up sooner. When she first came to Rose Valley Hills, her parents were at her side daily. It didn't take long before how she was raised by Marcus, or Hamilton, and Jennifer started to affect her relationship with her real parents. Therapy only compounded that issue.

In Cashmere's efforts to give Lei the space she needed to heal and move on from what they'd done to her, their relationship became more surface level than Lei would have liked for it to be. She'd gotten far closer to Ace, because of how safe she felt with Marcus when it came down to Jennifer. Regardless, Cashmere had been nothing but loving and kind toward Lei, and they both deserved a closer, more open relationship.

There were so many things, like men and friends, that she wished she could talk to her mother about. Her father and brother were solution focused. Any problem she had, all they cared about was creating a logical solution. They hadn't mastered the concept of emotional venting or talking just to get things out.

"What do you mean?" Cashmere asked, opening her crossed arms, and Lei appreciated the gesture of openness.

"I get why you don't try harder to connect with me, but I wish you would. I know I have my issues, our conversation today is proof that I still have work to do, but you're my mother. It would mean the world to be able to talk to you like this and spend time with you more often. I love Daddy and Cade, but I love you too, Ma. I want us to be closer."

As tears filled Cashmere's eyes, she pulled Lei into her arms. The embrace held all the warmth and security she needed.

"I love you too, Lei. I always have, and I always will. I didn't know you felt this way, but now that I do, Mama's gonna take it from here."

Cashmere's declaration caused Lei to melt in her mother's arms, and in that moment, her issues with Yandi completely left her mind.

thirty-three

Londen

"LEAVE THE CAR RUNNING," Londen commanded.

He was officially a free man, and the first person he wanted to see was Lei. As hard as it was to wait for her to get home, Londen did. It didn't seem wise to go to her office to see her publicly until they discussed how they would handle their relationship. Besides, Londen was adamant about speaking to Ace first. With the major secret he was keeping from Lei, they needed to discuss how they were going to handle that as soon as possible.

As anxious as Londen was to see Lei, he couldn't stick around long. He had a lot to do in preparation of the new life he was about to live. Since she was going to be a big part of that, Londen had to get ready. He appreciated Lei rocking with him while he was behind bars, and she would be rewarded for it, but things were going to be a hell of a lot different going forward. Women like Lei deserved the world, and Londen had every intent of giving her as much of it as he possibly could.

His driver, Keith, closed the door of Londen's Bentley after he stepped out of it. Some things still hadn't changed, and Londen had no intentions of driving himself around unless he absolutely had to. As he made his way to Lei's front door, he pulled in a deep breath.

Would Lei be happy he was out? Yes. What Londen was concerned about was how she would handle his proximity. It was no secret to him that she had demons from past hurt that kept her from fully surrendering to their bond. He'd never been the type of man to half ass anything, and that would include his pursuit of her. All Londen could do was hope that didn't cause a rift between them, because he was coming for her... and Londen was the kind of man that *always* got what he wanted.

After ringing the doorbell, Londen took a step back. He didn't realize he was holding his breath until she opened the door and became his release. Lei's eyes widened and she squealed. Just as she was about to jump into his arms, she stopped herself.

"I don't want to mess up your 'fit."

"Woman, fuck this shit." Londen tugged her close as he told her, "Come here."

If the choice was having her close or wrinkling the silk short-sleeved shirt he had tucked inside of his slacks, he'd choose her *every* fucking time.

"What are you doing here?" Lei asked, cupping the back of his neck and looking into his eyes.

"I'm out."

Her lips formed an *O* as she inquisitively looked his face over. Seconds passed as she processed his words.

"You're out? Of prison?"

Londen chuckled. "Yes, Baby. Your man is officially out on parole."

"Yay! Oh my God, babe! I'm so, so happy for you!" Her grip around him tightened, and Londen didn't mind at all. "Come in…"

Between the seductive tone of her voice and way she looked into his eyes, Londen wanted nothing more, but he had to resist.

"I can't. I wanted to stop by and let you know I was out, but I have a lot of things to do before I'm worthy of you."

As he placed Lei on her feet, she chuckled. Her hands rested on her hips as she looked behind him toward the Bentley.

"I don't understand."

"I know I did a lot for you while I was locked down to prove you wouldn't regret talking to a man in prison, but now that I'm out, I have to come harder."

She released an irritated sigh and rolled her eyes. "Londen…"

"Regardless of what you say, I'm a man, Baby. I have to be at a certain place in my life to be worthy of you. When I get to that point, I promise I'll be coming back here for you."

With a pout, Lei hugged him. "How long is this going to take?"

"Shouldn't take long. My staff is already in place, and I've been making money for the last decade. Just... need to have a few conversations and make a few moves, then I swear... I'm coming back for you."

Londen lifted her head and kissed her. The kiss was long and leisurely, lazy yet precise. So precise it had Lei reaching between his thighs and rubbing his hardened dick.

"Now you can't kiss me like that and leave me."

Londen groaned, feeling his dick harden against her even more. "I promise I'll be worth the wait."

"You always are." She gave him a sweet, quick kiss before softly pushing him backward. "Hurry up and go so you can hurry up and come back."

Londen shot her a wink, then walked away. He was even more motivated to handle his business. His arms craved having her wrapped inside, and his dick was begging to be smothered by her pussy.

♥♥♥

Ace stared at Londen in disbelief, which was not the reaction Londen expected him to have.

"It was you? All this time... you're the man that my daughter has been pining over?"

Londen's head bobbed once. "I have no reason to be facetious or fictitious, Ace."

"I know that I'm just..." Ace's head shook as he stared blankly. "I'm confused. How did me asking you to make sure the wrong man didn't connect with my daughter lead to you dating her?"

"You wanted her with a man who was worthy of her. A man who was righteous."

"Yes... that's true."

"So, who was a better man for her than me?"

Ace released a bark of laughter, then stood. He reached into the top drawer of his desk and set an old school pistol that, admittedly, was sexy as hell to Londen on top of it. His gun of choice proved the kind of calculated man he was—ensuring no shell casings would be left behind.

"Was it your intention to finesse me when I sought your help?"

"Not at all. I signed up for a profile to keep an eye out for her. I figured by studying her, I would know the kind of men who would want to pursue her. We matched, which was unexpected, and started talking. From our first letter, I was hooked."

Ace scratched the side of his head as he sat on the corner of his desk. "Does she know about Hamilton?"

"No, that's why I'm here now. Out of respect for you, I didn't tell her."

"But you're going to?"

"Eventually... yes. Before things become official between us, I have to tell her the truth."

Ace breathed deeply as his head shook. "I would appreciate a heads up before you told her, so I can prepare. I don't know how Lei is going to react when she learns I had Hamilton killed. She should know I would do anything to protect her and her mother, but that was the man she once considered her father."

"Look... I won't suggest I know Lei better than you, but I can say that I know her more intimately than you. We've talked about that situation a few times now, and each time, she lets me in on how it hurt or changed her. She's going to be upset, but she will understand. I'm not concerned about her being upset with you; I'm concerned about her holding it against me. You might have ordered the hit, but I'm the one that pulled the trigger."

"Then why tell her at all? If you fear this will cause a rift between you two..."

Londen's head shook as he sat up in his seat. "Nah, I'm not keeping this from her. She's been lied to and left in the dark enough. I'm not going to be another man who does that to her."

"But I was, huh?"

With a shrug, Londen stood. "Yeah, you were. You had your reasons and I respect you for it. I would do the same thing if I was in your position. Still, that doesn't make keeping this from her right. She deserves to know the truth, even if it hurts. I'd rather hurt her temporarily with the truth than do irrevocable damage because she finds out after we've been married with kids."

"Married with kids? Things are that serious between you two?"

Before Londen could stop it, a smile was spreading his lips. "For me, they are. I'll let her discuss that with you when she's ready. My intentions with your daughter are pure, though."

"I believe that." Ace stood. "You see what happens when anyone hurts her, so I'm not worried about you doing the same." Standing directly in front of Londen, Ace added, "Should that change, you know what your fate will be."

"I respect and accept that, and I will give you a heads up before I tell her the truth."

"Good. What are your plans now that you're out?"

"Honestly, sir, that's what I'm still figuring out. You

know how it is. I have a path I want to take, but it's not the one my family and friends are on."

"Well... you need to take the path that leads to your security and happiness, especially if you plan to be with my daughter." Ace returned to his seat behind his desk. "I know your father is still in the business and the Gabriels are too. Because you are so close to them, the temptation will be heavy. Do what's best for you, and you know you can always come back to the secret society permanently."

With a bob of his head, Londen said, "I appreciate the offer and will keep that in mind."

As he walked out, Londen considered if that was something he wanted to do. Realistically, he didn't have to work, so whatever he spent his days doing would have to be something he loved. The businesses he'd invested in over the years offered him a steady flow of residual income. This was an opportunity for him to do what he loved with food, but Londen didn't know if he would be fully satisfied with that.

Before he got locked up, his days were filled with excitement and adrenaline. Would he get the same pleasure from cooking? And even if he didn't, would that be a bad thing? Londen had to figure it out soon because he did not want to keep Lei waiting.

thirty-four

Yandi

MARCH

As much as Yandi didn't want to admit it, Tussi was right. For the last two weeks, she'd been ignoring Lei. The last time the pair saw each other, Yandi had gotten really close to taking her frustration out on Lei. It had never been

Yandi's intention to let her envy of Mercedes and Lei's lifestyle get the best of her, but them finding and connecting with men in prison who were better than the free men Yandi entertained seemed to be her breaking point.

The longer she ruminated on the extravagance of being spoiled by a rich nigga, the more infuriated Yandi became. There was a sense of loyalty that Yandi had toward Lei because she was the first woman in her life that accepted her just as she was. That loyalty, however, didn't outweigh Yandi's loyalty to herself. Before she could stop it, a seed of resentment was planted in her heart, and talking to Tussi only made it grow larger. Grace had Yandi avoiding Lei. No matter how she felt, she didn't want to get on bad terms with her best friend over something so silly. But she was becoming so hypnotized by hate that she was willing to do just about anything to make herself feel better, even if that meant betraying Lei.

"This might be a flawed way of thinking to a lot of people, but I'ma keep it a hunnid with you," Tussi continued, since Yandi was still silently pondering what he'd said. "At the end of the day, you gotta fall in love with yourself and your life. Regardless of who comes and goes, you gotta spend the rest of yo' life witchu. If you ain't pleased with who you are and what you got, life gon' be miserable as hell for you. I know you might not want to go against ya girl, but life is good enough for her. Don't worry about her. She got it made. You need to do what's best for you."

Yandi's head lowered, and her tears rapidly began to pour. "I didn't want to like your ass, but you get me. You're honestly perfect for me. If you weren't locked up, we could shake the world up."

"I feel the same way about yo schemin' ass." Yandi

chuckled, and Tussi followed behind. "For real, though. I do care about you, Yandi. We're one and the same. A lot of motherfuckers might not get you, but I do. And I'm telling you what you need to do. Humble yourself for the time being and make shit right with you and Lei. She's the key to me getting out of here, and when I am, it won't be a limit for us."

"I don't know, Tussi. If they find out about what I'm up to, I'm going to lose all my girls. I need you to guarantee me that this shit is going to work."

"Mane, fuck them. I promise it's going to work, and when it does, I can get out and get back to the money like I was before I got locked down. I'ma take care of you. You ain't gon' have to worry about nothing else."

Yandi thought about it for a second before agreeing with, "Aight. I'll do it."

"Cool. Get in there and act like ain't shit changed. I'll hit you up tomorrow."

"Okay."

After disconnecting the call, Yandi wiped her face and put a few eyedrops in her eyes. She retouched her makeup and applied a new layer of perfume before getting out of her car. The sooner she got Tussi out of prison, the better. The man she was dealing with now was paying her bills, but he wanted companionship in return. Usually, Yandi would be cool with that, but she was so disinterested in him, she could barely fake the funk.

The only reason she knew what her friends were up to was because Mercedes told her where she was headed, but she didn't extend an invitation for Yandi to join them. Yandi didn't blame her. Seeing as she hadn't spoken to Lei, it wouldn't be right for her to invite her to her home. Apparently, Lei was wrapping up a case and wanted to enjoy herself before giving her closing statement in the morning. This case had garnered a lot of attention, so Lei didn't want to be seen out drinking or doing anything else before the case was over.

Yandi knew it was risky just showing up, but she figured this would be the only way to get Lei to talk to her and hear her out fully. Last Yandi heard, Londen was out but he wasn't spending any time with Lei. If she was going to get back in Lei's good graces, she'd need to do so before Londen started coming around more often. Even if he didn't tell Lei about her visit, the vibe between them would be off, and eventually Lei would question why. She'd need to get her best friend back on her side and make sure no matter what Londen said Lei wouldn't believe him.

It took a second, but once Yandi knocked, Lei came to answer. It was clear her presence had caught Lei off guard because she gasped and jerked her head back. Gripping the door tighter, Lei looked around to make sure Yandi was alone.

"Hey," Yandi greeted. "Can we talk?"

Chuckling, Lei rolled her tongue around her cheek. "It's been weeks, Yandi, *now* you want to talk?"

"I needed time to get myself together. I wasn't in a good space, Lei, but I am now. So can we talk?"

"Yes, but not right now. I'm at the end of a very important case, and I don't need any distractions. Can I call you when it's over?"

"Yeah, sure. And um… good luck on the case."

"Thanks," Lei muttered quietly before stepping back and slowly closing the door.

That wasn't the reaction Yandi expected, but she wasn't

surprised. When Lei was deep in a case, she tried her hardest to maintain her focus. As long as she was willing to talk, that was all Yandi needed. Besides, waiting would give her more time to practice her story. The more believable she made it sound... the better.

thirty-five

Londen

BY HIS MOTHER'S REQUEST, Londen stopped by for dinner before going to chill with the Gabriel brothers. Londen hadn't planned to be so distant when he got out, but the conversation he had with Ace had been heavy on his mind. If he was going to live life differently, he'd need to make different choices and moves. As much as he loved hanging with the Gabriel brothers and the crew, it was too risky. Not only were they heavy in the streets, but a lot of them were reckless as hell. A fun night out could instantly be ruined because of one look or someone stepping on their shoe.

Londen felt the same way when it came down to his father. Before Londen's release, Simpson was adamant about how much work they could get done once he got out. It didn't seem to matter how much Londen said he was out of the game, Simpson believed it was just a phase.

It didn't help that he was missing Lei like crazy. So far, Londen had gotten a lot done. He'd checked in on all of his business investments, paid for his favorite beach suite at The Rose Valley Hotel, and met with all of his attorneys and financial advisors. Harem, his mother, urged him to stay with them, but Londen wanted his own space... and a small space at that. Too many rooms increased his anxiety. Plus, a lot of habits he'd started while in prison would inconvenience others, so he simply preferred staying by himself.

The only other thing Londen wanted to do was make sure his standing in Rose Valley Hills was still good. The last thing he wanted was for enemies to try to cause issues while he was with Lei. Alternating between Memphis and Rose Valley Hills for the bulk of his life had given him popularity in both places. Lei was the only thing keeping him in The Hills. If it wasn't for her, he would have stayed in Memphis the moment he was released.

Londen had already gotten his plan together for when he returned to Lei's life. He couldn't wait for the next three days to pass so he could see her. Now that he was released, he'd reconnected with her brother. Cade had his dealings with the Gabriel brothers, but he didn't come around as much as he used to. He was more strait laced than most in the crew, but it hadn't always been that way.

What Londen still hadn't pieced together was why Ace

had caught a body with a gun he'd used for other hits through others. Something was off with that, and it hadn't set well within Londen for the past ten years. Ace wasn't that reckless, and that was evident by the piece he had at his office. If Londen had to guess, he'd say Cade was the one who caught the body and Ace was covering for him.

Even if that was the case, Ace would never admit it. Cade had a lot to lose if he was ever charged with murder. Both men did actually. Londen could respect Ace taking the blame for his son, though, and now that he'd done time for the murder, it would never lead to a charge for either of them.

Pushing those thoughts out of his head, Londen opened the door to his parents' home. Immediately, the sound of juke joint music filled his ears. His nostrils flared as he inhaled the scent of soul food coming from the kitchen. Londen's steps increased in pace, hoping he could get a sample of whatever she was cooking.

"Damn, Ma. You got it smelling good as hell in here."

Harem's head tilted as she prepared for the kiss he always gave her on the cheek.

"It'll be ready in about fifteen minutes."

"What you got done that I can taste now?"

Harem chuckled as she stirred the cream sauce that she hadn't taken her eyes off. "Nothing. You know I don't allow tasting until it's done."

Though Londen sucked his teeth, he didn't bother arguing with her. Harem had been that way since he was a kid. Sitting at the island, Londen looked around the kitchen. He remembered a simpler time in the ghetto, wishing they could have a home that was as big as this kitchen. My... how times had changed.

"You talked to Matthew?" he checked.

"Not today. Probably won't call until the weekend."

"He good though?"

"As good as he can be. You know he doesn't have it as easy in there as you did."

Londen's eyes rolled toward the ceiling. He hated having these kinds of conversations with his mother. For whatever reason, she expected him to suffer while he was in prison just because his brother didn't have as much freedom as he did. As far as Londen was concerned, he'd earned the lifestyle he lived while locked up and his brother hadn't. It was Matthew's choice to avoid making connections, and it was also Matthew's choice to blow through all of his money and not invest. Granted, his family made sure he was straight, Matthew was a proud man. It was only so much that he would allow them to do.

"Where Pops at?" Londen asked, standing from his seat.

"Where he always is." She chuckled. "In the attic with them old records."

That got a genuine smile out of Londen. His father was just like him. They didn't like large spaces. Out of their eight-thousand square foot home, Simpson spent the bulk of his time in the closet-sized attic listening to his vinyl records. Londen was grateful that Simpson finally had enough money to live such an easy life. He wished his father would leave the streets behind, but the addiction of that lifestyle was hard to shake.

Londen made his way upstairs and knocked before stepping into the small space. Simpson stood and the two embraced.

"Wassup, son?"

"Can't call it. You good?"

"Yeah, I'm good. You gon' be here long?"

"Long enough to eat and chill for a little minute. I'm meeting up with the Gabriels later."

Simpson nodded and picked up his beer. "You want one?" he asked, pointing to the cooler that was next to his left leg. Londen extended his hand and accepted the beer his father offered. Before he could relax fully and take a swig, his father was saying, "I'm glad you're here, because there's something we need to talk about."

Though Londen had an idea of what his father was about to say, he wanted to give Simpson the benefit of the doubt.

"What's on your mind?"

"How long is this... going legit phase going to last?"

Before Londen could stop himself, he was releasing a frustrated breath. "Pops..."

"You were running things for me before you left. I don't trust anyone on my team the way I trust you. I need your mind. We could be making millions a month if you invested a little bit of time into this."

"Pops, if you can't trust your team the way you trust me, you need a new team."

"No, I need my son."

This was exactly what Londen was trying to avoid. He hated that his father even wanted to put him in this position, but it shouldn't have been a surprise.

"I would think you would want me to go legit. Ain't no amount of money worth me going back in, Pops. I'm sorry."

Londen stood, prepared to leave. At that point, he didn't care to spend time with either of his parents anymore. Love was one thing, respect was another. Every time they forced conversations on him they knew he wanted no part of, it made Londen desire closeness with them even less.

"I'll give you a month," Simpson said as Londen opened

the door. "Once you're out for a month or so, you'll be bored and want back in. When you do, I'll be here."

Not bothering to respond, Londen left as he shook his head. He wasn't even excited about the meal anymore because he'd lost his appetite.

thirty-six

Lei

THE WEEK HAD STARTED to go by in a blur. It took the jurors thirty-six hours to decide they couldn't decide. When they went before the judge, it was to let him know they were deadlocked. The judge declared a mistrial, and as much as Lei wanted a verdict of not guilty, she accepted it as a win. Cade surprised her but also reminded her of the kind of man he was when he told her he would not pursue a second trial. To celebrate, he threw a party and Lei went and thoroughly enjoyed herself.

After the great night she had, she had an even greater morning when Londen called and told her he had a surprise for her. He started her day having a private chef fix her breakfast, and she informed her she'd be making her lunch and dinner as well. Lei completed her meal and had a quick workout session before ending it with a swim.

Lunch was when things took an even better turn. Three women came over, who catered to her for hours in her spa. Her braids were taken out, and her natural hair was treated and styled in loose curls that came down to her bra before it was rolled. She was given a massage and mani-pedi that almost put her to sleep. The last thing was a session with a personal stylist that allowed her to pick out a week's worth of outfits for whatever Londen had planned.

By the time the chef returned to fix dinner, Lei was seated comfortably in her favorite Balencia bronze chaise lounge chair, ready to go to sleep. She didn't think anything could top what Londen had done... until he arrived. Lei was so relaxed her eyes were half shut. Once they settled on him, they opened fully.

"I'm not in the mood to be toyed with," Lei said, sitting up. "If you're not here for good, you need to go, Londen."

With that sexy ass chuckle she'd fallen in love with, Londen stuffed his hands into his pockets and slowly sauntered in her direction.

"I'm here for good. Can I stay?"

"Mhm," she agreed, lifting her arms for him. She'd been waiting two weeks to have him in her arms again.

Londen didn't waste any time picking her up and wrapping her legs around him. He sat in the lounge chair, keeping her legs wrapped around him.

"You're feisty when you want to be."

"You ain't seen nothing yet."

After placing a soft kiss to her lips, Londen told her, "I missed you."

"I missed you too. Thank you for today. It was so relaxing I was almost sleep."

"It's not over yet. We're going to have dinner, then head to the airport. That's why I told her to have you choose a lounge set to put on tonight."

Lei eyed him skeptically. "Where are we going?"

"New York, if you're willing. I know you have a thing about traveling, so if you don't want to, we don't have to, but I tried to make plans that would ensure your comfort. We'll be flying in a private jet, so you won't have to worry about crowds or sitting around for hours, and the hotel we're staying at is immaculate. The suite will have its own kitchen and gym, so we won't have to leave the room for anything but shopping if you don't want to."

Her mouth hung open as she smiled.

"Where are we going?"

"The Plaza."

Lei swatted his chest as she gasped. "Don't tell me you got the royal three-bedroom suite!"

"So you know it?"

"I do! I always said I'd go there to celebrate something really special. Fifty thousand a night is a pretty penny to spend just because."

"Well, I'm on that type of time, so get used to this kind of living if you're going to be with me."

His words caused her walls to throb as a low hum escaped her throat.

"I love the sound of that."

Leaning forward, Lei connected their lips, and it was

like her bottom set knew the routine. They were wet and ready by the time Londen had lowered her pants and panties. As soon as their centers were one, they both released content sighs. Lei rode him with a medium pace, vocally expressing the pleasure having him inside of her was building.

"Damn," Londen muttered. "Look at you. I wish I could watch you ride this dick forever."

"Now you can."

She smiled, but it turned into a sexy giggle when he hugged her close. His hand slipped down her cheeks and settled between them. As his finger massaged her ass hole, Lei moaned as her body heated. Londen sucked her nipple, causing her toes to curl and back to arch. Her pleasure fueled him to provide more. Londen was truly the best lover she'd ever had, and Lei couldn't wait to explore him even more.

thirty-seven

Londen

SEVEN DAYS Later

> Londen: I'm about to tell her.
>
> Ace: Thanks for the heads up.

ACE'S TIMING WAS PERFECT. Keith had just pulled into Lei's driveway, and Londen didn't want to end their time together without telling her the truth. The last week with her in New York was better than Londen expected. They got to know each other better, had a lot of nasty sex, and spent a hell of a lot of money in the shops on 5th Avenue. There wasn't anything about their time together that Londen would change... except it ending. If he had it his way, they would have stayed in their own little bubble in that suite forever.

Unfortunately, Lei had to get back to work, and Londen had to tie up a few loose ends. Word had gotten to him through Noah that Simpson was retiring men in his organization. The act in itself wasn't bad... the reason behind it was. Apparently, he'd been going around talking about how his son was home and preparing to take over. Londen was no fool. His father was trying to force him back in the business. He knew how Londen's mind worked. If Londen was aware of him getting rid of people, that would run the risk of more things going wrong. Someone would have to step up to run things, and it would have to be Simpson or Londen.

Simpson was a lot of things, but a man capable of running a seven-figure drug empire was not one. The most Simpson had done correctly was invest his money into product and workers. Things ran smoothly because of who Simpson employed, not because of anything he did himself. There was no telling how horribly wrong things would turn out if Simpson had to start making decisions and moves.

As much as Londen hated the move his father made, he respected it. Simpson was just like him—a man who was determined to always have his way. One of them would have to fold, though, and Londen was confident it wouldn't be him.

Before he could focus on his father, Londen had to get

the truth off his chest. As much as he wanted to make things official with Lei while they were gone, he couldn't. He'd never want her to feel as if he manipulated her into a relationship. Even if the truth meant their time together was over, at least Londen's integrity would remain intact.

Getting out of the Urus, Londen took slow steps toward the front door with Lei as Keith grabbed her bags.

"Why do you look so sad?" She gripped his chin, forcing his attention down to her.

"I am," Londen admitted, and the sight of her pout made him smile.

"Why, babe?"

"We'll talk when we get inside."

Lei clutched her chest. "You're scaring me."

"It's... it's bad, but... I don't think it's something you can't handle."

"Oh, God. Okay."

Londen didn't mean to alarm her, but he couldn't lie to her. Plus, they were seconds away from being inside, then she'd know the truth. Londen waited until Keith had her bags inside and was closing the door behind himself to say, "I don't want to go too far inside. You'll want me to leave after you hear what I have to say."

Lei chuckled, lifting her hands as her head shook softly. "Okay. What is going on, Londen? Do you have a family somewhere or something?"

"What? Of course not. Why is that the first thing you would think?"

"What else am I supposed to think? There isn't anything else that could warrant this reaction."

Londen pulled in a deep breath. "I killed Hamilton. Marcus. Whatever you want to call him. Your father ordered the hit, but I carried it out. I killed him, Lei."

Lei's mouth moved but remained silent from surprise. It looked like she was fumbling over her thoughts, blinking rapidly.

With an unfocused gaze, she asked, "You killed my father?" A quick no jerked her head. "You killed Marcus?"

"Yes. I didn't know who he was or why. Ace offered the deal, and I took it."

Clutching her throat, she looked away from him. "When did you find out?"

"In January, right after you told your family about the bet. Ace called and asked me to look out for you on the inside. Make sure you didn't connect with the wrong kind of character. I asked him then if you were the reason he ordered the hit when he mentioned his daughter. Up until then, I hadn't heard anything about you being back."

"So you... you started talking to me... because of my father?"

"Not at all, Baby." Londen took her hands into his, but she quickly pulled them away. "He told me to keep an eye out for niggas will ill intent, that's it. I matched with you because I was curious, and I pursued you because I wanted you."

Lei licked her lips and palmed her forehead. "Okay. Um... this is a lot. I need time to process this."

"Yeah... of course. You know how to get in contact with me when you're ready, and if you never are..." Londen used her chin to nudge her face in his direction. "I've enjoyed spending the last few months getting to know you." Her eyes sealed shut. "Everything I've said and done has been sincere. I want to spend my life with you, but if this is too much, I understand."

All she did was nod and gently push his hand down from her chin. Lei turned her back to him quickly, but he heard her sniffles when he opened the door. As much as Londen wanted to console her, he couldn't. Walking away from her was the hardest thing he'd ever done. She deserved time and space to process his actions, even if they were done before they met.

thirty-eight

Lei

SHE'D NEVER DRIVEN SO QUICKLY and recklessly in her life. Lei hadn't even bothered to cut the car off before she was hopping out of it. It was in park, and in that moment, that was the best she could do. Tumbling through the front door, Lei charged toward her father's den, sure that was where she'd find him. As soon as she burst through the door, the stark difference between their energies was evident.

While she was a massive ball of fire, he was calm and still.

"Is it true?" she asked through gritted teeth, chest heaving. "Did you hire Londen to kill my father?"

"*I'm* your father."

"You know what I mean!" she yelled. "Did you?"

Ace wiped his eye and sat back in his recliner. "Yes, I did. And I don't regret it at all."

With a chuckle, Lei ran her fingers through her hair. "How could you?"

"He took you from us. Did you really think I was going to let him get away with that?"

As she considered his words, she felt foolish. Did she really think he was going to let him get away with that? For some reason, she did. When nothing happened to Marcus immediately, Lei figured Ace would let it ride. It was smart of him to wait a month because no one considered he was involved. Technically, he wasn't. He had Londen, the man she was falling in love with, to do his dirty work.

"Why didn't you tell me?"

"I didn't want it to come between us. We had to learn each other. Me killing him would have ruined that."

She laughed as her eyes rolled. Nostrils flaring, Lei squeezed her chest. It felt like her heart was about to burst. All she wanted to do was run to Londen so he could make her feel better, but this was his doing. Sure, he didn't know he was killing the man that kidnapped her... and how crazy was she to be upset because he did? Father figure or not, what Marcus had done was wrong, and even if he hadn't been murdered, he would have paid.

"Did you plan on telling me at all?"

For the first time, Ace looked away from her. Slowly, his head shook. "No, I didn't. I didn't want to hurt you. I know that makes me like him in a sense, keeping something from you of importance, but that wasn't something I felt you needed to know. Londen wanted to tell you because he felt you needed the truth before you committed to him. But if it was up to me... no, Princess. I wouldn't have told you at all."

"He wanted me to know?" she asked softly, feeling some of her fire diminish.

Ace stood and slowly walked toward her, but he left a couple of feet of space between them, and Lei appreciated that.

"He did. He said you deserved to know the truth and that he wouldn't be another man who kept it from you." At the sound of that, Lei's tears began to fall. Ace reached in her direction, but she lifted her hands and kept him from consoling her. "If you blame anyone, blame me. Don't blame him. Londen handled this the best way he could. He held the truth while he was in prison to ensure he could protect you the way I requested, but he told you as soon as he could. He did not know who you were ten years ago, Lei, so please... if you want to be with that man... don't hold this against him."

"How can I not? He killed my..." Her voice broke. Looking away, Lei wiped her face. "I know you're my father, but Marcus was too. And as fucked up as what he and Jennifer did was, that little girl inside of me always longed for their love, validation, and acceptance. As much as I wish I could stop that, I can't. So it's really fucking with me to know that you had him murdered. Like... that's not okay, Daddy. Not at *all*."

His chin lowered to his chest, removing eye contact. Ace's sagging posture straightened, but his toneless responses continued when he said, "I respect that. I know it's going to take you some time to accept what I did..."

"I will *never* accept what you did. Are you kidding me?"

"Fine. You might not accept it, but this is not going to ruin our relationship. I've already lost twenty-six years with you, Lei. I'm not missing out on anymore time. So whatever I have to do to fix this, I will."

Her mouth opened, but she was in such a state of disbelief that nothing came out. Releasing a low chuckle, Lei weakly left the room... grateful her mother hadn't heard their exchange. Otherwise, she'd want her to stay and try to hash things out. In that moment, all Lei wanted to do was sleep—and that made her feel like she was finding out about Steven and Regal, along with being kidnapped all over again.

thirty-nine

Londen

AS HAPPY AS Londen was to see his sister, he couldn't devote too much of himself to anything she was saying and doing. She'd been in town for two days, and already, she'd already set up a YouTube channel and social media pages for his cooking. Megan had also created a schedule for him and connected him with a photographer and social media manager. Both would come over when he was cooking to take pictures and videos of his dishes, then set them up on his profiles and channels. Londen had gone this long without being on social media and he didn't want to change that now.

"Where's your head, Londen?" Megan asked, bumping his shoulder with hers.

He hadn't even realized when she'd come out to the patio with him. What Londen loved about his suite was that the bedroom and living room had large views of the beach. Every time he stepped out onto the patio or went down to the beach, peace consumed him. Londen was so excited to experience this with Lei after hearing about how much she loved Sausalito, and now, he wasn't sure if he'd ever have the chance.

"Lei," was all he offered.

"Have you heard from her yet?"

Londen continued to look straight ahead as he shook his head. "Nah. I haven't tried to call or text her. I want to give her space."

"That's a good idea, but you should still let her know you're here. Just a simple text to remind her makes all the difference in the world."

With a sigh, Londen considered his sister's words. Though his parents knew he was seeing someone, no one had met Lei. Hell, they hadn't had a chance. As soon as they came back from New York, it was over before it could even begin. Maybe it was best that way. The last thing he wanted was to create an image of a happily ever after fairytale that would never come to fruition.

"I'll see."

"Boy, text that girl!" As she punched him in his arm, Londen chuckled.

"Aight, aight. Damn. But if she tells me not to reach out to her anymore, that's on you."

"And I'll take that charge, but if you were as close as you said you were, and she has the character you described, she's not going to say that."

Londen looked at his sister for a few seconds before pulling his phone out of his pocket.

> Londen: Just want you to know I'm waiting for you. I'm ready whenever you are.

To Londen's surprise, Lei texted him back and told him to send her his location. As soon as he did, he texted her the room number.

"She's on her way," he said in disbelief.

"See! I told you. You owe me."

"Mhm." Londen wrapped his arm around her shoulders. "I'm glad you're home, sis."

"I am too. It wasn't the same without y'all. Without you. You kept me sane growing up with the crazies."

Londen chuckled, but he couldn't really argue with his sister. Their parents had an unnatural way of raising them, evident by his father's insistence that he export drugs. They gave way more freedom than Londen believed they should. He loved it in his younger days, but eventually, he started to crave structure. One thing his parents didn't play about was their education. Even with them being in the streets, Simpson still wanted his sons to get a degree.

"Have you let them know you're here yet?"

"I told them today, and they want us to come over."

"I'm not tryna deal with their asses tonight."

"Duh, that's why they want me to get you to come. They know you can't say no to me."

"I'on know about all that, Meg. The last time I went over there, it was one blow after another. I'm not trying to spend my days dealing with that toxic shit. If they can't accept my choices and the way I live, they don't have to be in my life."

"I hear you, and I respect whatever decision you make, but I think they don't understand how much that bothers you." Londen sucked his teeth and headed back inside with Megan following close behind. "Hear me out. You might tell them no, but you don't actually express your boundaries, Londen. It wasn't until I told Mama straight up, I was tired of her talking negatively about me leaving so young, and if she continued to do so, I would no longer talk to her, that she stopped. Same thing with Daddy before I left. He kept insisting that I go to the University of Memphis, and I told him whether he paid for my tuition or not, I wasn't going. When he realized I was serious, he left me alone and still paid. Tell them how you feel about what they're saying and what you expect from them, and I promise things will change."

"It might be that easy with Mama, but I don't know about Pops. There's a lot at stake right now. He's going to drill me about this until he gets his way."

"Are you going to let him?"

Londen scratched his head as he considered her question. If things were over with Lei, he had less to lose. Going back to the streets would be a good distraction. What reason would he have to live right and be legit without her?

"Honestly, sis, I don't know. A part of me wants to stand firm and stay legit. The other part of me is starting to waver."

"Well, if my opinion matters, I think you should stick to your guns and stay legit. He's been doing just fine without you. Live the life you want, Londen, and don't let him or anyone else make you shift gears."

Londen couldn't deny how happy he was to have his

sister back home. Their relationship didn't require they talk daily, but when they did, they always lifted each other up. It just so happened this time around, it was his turn to be lifted up, and he appreciated flying on her wings.

They chilled for another hour before there was a knock on the door.

"That's her," Megan whispered. "You want me to leave?"

"Let me see what she on first. Go outside."

"Outside?" Megan repeated loudly as they stood, looking just like their mother. They shared the same walnut brown skin, round faces, and thin lips. "I ain't no damn dog."

"Girl, just go chill on the patio for a second. Or go down to the beach."

"Fine," she grumbled. "But I want to meet her."

"Aight."

Londen waited until she was on the patio and had closed the door before he went to let Lei in. With his hand on the knob, he closed his eyes and took in a calming breath. As soon as he opened the door and set eyes on her, Londen released, like he always did at the sight of her.

"Hey," he spoke, opening the door wider so she could step inside.

"Hi."

Cupping her hands in front of her, Lei took small steps toward him. He allowed the door to swing shut on its own, unable to keep himself from wrapping his arms around her. Even dressed down in a sweatsuit, Lei was beautiful. Her hair was pulled into a bun and her face was lightly made. Chunky hoop earrings dangled from her ears, and the diamond crown necklace he gave her hung from her neck.

"I don't want to hold the past against you. I want to be

with you. It's going to take me some time to get over this, but we're worth the work. I'm..." Her mouth twisted to the side and eyes shifted briefly. When they landed on Megan, her brows wrinkled as her grip around him loosened. "Why didn't you tell me you had company?"

"That's my sister Megan."

"Oh. I can come back later."

"Nah." Gripping her chin, Londen regained her focus. "Finish what you were saying."

Lei's hand slid down his chest. "I was saying..." she whispered, smiling a small smile. "I'm falling in love with you. I-I am in love with you. I love you, Londen."

Her statement made him feel taller, bigger... better. Expanded lungs pulled in deep, satisfied breaths.

"Say that again." When Londen lifted her into the air, she squealed. Once he had her legs wrapped around him, Londen smacked her ass. "Baby."

"Hmm?"

"Say that shit again."

Cupping the back of his neck, Lei brushed her nose against his. "I love you."

Londen moaned as his dick throbbed. He carried her over to the patio, where he opened the door and handed his sister his wallet. "Here, get some cash and go somewhere for a few hours. Call me before you come back."

"Hi," Megan greeted with a wave. Her smile was wide and bright, and Londen knew she'd never let him forget this assist.

"Hi. I'm Lei." Lei extended her hand. "It's nice to meet you."

"You as well. Welcome to the family."

Not bothering to let them say anything else to each other, Londen carried Lei to his room. She laughed at his urgency, and Londen really didn't give a damn. After locking the door, he placed her in the middle of his bed.

"Babe, wait until she leaves."

"Fuck that. I haven't seen you in two days, and you just told me you love me." As Londen pulled her Jordans off, Lei covered her face. "You need to get off your birth control."

At the sound of his statement, Lei lowered her hands. "Huh?"

"You heard me, Baby."

"Why?"

"Didn't you say you wanted to be pregnant by the end of the year?" She nodded. "So get off your birth control."

"And you're okay with us not being married?"

He wasn't, but Londen knew that would come.

"I know your past makes it difficult for you to value that right now, even though I know it's going to happen. We'll go in the order you need us to."

Pulling him down to her, Lei connected their lips, and Londen was happy to hear the front door closing.

"Hey," he called softly, looking into her eyes. "I love you."

♥♥♥

Making love to Lei for hours had completely drained Londen of his energy. When he woke up, it was to the sound of music and the smell of candles. He went into the living room, finding his woman and his sister dancing as if they'd been friends for years. That was a sight Londen loved to see. He took a quick picture of them before heading toward the kitchen to fix them all something to eat. He'd decided not to go to his parents' house and was glad Megan didn't either. This moment, with just the two of them, was perfect for Londen.

Lei's arms wrapped around him from behind, and the gesture combined with the sound of her sweet voice as she asked, "Will you be my man?" made Londen's heart squeeze.

He turned in her arms. "You sure you ready for that, Baby?"

Lei nodded, giving him a lazy smile. There was no telling how many bottles of wine they'd gone through.

"Absolutely."

"I would love to be your man. You know that's all I've been waiting for."

Lei stood on the tips of her toes and gave him a quick kiss before grabbing another bottle of the wine Megan had brought back off the counter, then headed back to the living room. She poured them both a glass before they took a few pictures and returned to their makeshift dancefloor, and Londen was convinced nothing could make that moment better.

forty

Yandi

APRIL

Every day that went by without Yandi hearing from Lei only fueled her anger and resentment. And when she saw Lei's life being played out through social media—her family fun, time with Infinity and Mercedes, being absolutely spoiled by Londen—Yandi's envy grew.

By the time two weeks had passed, Yandi had made up in her mind that she couldn't play nice the way Tussi wanted her to. Tussi didn't seem to care about how Yandi got close to Lei as long as she did, so when she shared that news, he came up with a plan that was so sinister Yandi had to consider just how dedicated to it she truly was. The only thing that made her agree was Tussi's confirmation that no matter how things played out, no one would ever know she was involved.

It just so happened, after Tussi and Yandi established the new plan, that's when Lei called. Almost like fate, Yandi agreed to meeting Lei at her favorite restaurant on the beach. It wasn't lost on Yandi that Lei asked to meet her in public. That further confirmed she'd made the right choice. If Lei was about to end their friendship, Yandi wouldn't have any more loyalty toward her.

While she waited for Lei to arrive, Yandi browsed her socials. As soon as she saw Lei pop up on Facebook, her eyes rolled. Apparently, Londen had already started to shower her with gifts for her birthday. Every day for the next month, until May seventh, she was going to receive a gift. Yandi had to stop herself from gagging as she watched Lei open the box that held tickets to a play that she had been raving about seeing. It irritated Yandi more to hear Infinity and Mercedes in the background. Yandi's heart dropped when she heard Londen say, "The fact that you're so happy about something as simple as tickets to a play will always motivate me to go hard for you."

"Babe, I don't care how small or big the gift is. I'm just grateful you thought of me," Lei replied.

"I think of you daily. That won't ever change."

Yandi's eyes rolled as she clicked out of the video. Apparently, whatever Lei did to thank him for the play tickets off-line motivated Londen to one up himself. Today's gift was a flight to Greece, where the first recorded play was done. Lei cried and jumped into his arms, and the display of love and gratitude had Yandi releasing a low growl as she chunked her phone onto the table.

"That's supposed to be me," she whined, though she'd never be so excited about something as boring as a play. A trip to Greece, however, would do.

Her phone vibrating on top of the table gained her attention. Yandi didn't realize how upset she was until she accepted Mercedes' FaceTime request and saw the frown on her face. She tried to quickly soften her features, but it didn't help.

"Who made you mad?" Mercedes asked with a teasing tone.

"Girl, Lei," Yandi confessed. "She got me waiting up here for her and her ass is late. She's probably fucking around with Londen's ass."

"I mean... she might be. That man is going hard for her since her birthday is next month. I wouldn't want to leave his ass, either."

Yandi's eyes rolled as she all but snatched her drink from the waiter before he could set it down. She took a large gulp of the ginger mule before replying.

"Whatever. She acts like she ain't never had a nigga to do shit for her before. It's really pathetic."

A few seconds passed before Mercedes chuckled and shook her head. Pulling her wavy hair out of her face, Mercedes pulled in a calming breath.

"You sound like a true hater right now, you know that? I don't know what the fuck is up with you, but I don't like it."

"I'm just saying... it's not a good look. That man is

clearly buying her. Ain't no telling what kind of abuse he's going to put her through."

Mercedes scoffed. "So you're a hater because you're concerned? *That's* the excuse you're going with?"

Yandi laughed, sitting up in her seat. Anger was coursing through her body, and it needed to be moved around.

"Because I'm looking out for my girl, I'm a hater?"

"You're not looking out for your girl, you're being a fucking hater, and I don't tolerate that shit."

"How am I being a hater?" Yandi yelled. "Because I'm tired of seeing her post all the shit he's buying her? I'm supposed to be happy about that? That's not the love she was supposed to find. She found a sponsor."

"And you would know all about that, wouldn't you?" Mercedes chuckled again under her breath before releasing a low, "Whew," and scratching her ear. "You know what, I've known you far longer than I've known Lei, but I'm not going to let you disrespect her like this. Lei has been nothing but good to you. She always takes up for you and has your back. When everyone else talks shit about you, Lei is the one who comes to your defense. At one point, she swore you could do no wrong. For you to sit there and call her pathetic because she's happy and being spoiled by a man knowing what she's been through..." Mercedes' head shook as her top lip curled. "*That's* pathetic. That girl is in love, and Londen loves her too. He doesn't just buy her shit, but even if he did, if that's how he expresses his love, that's *their* prerogative. You're just mad because Londen is doing all of this for her and not you, and don't think I didn't hear about you trying to go after Noah too. I let it slide because I know that's just how your ho ass is, but quite frankly, I'm disgusted by the sight of you. I'm done with your ass, Yandi.

You are *not* a good person and I'm tired of trying to pretend as if you are."

Before Yandi could respond, Mercedes was ending the FaceTime. Yandi's eyes blinked rapidly as she stared at the wallpaper on her phone. Standing, she gripped the edge of the table as her leg shook. She looked out into the ocean and shook her head. Regardless of how things played out with Lei, her friendship with Mercedes was officially over... which meant her friendship with her sister, Lexus, was over too. Without them, there would be no Infinity. Now, Yandi would have no one. No one but Tussi.

This plan *had* to work.

"Hey." The feel of Lei's hand on her back caused Yandi to tense. "Are you okay?"

"Ye-yeah, I'm fine."

Yandi sat down, and Lei took the seat across from her.

"How are you?"

"I'm okay, just a little frustrated but I'll be good. How are you?"

"Really good."

Lei's grin had Yandi gritting her teeth. The waiter came to take Lei's order, but she told him she wouldn't be staying long.

"So, what's up?" Yandi asked. "If you're not staying, that's not a good sign."

With a small smile, Lei pulled hair behind her ears. Resting her elbows on the table, she looked out into the ocean.

"I love you, Yandi, but I think it's best if we end our friendship." The women locked eyes. "I heard about you trying to get with Londen and telling Tussi my business. On top of that, you've been acting really strange lately. You know I don't do drama. I've dealt with enough bad shit in my life. Finally, I'm at a really good place. I don't want any energies around me that don't seem sincere and that I can't trust."

"So that's it? Our friendship is over just like that? You're going to choose that man over me?"

Lei chuckled. "I'm not choosing Londen over you. *You* choose a man over *me* when you risked our friendship to get him. Even when Infinity tried to warn me about you having ill intentions with the bet, I gave you the benefit of the doubt like I always fucking do. How do you repay me? By betraying me, knowing what I've gone through."

"You act like you're the only one that's been through some shit," Yandi said as calmly as she could. "You aren't so good of a person that you're immune to struggle and heartache, Lei."

"You're right." Lei stood, expression hardening. "But what I *am* immune to, is keeping people in my life who don't deserve to be here. Goodbye, Yandi."

It took all the restraint Yandi had to not follow Lei and push her down the stairs. Instead, she remained seated and ate her meal alone to ensure she had an alibi. A few minutes after Lei left, Yandi received a text from an unknown number that told her it was done, and a sense of peace immediately filled her. As she was leaving the restaurant, Tussi called just as he said he would.

"Yan," he called after she accepted the call.

"It's done."

A few seconds passed before Tussi disconnected the call, and a wide smile spread across Yandi's face.

forty-one

Lei

DAYS *Earlier*

"I NEED THE TRUTH, *Daddy. All of it.*"

Lei's request was bold. There was a chance the truth would make her feel even more disconnected from her father, but the risk was worth it. She hadn't seen Londen for two days, and the distance was torture. Though there was no part of her that wanted him out of her life for good, Lei didn't know, realistically, how she'd be able to look at him and not see the man that murdered her father. That, however, was her personal issue. Because the truth was, Marcus wasn't her father; Ace was. Marcus had taken her from her family, causing them to grieve for over twenty years. If Lei was in her mother's shoes, she would have begged him to punish the man that took their daughter away. The logic of her mind was at war with the love in her heart, and Lei was determined to make sure the right voice won.

"Are you sure, Princess? Because we often think we want the truth, but those are words you'll never be able to escape."

Taking his warning into consideration, Lei nodded.

"Yes. Tell me everything."

"Okay."

With a sad smile, Ace accepted the cigar she offered, then he poured them both two fingers of cognac. Lei hoped the gesture would ease his nerves. She couldn't imagine the conflict that filled her father. To be stuck between sparing your daughter of pain and killing the man who was responsible for filling him and his family with so much of it was no easy space to be in. And now, with the truth coming out so many years later, even more was at risk. Had Lei found out immediately, she probably would have walked away from Rose Valley Hills. Now, she was too invested in this town and the people in it to let something from her past destroy the life she'd built.

"You know that the secret society was established here in Rose Valley when the town was founded," Ace started. "Though a lot of what we do is for the betterment of our town and its residents, that doesn't come without a fair share of danger and issues. To keep our hands clean, the founders of the secret society came into agreement with three families who were in the streets. The Gabriels, the Santanas, and the Omegas. In exchange for the protection of those in the secret *society and the handling of any issues its members might face, we give those three families free rein in the streets just as long as they keep it under wraps. They also get to have input in certain laws and regulations politically and professionally for the risks they take. Now this only applies to the things they do in The Hills, not in Memphis or any other city and state in the south."*

Ace took a puff of his cigar. *"When your mother and I divorced, before you were born, it was because she didn't like how blurred the lines were getting between the secret society and those who were in the underworld. The good mingled a bit too much with the gritty. Drugs were being exported through Memphis and Rose Valley and our image became tainted."*

"Why would that cause a divorce between the two of you?"

Ace looked away briefly, running his hand up and down his thigh. *"I... I blurred the lines, Princess. There was a really long period where instead of seeking to do good, I did what our founding fathers considered evil. The money that we have is not just from our legal businesses and generational wealth; it's from a period where I was in the streets selling drugs and guns too. For quite some time, your mom was patient with me. It wasn't until we learned my name had been mentioned by an informant to the FBI that I realized I needed to get out. That was easier said than done. The supplier that I was working with didn't want me to stop. He believed I had enough freedom to make him consistent money. After a few months of him muscling me into staying, I permanently ended the situation."*

Her expression was slack until she poked her cheek with her tongue. At one point, Lei vowed to share information of any crimes so those responsible would be punished. Now, casual conversations with the men in her life were becoming tests of her loyalty to them or to the law. While it was never a choice Lei wanted to have to make, the choice was easy. She'd choose them *every time, even if that meant accepting their crimes and keeping their secrets.*

Their eyes disconnected for a brief moment as she looked around, like the answer to the question she wanted to ask was written on the walls... because she wasn't quite ready to hear him say the words yet.

"You... killed him?"

Ace nodded before taking a sip of his drink. "I did. After that, I got out and promised your mother if she gave me another chance, that she'd never have to worry about that lifestyle appealing to me again."

"And it hasn't?"

"It has..." *Ace smiled softly, and Lei couldn't help but mirror it.* "But I've resisted. Fast forward to right before you came back. The son of the supplier I killed to secure my freedom came to the States, to Rose Valley, to avenge his father's death. When he realized how heavily protected I was, he went after someone close to me... your brother."

Lei tugged her bottom lip between her teeth to avoid gasping. Instead of hearing her father's past, she felt like she was listening to a juicy book.

"Cade defended himself, as he'd been taught to, and he killed him."

"Oh my... wow."

"It happened so fast, I couldn't get anyone on it. And I don't regret that because Cade did what he needed to do to stay safe, but the gun he used... I had to find a way to connect it to others to avoid him ever being fingered for the murder."

"How did you do that?"

"I gave it to the head of my security, who used it and the remaining bullets for hits. Turns out, he gave the gun to three men, one of which was Londen. He used that same gun to kill Hamilton."

Her chest tightened and mind raced.

Finally, the pieces were starting to connect, but Lei still wasn't sure where her father was going with this.

"I remember Londen saying he was serving time for a crime he didn't commit. Is this what he was referring to?"

Ace nodded. "Yes. Apparently, the last time that gun was used, it was discarded of by a man who had little experience. It was found, and mostly all the bullets were connected to previous murders with no suspects."

"What changed?"

"There was a young man who had just gotten picked up with several possession charges. In order to lighten his sentence, he gave names of other dealers and murders that he knew for sure could be proven in court. One of the names he gave was Londen's. I'm not sure why or what he said, but that's what shifted the district attorney's attention to Londen. Now they couldn't prove Londen was tied to any murders because he was very clean, but they could prove that he was connected to me. They put two and two together about Cade killing my supplier's son and suggested I was involved. Hamilton was in that lineup as well. When he was murdered, he had a warrant for kidnapping you. Before Hamilton could be found and picked up..."

"Londen had killed him," Lei muttered. "So that would have been three murders attached to you and possibly Cade too. They weren't going to go after Londen because they had no real proof. They were going to try to get him to snitch on you."

"Exactly, but that's not the kind of man Londen is. He would do the time before he snitched, and that's what he did. He felt as if it was more important that I be free than him. Plus, he had several bodies that he could potentially be charged with, and the prosecutor over the case made that clear. Their case with Luis was weak, which is why he was able to get the small amount of time he did. Had he not confessed or turned on me, there would

have been a target on his back. If they found any evidence against him, they'd want to give him life or death. So it was self-preservation but it was also his way of looking out for me. In exchange, I looked out for him while he was locked up. Every year, January first, I had half a million dollars deposited into a bank account for him. We didn't speak after he started serving his time. I did, however, reach out when you mentioned the bet. I told him I didn't want you connecting with a man in there who would bring you more harm than good, and he agreed. I just... I want you to see how interconnected things can get doing what I, what we, do. And regardless of what happens between us, I never want you to think Londen didn't have good intentions when it came down to you."

Ace leaned forward and wiped the tears from her eyes.

"He's been looking out for our family for years. I trust him with you, and that doesn't come cheap. Please... don't let my choice end your relationship."

"I won't," she promised. "I already felt like I wanted to get over this so we could be together, but now I really do. There was always something special about Londen to me. He's always seemed..." Her head shook as she tried to find a word that was worthy of him. *"Irresistible to my being. Like... something that I simply could not avoid. I've closed myself off to love because I didn't think I'd ever feel safe and secure with a man after what Marcus and Steven did, but Londen has been looking out for us before we even met."*

Sniffling, she released a shaky breath.

"I hope you can one day forgive me."

"I already have, Daddy. I know you didn't do that to intentionally hurt me, and I don't blame you for it. I wanted Marcus to be punished, and I wish he could have just served jail time, but I'm emotionally intelligent enough to know how you handled that betrayal toward you and Ma had nothing to do with me. So

yes, it hurt, but how you handled it... that was your right. I don't have to accept it or respect it, but I accept and respect you, so we'll be fine."

Ace stood and pulled her into his arms. "Thank you, Princess."

He held her close, causing Lei to smile. When he released her, Lei asked, "Hey, do you happen to know the name of the person that gave Londen's name? I know it's a long shot, but..."

"Yeah, I know. It was some lower-level dealer named Tussi..."

forty-two

Lei ♥

THE PRESENT

GROGGILY, Lei shifted in her seat. With a groan, she jerked in the seat. Panic filled her when she realized her hands were tied behind her back, and her ankles were tied to the legs of the chair. As she released a squeaky yelp, Lei continued to try to loosen whatever was binding her wrists unsuccessfully. The last thing she remembered was leaving the restaurant after talking to Yandi. She touched her door handle, and by the time she sat inside of the car, she was drifting off to sleep.

"Stop fighting. You're not going to get out."

At the sound of a deep voice, Lei's movements stopped.

Since there was something in her mouth, she couldn't speak clearly. Her words came out like muffled hums that forced him to pull whatever was stuffed inside of her mouth out.

"Who are you and why did you take me?"

He lowered the covering from her eyes. Lei looked his face over intently. He was vaguely familiar, but she couldn't place why. There was no doubt in her mind that she'd never seen him before, but his features were familiar. From his tall, lanky frame that was covered in medium brown skin to his almond-shaped eyes and long nose.

"I'm not going to tell you my name, but I will tell you that you're going to stay here until your father gets Tussi out of prison."

"Tussi?" she repeated. *Tussi.* That's why he looked familiar. Their features were distinct. Whoever this man was, he was related to Tussi. Why had he conspired with Tussi to kidnap her? *Kidnap.* Lei chuckled. "Just my fucking luck."

His eyes narrowed as he frowned.

"The hell is so funny?"

"Believe it or not, this is not my first time being kidnapped, and with my luck, it probably won't be the last."

Lei laughed again, and it was the only thing keeping her from being filled with fear.

"Aye!" he roared, making himself eye level with her. "I

don't know what your problem is, but ain't shit funny about this."

Reeling back her laugh, Lei nibbled her bottom lip as she stared into his familiar eyes.

"I don't know what Tussi offered you in exchange for taking me, but when my man and daddy find out about this, it won't be worth your life."

"That's my fucking brother. He didn't offer me shit. I'm going to do whatever I have to do to get him out of prison."

"How do you think taking me is going to accomplish that?"

"I don't know, but Tussi seems to think your father has enough pull to get him out. So until that happens, you're staying here with me."

The gravity of the situation began to settle within Lei's spirit. Her bladder loosened but she clenched and gulped a large breath to soothe her nerves.

"Look..." Her voice lowered as she quickly took in her surroundings. The living room she was being held in was large and filled with vintage furniture. There was a brick fireplace off to the right by the front door. Directly in front of her were several religious themed photos surrounding an older model TV. Had he brought her to an older family member's house? "I don't know why Tussi thinks my daddy has that kind of pull but he doesn't. He can help people who are locked up, but he doesn't have the power to get them out."

"That sucks for you, then. If he can't get him out, you're dying here."

Lei's heart dropped as he began to walk away from her. "Wait!" she yelled. He stopped walking but didn't bother to go back in her direction. "Even if my father did have those kinds of connections, Tussi already has a deal on the table.

He's only serving twenty-five of his sixty-year sentence. They aren't going to come down any more on that. He *has* to do that time."

His head tilted to the side. With a focused gaze, he crossed his arms over his chest.

"What do you mean, he's only doing twenty-five?"

Licking her lips, Lei realized a way to possibly swing this in her favor. Tussi obviously hadn't informed his people of him being an informant, and if he hadn't, that was for a reason. All Lei could do was hope that reason was bigger than whatever was motivating this man to keep her.

"Tussi is an informant. He had his sentence drastically reduced by giving information on other dealers and murderers. From what my man told me, he's also getting favors while he's locked up by letting the warden know of things happening in his pod with the other inmates. For his protection, the deal that he made is sealed... but he's getting out in about fifteen years."

Slowly, the man walked in her direction. "You're lying. Tussi ain't no fucking snitch."

"I'm sorry, but he is. I can understand why you don't believe me, but he is."

Pulling his gun from his hip, he shoved it in her face. "That's a bold accusation, bitch. Unless you have proof, I might have to put you down now. Give me names or a copy of the deal he made."

Lei's eyes closed as her heart palpitated. She pulled in short, choppy breaths as her breathing increased. When she talked to her father and he told her Tussi was the informant who snitched on Londen, it made a lot of sense. Once she and Londen made up, she told him about her conversation with Ace, and Londen confirmed everything her father had said.

Londen didn't know immediately that Tussi was the reason his name began to float around, but when he did find out, he tucked that information away until it became useful to him. Londen knew every person Tussi had snitched on. He didn't go into great detail because it was useless information at that point, but he did tell her that two of the biggest fish Tussi gave up were a dealer from his old hood that he worked under, and his own brother.

"I don't have any proof, but I can share two names. If you want proof, call my dad. My man doesn't answer numbers he doesn't know, but my daddy always will."

"Give me the fucking names," he ordered through gritted teeth, putting the gun so close to her face it grazed her nose.

"Ma-Marco and D-Deon," she stuttered, craning her neck to put space between her and the gun.

It didn't matter, though, because the man slowly lowered it.

"What you just say?" he whispered.

Gaining more confidence, Lei pulled in a deep breath and said, "Marco and Deon," a bit louder.

"Give me your dad's number. If he has proof to back up what you're saying, I'll let you go ASAP..."

forty-three

Londen

WHEN MERCEDES ASKED Londen for a menu and cooking instructions for a cooking and cocktails party she wanted to have, he happily agreed. He even offered to give her a lesson before the party so she could help her guests and she was glad he made the suggestion. Though Londen offered to do it for free, she insisted on paying him something. He hadn't even considered what to charge for something like that. As soon as he arrived at her home, she was handing him a golden envelope that he hadn't looked inside of yet, but Londen could tell the stacks of cash were thick.

While they discussed the upcoming party, no other topics were on the table. It wasn't until they wrapped up the planning that they began to talk about their personal lives. He listened intently while Mercedes gushed about Noah and how she hoped he would be out soon. There was a great chance that he, too, could be out in a few months. Londen didn't want to get her hopes up though, so he chose not to allude to that fact. It was when they started to talk about Lei that Mercedes' tone shifted. As she walked him to the door, she told him...

"So, Lei and I have never really called each other friends, but doing the bet changed that. We talked a lot and got really close. I care about her and... I wanted to warn you about something."

Londen turned to face her instead of opening the door. "Warn me about what?"

"Yandi." Mercedes looked away briefly and squeezed her arm. "I stopped talking to Yandi today because I didn't like how she was talking to and treating Lei. She's been giving me bad vibes and the last straw was her bashing Lei for posting about you on her page. Lei told me she was going to end their friendship, but Yandi still needs to be watched. She can be scandalous when she's hurt, and if she doesn't want the friendship to end, there's no telling what she will do."

"I appreciate the heads up. Even before I got out, I didn't trust her. I warned Lei about her myself. Hopefully, Yandi won't try no funny shit, because if she does, she can be handled just like a nigga would."

Mercedes chuckled. "That used to be my girl, but I don't

blame you. Protect Lei at all costs. I would want my man to do the same for me."

"Oh, don't worry. Noah will."

Mercedes blushed as he opened the door. They said their goodbyes, and Londen slowed his walk at the feel of his phone vibrating in his pocket. He held his hand up toward Keith so he wouldn't open the door of the Bentley as he accepted Ace's call. They were on good terms, but not the kind of terms that called for casual conversation.

"You good?" was Londen's greeting.

"That pussy ass motherfucker had his brother take my princess."

His chest caved and legs grew weak as a chill shot down his spine.

"What? Someone has Lei?"

"Tussi's brother. He told him to kidnap her and keep her until I had him released from prison."

"Aw, that nigga want his whole fucking bloodline to die," Londen decided, hopping into the car.

"Don't move too recklessly. I'm already on it. Lei told him I didn't have that kind of power, and even if I did, because he's serving a reduced sentence as an informant, there would be nothing I could do."

"Fuck. Vernon didn't know Tussi snitched on Marco."

"Exactly. He told her if I could get proof, he'd let her go now."

"Where you at?"

"I'm headed to my office. I had the prosecutor who handled his case to forward a copy of the deal to me. As soon as I have it, his brother is going to give me a meetup location."

"Don't leave until I meet you there."

After disconnecting the call, Londen gave Keith the

address to Ace's office and told him to drive as if his life depended on it. It didn't matter how much he told himself to remain calm, all he could think about was getting locked up on a petty charge just to handle Tussi *himself*. What surprised Londen most was the extreme at which Tussi had gone to get to Lei. He guessed since there was no chance she'd give him any play romantically, Tussi decided to take what he wanted... literally. There was no doubt in Londen's mind that Yandi was involved, especially after his conversation with Mercedes.

The entire ride was done in a blur. By the time they arrived, Ace and Cade were outside, waiting for him. Londen hopped in the back of the truck, not bothering to say or ask anything. As long as Ace had what was needed to secure Lei's freedom, Londen would handle the rest.

forty-four

Lei

SQUEEZED between two people in the back seat of a car, Lei shook like a leaf in the wind. She had no idea where they were taking her, but there was no doubt in her mind that her father would be there waiting. Before her mouth, ears, and eyes were covered again, Lei heard the man who had taken her, speaking to her father on the phone. Their conversation ended with Ace sending him proof of what Lei had said. As soon as it came through to his phone, he was heading to the back of the house and telling two more men they needed to go.

Lei didn't know how long the ride had been, but it seemed like forever. Before she could gather herself, she was being pulled out of the car and carried away. They'd warned her not to scream or try to bring attention to them, and she agreed. In her line of work, Lei knew all too well the consequences of trying to play hero. She was placed on concrete before her hands were pulled behind her and wrapped around a pole.

"Your dad is on his way to get you. As soon as my guys confirm he dropped the papers off where I told him to, I'll leave and tell him where he can find you."

Nodding rapidly, Lei wished he would pull whatever was in her mouth down so she could speak. She wanted to ask what he planned to say or do with his brother now that he knew the truth. If he was upset enough with Tussi snitching to let her go, she wondered what else his brother would do. Lei could hear the hurt and anger in his voice when he talked to her father about how he refused to believe Tussi was the reason their other brother was in jail. Worse, Marco was serving a life sentence for murder.

"I'm sorry to have brought you into this," he continued. "I was so loyal to my brother that I didn't ask questions." With a soft sigh, he sat close enough to her for her to feel his body against hers. "Your people are probably going to come after me, and I don't blame them. Hopefully, me returning you unharmed will get me some kind of grace. If not, I accept my fate. I don't regret trying to help my brother, but I will regret losing my life for a fucking snitch."

After sucking his teeth, he stood and answered a call with, "Is it there?" A beat of silence passed before he said, "And you can tell it's real?" He cursed under his breath.

"Aight. Y'all meet me back at the spot. I'm about to send him the location so he can get her."

He disconnected the call, then told Lei, "I'm going to send him to you. It shouldn't take him long to get here. Maybe two minutes tops. And I promise after this, you won't have to worry about my brother bothering you ever again."

Whether he promised that or not, Lei knew that would be the case. Still, she bobbed her head, grateful this was almost over. Things could have taken a turn for the worse. Even after finding out that Tussi was a snitch, his brother could have still been loyal to him. Lei was just grateful that Tussi had snitched on his other brother, otherwise, Lei didn't know what would have become of her as time progressed. She knew her father had a lot of power and influence, but she didn't think he would have ever been able to do what Tussi was asking of him.

While Lei waited for her father to arrive, she thought about how she'd gotten into this predicament, anyway. It didn't seem like a coincidence that she was taken after meeting Yandi. Yandi and Tussi were talking, so was it a far stretch to think Yandi was involved? If she wasn't, Lei believed Yandi knew what he was planning and didn't bother to warn her. Was that what she'd been wanting to talk to her about and because Lei ended their friendship, Yandi kept it to herself?

As she rested her head against the pole, her mind raced with a million thoughts. The one that screamed louder than most was the fact that yet another person she trusted and cared about had betrayed her. Before meeting Londen, this would have triggered Lei to the point where she reverted to her shell and didn't want to engage with anyone. Now, she wasn't as fazed because betrayal, unfortunately, was a part of life. What her mother had said was true—trying to avoid hurt was like trying to avoid the sun. All she could do was remove those from her life that were unworthy and keep it moving.

At the sound of tires screeching, Lei's shoulders perked as she hummed. The sound of feet trampling toward her mimicked the sound of her heart beating against her rib cage. While one pair of hands removed the cover from her eyes, mouth, and ears, another pair was cutting the bondage around her arms and ankles. Gritting her teeth, Lei tried not to cry at the sight of her three favorite men. Ace was pulling her off the ground first, lifting her into the air and swinging her around. Her eyes landed on Londen, who had pulled his arms behind his back to avoid reaching for her.

Not being sure if she'd live or not had given Lei more value for life and everyone that was in it. She didn't just want Londen to be her man; she wanted him to be her husband. The past had robbed her of enough... it wouldn't rob her of her future too.

"I would have died if something happened to you," Ace declared.

"Thank you for coming to get me."

"I always will. *We* always will."

Once he released her, Cade pulled her into his arms. "What would I do without these hugs?"

Lei giggled as she swayed against him. "Let's pray you never have to find out."

She expected Londen to make his way over to her, but he didn't. He stayed behind, staring at her with those dark, lazy eyes. Sniffing under her armpits, Lei asked softly, "Do I stink? I don't know how long I was with them."

Cade chuckled as he grabbed her purse off the ground

and handed it to her. She checked to make sure everything was inside. Finally stopping to process her location, Lei realized they'd taken her back to the beach and dropped her off under the restaurant she'd met Yandi at. Because of its design, there was a large area of space for people to walk under on the side of the building by the trash cans. Now she was even more convinced Yandi was involved.

"We'll give you two some privacy," Ace offered when Londen remained silent.

"Are you... okay?" Lei asked, taking a small step in his direction.

"If I would've lost you..." His head dropped and shook.

"Baby."

Closing the space between them, Lei wrapped her arms around him, and Londen held her tightly. He kissed her forehead, and the moment she felt his tears on her skin, her eyes watered.

"I would've painted this town red trying to get to you, Lei."

"But you didn't have to. I'm okay, babe."

"Are you?" His hands cupped her cheeks, and he lifted them from his chest to look into her eyes. "Because if they did *any*-fucking-thing to you..."

"They didn't." Lei chuckled nervously as she wrapped her hands around his wrists. "He was actually nice after I told him about Tussi. Well, after I gave him the names. Before that he was a little aggressive, but they didn't mishandle me in any way."

"Good. I'm taking care of Tussi, and I need to discuss what we're going to do with his brother with Ace."

"Look... I know what he did was wrong, but can you please spare him? I'm 100 percent okay."

"Nah. Everybody involved with this shit gon' pay.

Including your girl. I know she had something to do with this."

His posture hardened and grip on her cheeks tightened.

"Unfortunately, I agree. I was snatched right after I left her table. I want to ask her to confirm, but I'm pretty sure she set me up. How long was I with them?"

"Just a few hours. Ace called me when I was leaving Mercedes' house after setting up her menu for the party."

Lei ran her hands down her face. "I just want to go home, take three showers, and sleep for a few days. I need to forget this ever happened."

"We can make that happen. I'll take you home and get you settled in before taking care of this."

"Can it wait?" Lei wrapped her arms around him. "I don't want you to leave me tonight."

"I can wait if you want me to."

"Good. Because... not knowing if I was going to make it out of there alive changed my perspective, Londen. I know I've been hesitant about marriage and wanting to move slow, but I want everything life and love has for me. So... whenever you want to propose... I'd say yes."

For the first time, Londen smiled. "You lucky your people in the truck. Otherwise, I'd press you against this wall and dig inside your pussy."

When his lips lowered to her neck, Lei chuckled. "Thank God I got your lips on me. You were scaring me for a moment."

"Honestly, I didn't want to touch you and this moment become a dream. I didn't want to wake up in the car on the way to you."

"Well, I'm real, and this moment is real... in more ways than one. I hate this happened, but I'm also glad it did. It showed me that Yandi is not to be trusted but it also showed me how crazy my family is and how lucky I am to have you as my man. I really do love you, Londen, far quicker than I knew was possible."

"Baby," he moaned, lifting her into the air. "Let's just walk to my place now. I'll take you home later."

Lei's giggle was cut off by his lips connecting with hers, and she had no complaints about his plan at all.

forty-five

Londen

WHEN LEI INVITED Londen to her parents' house for family dinner, he was surprised. Though they were in a committed relationship, the invitation seemed to make things more official. He enjoyed his time with them, but the visit was bittersweet. Londen didn't know when he'd be able to have her around his family... well, his parents. She and Megan were practically best friends already, texting every day. Londen was grateful for that and hoped the connection would give his sister a reason to come home more, but he wouldn't blame her if she didn't.

Londen's hesitance to have Lei around his parents stemmed from the guilt that consumed him whenever he was around them. With his mother, she guilted him about his brother, and his father guilted him about the business. There was no part of him that wanted Lei to experience the shift in his energy or the dynamic change in his character when addressing his father. The gentle gangsta who never shied away from taking control with her turned into a little boy who struggled to make clear boundaries with the man who raised him. All he could do was pray that one day his issues with both of them would be resolved so they could meet the woman he planned to spend the rest of his life with.

Before dinner, Londen was given a grand tour of Lei's parents' home. It was... luxurious... to say the least. With all Londen saw, they didn't have to leave home for much of anything. They had two living rooms, ten bedrooms with attached bathrooms, several common areas, two kitchens, a gym and game room. Home offices were in the backyard, and there was a space for detailing their cars off to the side. A smaller home was on the opposite side, equipped with a bar and small convenience area that had just about everything they would need from the grocery store.

From the way they were living, Londen couldn't help but wonder if Ace was really out of the streets. If his business investments and wealth from founders and the secret society provided this type of wealth, that was all the more reason for him to join.

As he and Lei were preparing to leave, Ace asked to speak with him privately. They went outside to his home office, which looked more like a chill area than anything else. To Ace's credit, there was a small writing desk in the corner with a laptop on it, but it didn't look like he did much work in there at all.

"You good?" Londen confirmed as Ace closed the door behind them.

"I'm great. Have a seat." Ace waited until they were seated in the two burgundy chairs that were facing each other, with a small, round table between them to continue. "As thanks for what you've done over the years and recently, plus a way to welcome you into the family, I want to offer you an official position in the secret society. Not just doing hits as our freelance security, but a salaried position that will be yours until retirement, should you accept."

Leaning forward, Ace pulled the small burgundy and gold box closer to him. He opened it and pulled two Cuban cigars out. Londen was familiar with the brand; it was the same kind Lei smoked. She was always so fucking sexy with her cigars and cognac on Fridays. There was nothing more attractive to him than a woman who did exactly what she wanted, no matter what others thought. Lei was in tune with her feminine and masculine energy, and he loved every facet of her. From the layer that could smoke, play pool, and talk shit with him to the layer that loved shopping, being pampered, and spending time with her girlfriends.

Ace extended a cigar in Londen's direction. He accepted it and lit it as Ace continued.

"Should you accept the position, I'd need you to move to Memphis. I've always wanted Lei involved in the secret society's legal department for several reasons, the most important being it would keep her and Cade from competing, and it would also set her up with permanent wealth beyond what I give her. I believe if you joined, she would too. I don't want her to return to Memphis, but I know I can't hold on to her so closely just because I missed the first part of her life. Taking these new positions would be a great new start for the both of you."

"I respect your reasoning. What position do you want me to fill?"

"Well, I know you wanted to be a profiler for the FBI, but your father gave you to the streets before you could take that path. In Memphis, you can head the criminal profiling and private investigation division. The truth of the matter is, things are getting worse there and a lot of our services are being requested."

Londen thought he was hearing things. He refused to believe Ace had just offered him a position to do what he'd always wanted to do. Sticking his finger in his ear, Londen wiggled it, as if there was something inside that he needed to clear out.

Ace chuckled before puffing on his cigar.

"I don't think I heard you correctly, Ace."

"You did." He laughed softly and sat up in his seat. "You would have to go through two years of additional training since you already have a degree, but if you want the position when you're done, it's yours. You can do the training here, but you'll have to move to Memphis when it's complete. Our division will work directly with the FBI and MPD. We will get our cases directly from them, but they won't have a say in our tactics or who we hire."

Rubbing his hands together, Londen swallowed hard and blinked his glossy eyes.

His voice was so thick with emotion, it almost sounded choked when he said, "Wow. I... I don't know what to say."

"You can say you accept."

His laugh was light as he nodded in agreement. "Of

course. Yes. Thank you. I'm grateful for the offer and the opportunity."

Standing, Londen put the cigar out and shook Ace's hand. As happy as he was, there was also a part of him that was unsure. Ace might have wanted Lei to move and work within the secret society, but Londen didn't think she'd be willing to move to Memphis. Sure, she'd visited him, but that was because she didn't have to go deep into the city. Who was to say she'd go back to the place where she suffered for the sake of a job and her relationship? Londen didn't know, but he damn sure hoped she would.

forty-six

Lei

LEI HELD JACK'S HAND, inspecting it carefully. Jaqueline Smith had quickly proven why she was *nothing* to fuck with. Londen had reached out to her and told her he had a situation he needed her to handle, because he refused to ever let Lei get her hands dirty. Jack drove down from Memphis with no hesitation. All it took was a brief overview of what happened, and she was pulling up to Yandi's house to render the punishment she deserved.

The only reason Yandi was still alive was because Lei asked for her life be spared. She already had Marcus' death on her conscience... Yandi couldn't be the second. From what Jack described and the look of her hands, there was no doubt in Lei's mind that she'd done some serious damage to Yandi, who had confessed to the role she played in hopes that it would cause Jack to be gentle.

The cuts and bruising of Jack's hand caused Lei to wince as she released it.

"I'm grateful for what you did, but it looks like that is painful."

"It's nothing. You should see that bitch's face." Jack nonchalantly took a sip of her drink.

They'd met at a bar of Jack's choosing before she headed back to Memphis.

"Did she... was she... remorseful?"

"No. She admitted to what she did because she wanted to save herself, but she didn't apologize or say she regretted it or anything like that. I thought Londen being there would help her speak her truth, and it did, but even still... she just made it about herself."

That shouldn't have disappointed Lei, but it did. For once, she hoped her friend would have realized how flawed her actions were. Unfortunately, that wasn't the case.

"Hey," Jack called, pulling Lei out of her head. "I know we aren't close, but fuck her. Anyone who hates themselves enough to reflect that hate onto you is not worthy of your concern and sympathy. Fuck her."

Jack's words caused Lei to smile and nod her head in agreement. "Thank you. I really appreciate the sentiment. And we'd be a lot closer if you came to The Hills more, though I understand why you keep your distance."

Jack sighed and lifted her Jack and Coke to her lips. "It's

just not safe for me to be here for too long. Not right now, at least." She checked the time on her Rolex before standing. "Speaking of which, I need to get back to Memphis."

"Okay. Thanks again." When Jack went into her wallet, Lei stopped her immediately. "No, ma'am. The least I can do is buy you a drink. Put that away."

"Aight, I got you next time you come to Memphis. Just hit my line."

Lei agreed, but she didn't see herself returning to Memphis any time soon. Going to visit Londen was hard enough, but he was her reward. Now, she had no reason to go... not even the potential budding of a friendship with a badass like Jack.

♥♥♥

The last time Lei spoke to Londen, he was telling her that Noah could not handle Tussi. He was more clever than they gave him credit for. By the time his plan was put it motion, Tussi was being transferred out. They had no way to find him at the moment, which led Noah and Londen to believe he was being heavily protected. If his name was being kept out of databases, Tussi had finally found a way to exercise his power.

That wasn't a surprise to Lei. Because he was an informant, certain measures were taken to ensure his safety. If he had any doubts that his plan was going to work, all it would take was one word to the warden that his life was in danger and Tussi would be immediately moved.

All he'd wanted was his freedom—he'd just gone about it the wrong way—and unfortunately for Tussi, things weren't *anywhere* near over. He may have been missing now, but Londen was determined to find him. As Lei requested, Tussi's brother was left alone... until they found out Tussi was gone. His immediate release of her when he found out about his brother had earned grace, but that grace ended when they needed to send a message to Tussi.

Vernon tried to assure them that his death wouldn't sway Tussi, but Londen thought otherwise. He hadn't been killed yet, but he was being held, and Londen was confident his funeral would be the only thing that would make Tussi show up.

Though the experience was traumatic, Lei hadn't lost any sleep over it. She was just glad no harm had come to her. Reflecting on the only positive thing that came out of this, her change in perspective, was what filled Lei with peace.

As she let herself inside of Londen's place, she wondered when he would be coming home. Her case load was light, and that was intentional. After the mistrial with Garrett, Lei needed a break. It was the most mentally taxing case she'd ever had. As much as she tried not to bring work home, some cases would haunt her and demand she give as much time to them as she possibly could. Garrett had taken something out of her that Lei hadn't been able to get back, and with everything else going on in her life, Lei was okay with that. She was financially comfortable enough to pay her staff and not take any cases unless she wanted to. Until that happened, Lei was enjoying the rest.

The first thing that caught Lei's eye was the setup on the living room table. With a large smile, she scurried over. Grabbing the large bouquet of red roses, Lei inhaled their scent before putting them down and giggling at the sight of her favorite sushi roll with a small side of kimchi. Lei picked up the handwritten letter and sat down to read it.

B. LOVE

Baby,

I know we don't have to write each other letters anymore, but I want to. I never want to stop putting forth the effort and doing things to keep that beautiful smile on your face. While you wait for me to return, I want you to ruminate on just how much I love you. We've been in each other's lives for almost four months, but it feels like four lifetimes. I cherish the time we took getting to know each other through those letters. There were things I got to know about you that I probably wouldn't have taken the time to learn if I was free, but I'm glad I did because they equipped me to love you and take care of your wants and needs.

Don't be upset with me. I know you wanted to take me out tonight, but you should know I'm not going to let you do that. You can plan our evening, but I'm paying for everything. There's nothing more that I need than your presence. Whatever else that comes tonight will be extra.

With how things have progressed since I've been out, I want to take a moment to make clear my intentions with you. I've always told you I wanted you and wanted children, but I also accepted those things might not come immediately. By year's end, you won't just be winning that bet, but you'll also be my fiancée and my wife by next year. I still need to throw something Lexus' way for suggesting the bet because if she hadn't, I wouldn't have you, and you truly are the best thing that's ever happened to me.

You complement my energy and make me feel like a man. You make me feel needed and wanted. I love how respected and accepted I feel when I'm with you. In our communion, I've laughed and smiled more than I have in my adult life. It isn't because I've been unhappy; it's because I haven't had a reason to express myself. That changed with you. You make me feel safe. You make me feel whole. You make me feel loved.

I'll see you soon.

. . .

PLACING the letter on her chest, Lei released a content sigh. Lei was sure she'd never be open to love again, but being loved by Londen made her happy she'd taken the risk.

🩶🩶🩶

"So when were you going to tell me about this?" Lei

asked, pointing at Infinity's date for the evening. For their date night, Lei planned dinner and a trip to the casino. It wasn't the most extravagant thing, but Londen loved gambling and winning big, so she knew spending the evening there would put a smile on his face. Lei hadn't expected to run into her best friend, and she certainly wasn't expecting to find her with a man.

Though he was attractive, he certainly wasn't Infinity's type. Not physically, at least. He was more clean cut than her brother, and that was saying a lot. Cade was rough around the edges, but he didn't look like it—at all—and that was his superpower.

"Well, it's not serious enough yet for me to talk about him. I knew if I did, you'd get excited. Plus, I didn't want you thinking I was a hypocrite."

"Why would I think that?"

"Because I told you I wasn't going to date your brother because he isn't my type, and you can tell just by his looks that Sean isn't either."

Lei's eyes casually scanned Sean's frame as he talked to Londen. The two had quickly bonded over talks of table games, which didn't surprise Lei. Londen was a good judge of character, but more than that, men could become the best of friends instantly if they had something in common.

"Well..." Squeezing the back of her neck, Lei chuckled. "Now that you mention it... He doesn't really look like your type, but I wouldn't call you a hypocrite for that. It does make me think there's another reason you don't want to give Cade a chance, but that's your prerogative. You don't have to date anyone you don't want to. If you're happy with Sean, that's all that matters to me."

A smile spread Infinity's lips. "I really needed to hear you say that. Honestly..." Infinity rocked on her heels.

"There *is* a reason that I don't want to date Cade that I haven't shared with you. I don't want a relationship with him to come between me and you. Cade is charming and flirtatious and not serious about women at all. I feel like he likes me as much as he does because I don't give him any play, but I don't know. I just value our friendship too much to risk it for something as fickle as love. I'll probably always be attracted to Cade, but I'll never take it there with him because I love you. Nothing will ever be worth losing you."

Lei's bottom lip poked out as she fought back her tears. Pulling Infinity into her arms, she whispered into her ear, "I love you so much. Thank you for holding our friendship this sacred. I promise I'll be the best friend ever, and you'll never regret this." Lei cupped Infinity's chin as she told her, "But you should know I value you just the same, and I won't let anything come between us either. If you truly wanted to give something with my brother a chance, we're all mature enough to have clear boundaries. I'm going to support whatever makes you happy, whether that's being with my brother or not."

They hugged again, and the feel of a hand grabbing her ass caught her off guard. "Damn, can I join in?"

As Lei turned to face the stranger, Londen was making his way over. Before she could address him, he was being knocked onto his side. Londen's fist connecting with the side of his head knocked him out instantly.

"Did you really just grab Baby's ass?" Londen asked, as if the unconscious man could answer. "Niggas get killed for less fucking with me."

The hard kick Londen sent to the man's temple was so loud Lei was sure she heard his skull crack.

"Shit!" she yelled, grabbing Londen's hand. "Okay. We have to go *now*."

Though Londen didn't fight against the grip she had on his hand, he grumbled under his breath about finishing the man off the whole time they walked off. Lei's insides burned as her body shook. She couldn't believe what had happened so quickly. One minute, she was sharing a beautiful moment with her best friend and the next she was watching her lover almost kill a man. And if Lei was to be honest with herself, she knew there was a good chance the man was dead if not severely hurt.

As upset as Lei was over Londen's lack of self-control, she maintained her composure. If she said something now, they would end up arguing, and they hadn't done that yet. Though Lei knew all couples had disagreements, she hoped she and Londen continued to have peace.

"Leaving already?" Keith asked, opening the door for her.

She gave him a nod and a small smile, afraid her voice would shake if she talked.

It wasn't until they were out of the parking lot and heading into traffic that she told Keith, "Take me home, please."

She saw Londen look at her out of the corner of her eye and chuckle, but he didn't say anything to her. Instead, he told Keith, "Go back to my place as planned."

Pushing her hair out of her face, Lei looked over at him. "I want to go home."

"Why?"

"Because I don't want to argue with you."

"Why would you?"

"That was... stupid. We were in a room full of people, and you damn near killed that man. Hell, he might *be* dead! Are you out of your fucking *mind*?"

"Pull the car over," Londen commanded, and only a few

seconds passed before Keith was pulling over on the side of the road. When he got out and gave them privacy, Londen continued. "Two things," he started calmly, looking over at her. "You do not curse at me or raise your voice, nor will you ever disrespect me, especially in front of someone else."

"I told you I wanted to go home."

"And I asked you why. You could have answered with the same calm tone I'm using with you without cursing at me. So we're going to try this again." When Lei huffed and crossed her arms over her chest, he added, "And you're going to lose the fucking attitude too."

Lei looked out of the window and stared out into the night sky. She took deep breaths, hoping they would calm herself. Getting to the root of her true issue, she asked herself why she was truly upset. For her, anger was often a safer expression of her true feelings. And in that moment, her true feeling was fear. Eyes watering, Lei allowed her shoulders to drop.

"I just got you, baby. You can't go back to prison... especially over something so silly as a man grabbing my ass."

Londen took her hand into his and kissed it. Lowering it onto the seat, he held it and stroked it with his thumb.

"Look at me, Lei." Slowly, she turned in his direction. "I'll die before I ever let anyone violate or disrespect you. I don't give a fuck where I am or who it is. No one will ever get away with that." Londen's grip on her tightened as his breathing turned shaky. Just the thought of someone violating her was getting him riled up again. "I apologize for putting you in fear of losing me, but you can trust that I'm not going to do anything to go back to prison. Not that it changes anything, but I know the owner of this casino. All I have to do is call him and he'll have the security footage wiped, so I'm good. Even if I didn't know the owner, I'm not worried about that sending me to prison."

"You might not be, but I am. All I could think about was losing you. My life has been so much better with you in it. I do apologize for yelling and cursing at you, especially because you were protecting me, but I couldn't help myself. That fear came out as anger, and you didn't deserve that."

"Com'ere," he requested, tugging her hand gently. Unbuckling her seatbelt, Lei straddled his lap. He placed his hand over her chest, holding it there until her heartbeat steadied. The longer she stared into his eyes, the calmer she felt. "I love you, and I'm going to protect you. I can't apologize for that or tell you it won't happen again. What I can say is that I'll try not to react so quickly physically, but I'll go to war with God behind you, so it's really off with these niggas heads while we're on earth."

Tugging her bottom lip between her teeth as she smiled, Lei rested her forehead on his.

"I love you too. You're so gentle with me I forgot who you are," Lei admitted.

"And who am I to you? Did I scare you?" Between the hesitance in his tone and concern in his eyes, Lei's heart squeezed.

"Not at all. I was scared for you, but I wasn't scared of you. All I could think about was how many witnesses there would be if charges were pressed against you. Even I wouldn't be able to talk you out of that."

Londen chuckled. "Good. It would break my heart if you no longer felt safe with me."

"I feel safer with you. Honestly, it was a little sexy."

"Yeah?" The sight of him licking his lips as he gripped her waist had Lei swallowing a moan.

"Mhm." She rocked her hips against him and sucked his

bottom lip into her mouth for a deep kiss. When his hand slid under her shirt, Lei pulled away. "What about Keith?"

"He's not going to get back in until I knock on the window."

"Babe, we can't leave him out there long!"

"Then you'll need to cum quick…"

forty-seven

Londen

MAY

"I could do this shit for hours," Londen muttered against Lei's ear before kissing it.

With a giggle, she turned slightly to place a sweet kiss to his lips.

"I haven't done this for pleasure in years. You make all things better. This is so much fun!"

They'd randomly decided to turn a room in her home into a music room. Londen had been dying to play something with her after finding out about all the instruments she played. There was a grand piano in her sitting room, but Lei admitted she never played it. Apparently, her experience with Hamilton and Jennifer ruined instruments for her. Londen could understand that, but he was grateful that playing with him corrected that traumatizing time in her life.

Trying out a keyboard led to them playing together so well they'd garnered a crowd. The more they played, the more Londen's mind shifted to other things. He'd never felt so compatible with a woman before, and their differences balanced each other out. Londen was trying his hardest not to rush and propose because he was sure they had forever together, but every day that passed he wanted to legally make her his more and more.

They ended up playing a little while longer before making their way over to the drums. After deciding on two sets, they headed to the front to check out. Their order was so large it would have to be delivered by truck and Londen was okay with that.

After checking out, they headed to the ice cream shop next door. Lei got a classic strawberry waffle cone while Londen was more adventurous with a kitchen sink mix that was every flavor mixed up. Sitting across from each other, Londen looked her face over intently as she licked her ice cream. The visual was filling his mind with naughty thoughts.

Clearing his throat, Londen shook the thoughts away.

There was something he'd been needing to talk to her about and he couldn't put it off any longer.

"Baby," he called, gaining her attention. She was so deep with her ice cream she hadn't bothered looking up at him or their surroundings. That didn't matter though. As long as she was with him, she was always safe.

"Hmm?" she called, rolling her tongue across the top of the ice cream.

"I need you to eat with a spoon while I'm trying to talk to you. All I can think about is your tongue swirling around my dick."

Lei's head flung back as she laughed. "I most certainly can slurp you up later, but what's on your mind?"

"Ace offered me a very good position in the secret society. I'll get to do what I love, criminal profiling."

Lei's eyes widened as she gasped and lightly smacked the table. "That's great, babe! Congratulations."

"Yeah, thank you. I would have to do two years of training, but the job is mine."

"Yay, I'm so happy for you! I remember you talking about how that was what you truly wanted to do with your life. I figured you would be happy doing just about anything, but nothing would probably fulfill you the way this will. This just made my day."

Londen smiled bashfully. "There's... something that has me hesitant to take the job."

Her hand lowered as she stared at him with a confused expression. "What would make you not take the job?"

"It's in Memphis."

"Oh." She lowered her ice cream completely into its container.

"Eat, Lei."

"You're not going to turn this down for me, are you?"

Londen shrugged as he picked up her ice cream and handed it back to her. "I don't know. If we're going to get married, I have to take your future into consideration as well. I don't know if I want to make a three-hour commute twice a day going from here to Memphis, but I couldn't ask you to go back to the place that holds so many bad memories for you. You've always expressed how much you love your home and the life you've built here. I can't take you away from that."

Lei stood and walked over to his side of the table. She took his hand into hers.

"First, I appreciate you considering me in your future in such an important decision, but I can't let you turn this down. This was something that you wanted before I came into the picture."

"It is, but the best relationships have compromise."

"They do," Lei agreed quickly... softly. "But a compromise would be me going to Memphis with you, not you turning down the opportunity to do what you love."

"Lei..."

"I can keep my house here, because I'm sure we'll be coming back often. It'll be where we can stay on weekends and holidays when we come. And as far as my trigger with Memphis, it's time I worked through that, anyway. It's been over ten years, and I've been working steadily to release the power they and that city has over me. By cutting Jennifer off, I already feel so much lighter. I don't think it's going to be easy, especially with the anxiety of running into them, but I'm going to do whatever it takes to make this work because I want us to work. If you were going to sacrifice this for me, there's no doubt that I'm going to take this move with you."

Cupping her cheek, Londen covered her lips with his.

The coldness and sweetness of the strawberry ice cream were both refreshing. With his lips still connected to hers, he told her, "Just when I think I can't love you anymore, you give me a new reason to."

With a smile, Lei wrapped her arms around his neck and pecked his lips. "Thank you for being a safe love. Thank you for providing the security I needed to open myself up to this again. I love you so much, babe."

Londen moaned against her lips before declaring, "I love you too."

forty-eight

Lei

THE RIDE to Memphis was more draining than it had ever been. Lei was tired as hell by the time they'd arrived at the address Jennifer had given her. After hearing about London's job opportunity, Lei reached out to Jennifer and told her she needed to see her. Without asking any questions, Jennifer gave her the address and told her she could stop by at any time.

Lei waited until the following weekend to head that

way, and she was glad Londen had come with her. Even if he hadn't, she knew she needed to make this trip. Before she permanently returned to Memphis, Lei was determined to look her past in the face.

"Are you sure about this?" Londen asked, taking her hand into his as she stared at the house.

"Yes. I need to know that I can see them and not break down. If I can do that, I can come back to Memphis and be okay."

"Okay, but if you get uncomfortable at any point, we can leave."

Lei nodded her agreement as she breathed deeply. With the way she was feeling, Lei didn't plan on staying long, anyway. Between her tiredness, tender breasts, and cramping, Lei was ready to crawl into her bed and sleep the discomfort away. If Simone and Destiny knew she'd come to Memphis without seeing them, they would have a fit, so Lei was going to try to see them before they left for Rose Valley Hills. If her symptoms didn't get any better, they'd just have to be upset.

Keith opened the door for her, and Lei held Londen's hand tightly. It was the anchor she needed. They made their way to the front of the house, where she took her time ringing the doorbell to further calm her nerves.

The moment Jennifer opened the door and Lei laid eyes on her, her heart stopped. With watery eyes, she stared at Jennifer as if she was looking at a ghost. It was evident Jennifer didn't know what to do, because she reached for Lei, then quickly pulled her arms away.

"It's so good to see you, Roy. Please, come in."

"It's Lei," she reminded, slowly stepping inside.

"Right, yes. Sorry."

With a nervous chuckle, Jennifer closed the door behind them.

"Londen Graham." Londen shook Jennifer's hand, pulling in her energy to get a feel for her.

"It's nice to meet you."

Lei could tell Londen had no plans of returning the gesture, and that made her smile. The longer they stood there, the less it felt like there was an elephant on her chest. The warmth that was radiating out slowly began to dispel.

"Would you... like to have a seat?" Jennifer offered. "Can I get you anything?"

"No, we won't be long. I really just wanted to set eyes on you. We're going to be moving back to Memphis in a couple of years, and I wanted to see how I would react to seeing you."

Jennifer's hand flew to her chest. She smiled widely. "You're coming back home?"

Lei's head shook. "Rose Valley Hills is my home, but yes, I'll be coming back to Memphis."

"I have to ask..." Jennifer looked from Lei to Londen back to Lei. "Is there any chance of us establishing a relationship when you come back? I know you said it was best for you if we didn't talk..."

"And I still feel that way. I feel like we're at a good place now. I've forgiven you and Marcus, and even Regal, but I don't have to allow you into my life to prove that."

Jennifer's smile wavered. "I understand." She released a heavy breath and looked around the entryway. "Regal and Royalty are in the living room if you want to see them too. Steven is out back getting ready to grill."

"Royalty," Lei repeated, voice thick with emotion. "I still can't believe she named her baby after me."

"I know what she did was wrong, but..."

"Jennifer, please," Lei interrupted, lifting her hand to stop her. "I didn't come here for that."

Nodding rapidly, Jennifer took a step back. "Okay. I'll um... go and get them if you don't want to come in any further."

"That would be great, thank you."

Lei didn't pull her eyes away from Jennifer until she was no longer in sight. She jumped slightly at the feel of Londen's hand on the small of her back.

"You good?"

"Yes," she almost whispered. "My heart's beating like crazy now. Regal is... different. I've been talking to Jennifer, but not Regal. I don't know how this is going to be."

"I think it's going to be easier than you realize. Surprising but easier. You've had quite some time to process this, and you're a hell of a lot stronger than you think. You've got this, Baby, and even if you don't... I got you."

Londen wrapped his arms around her, and just as they kissed, they heard, "Ooh, they kissing!" in the background.

With a chuckle, Lei turned to face Regal, Royalty, and Steven. At the sight of Royalty, Lei's knees almost buckled. She was the spitting image of Regal when she was a child. Regal still looked the same... just a little bigger with longer hair. Lei couldn't allow her eyes to focus on Steven long enough to even process his presence. He was such a nonfactor to her, she hoped to completely erase him from her memory one day.

"Well, hello there," Lei greeted, locking eyes with Royalty.

"Hi."

"Hey, Roy," Regal greeted while Steven wrapped his arm around her waist.

"Royalty," he spoke.

Looking from one to the other, Lei gave herself time to process what she was feeling. It wasn't love or hate—it was indifference. All this time she feared exploding or shrinking if she ever crossed paths with these people again, but they meant so little to her now that she looked at them as if they were strangers.

"Wow," Lei whispered as tears filled her eyes. "Hey. Um..." Her head shook absently as she gave Jennifer her attention. "Thank you for this. It was exactly what I needed."

Lei turned abruptly to leave, and Jennifer followed close behind.

"Wait, that's it? You're leaving already?"

"Yeah. I came, I saw, and I felt... nothing at all." Lei's chuckle was light as she grabbed Londen's hand. "I feared seeing y'all would fill me with all these negative emotions, but I didn't feel a damn thing looking at them, and I truly thank God for that."

Stunned, Jennifer stood there with her mouth partially opened as they walked away.

"Royalty!" Regal yelled, jogging toward them. "Um... I just... wanted to say sorry again. There was no room for talking when you found out, and that's on me. I never should have done something so horrible to you. Trust me, I've paid for it." She looked back toward the house. "That man has taken me through it every year that we've been together, and I know that's my karma for what I did to you."

At the sound of Regal's confession, Lei's heart grew heavy. It felt like she had a lump in her throat, trapping words her heart needed to say even though her mind didn't want her to.

"Regardless, you don't deserve to be mistreated for ten years, Regal. If he's not doing right by you and your daughter, leave him."

Regal chuckled as her eyes watered. She looked into the distance as she said, "It's not that simple, but thank you."

Lei stared at her for a few seconds before taking Regal's hand into hers and squeezing it. Regal finally looked into her eyes as her tears began to fall. It was then that Lei noticed the purple bruise under her eye that her makeup was trying to cover up.

Lei's nostrils flared and lips curled as she gritted her teeth.

"Did he... Is he putting his fucking hands on you?" Lei seethed, looking toward the door as if she could see him.

"When he's not cheating... yes."

"Regal," Lei called, pulling her into her arms. "Girl, we don't have to be close for me to want better for you. You need to leave him. If not for yourself, for your daughter. Is this the normal you want her to grow up seeing? Do you want her attracted to boys like Steven who are going to treat her the exact same way?"

"I don't know what else to do!" Regal whisper-screamed. "He's all we have, Lei. I didn't finish my last year of college because I was pregnant with Royalty. I haven't worked in the past ten years. He makes all the money and... I'm just... stuck."

Londen's breath came out low and hard as he stepped toward them. "Do you want me to handle that, Baby? Because you *know* I fucking will."

Lei's eyes squeezed shut as she considered Londen's request. "Not while their daughter is in there."

"What is he talking about, Royalty?"

"It's Lei," she corrected. "And does Steven have life insurance?"

Her mouth dropped, and eyes protruded in surprise. "Yes, but... you can't..." She looked at Londen. "He can't kill him. That's Roy's father."

"Girl, fuck that. If that man is putting his hands on you, he deserves to die. Take that life insurance and start fresh with your daughter. When you're ready for that, Jennifer knows how to get in touch with me."

Lei gave Regal another brief hug before walking away. While she still had no desire to be in their lives, she wouldn't ignore what was going on with Regal. There was a great chance Regal would never reach out for help, and if that was the choice she made, Lei was more than okay with that. If she did call, though, Lei would allow Londen to do whatever the hell it was he wanted to do to Steven.

Londen waited until they were in the car to ask, "Are you really good?"

Sniffling, Lei nodded as she wiped her tears. "I am, and these are happy tears. It feels so freeing, no longer allowing fear and pain to hold me back. And knowing the bullet I dodged with Steven..." She chuckled as her tears fell more frequently. "This gave me the confidence I need to start a new life here with you."

"I'm glad because I wasn't going to do this without you."

"Thankfully, you won't have to."

Lei's head tilted back, and she closed her eyes as a smile rested on her face. It felt like she could finally close that chapter of her life, for good, and Lei was so... so happy about that.

forty-nine

Lei

LATER THAT AFTERNOON

As excited as Lei was to be with Simone and Destiny, she couldn't focus for anything. Her mind kept drifting back to Regal and the hopeless look on her face. To Royalty and how happy she appeared to be. Lei couldn't imagine how much of an expense Regal was paying to raise a happy, healthy daughter with Steven. Though Londen promised not to handle Steven until Regal reached out, a part of Lei wanted to have him take care of it now and just bless Regal with enough money for a fresh start herself. If she did that, though, Regal would be the one carrying hate in her heart for Lei, and Lei didn't want to be on the receiving end of that.

Unfortunately, a woman wouldn't leave until she was ready to. All Lei could do was hope Regal made that decision before Steven made the decision for her to leave this world.

"Hey," Simone called softly, squeezing Lei's hand. "Are you okay? You look like you have a lot on your mind."

"Yes, and I do, but I'm good. Just... can't get Regal's face out of my head."

Simone's eyes rolled and Destiny chuckled. "Fuck her and whatever she's going through. She deserves it for what she did to you."

Lei hadn't mentioned what transpired because she wasn't the kind of woman to spread another woman's business. "That's not true, Simone. She deserved to be punished, but not like this and not this long."

That caused Simone's smile to fade while Destiny asked, "Uh oh. Is she going to be okay?"

Lei's mouth twisted to the side as her head shook. "Honestly, I don't know. I'm trying not to worry about her, but that's hard to do. I'm a fighter and advocate for those who can't defend themselves. She's asking me to do nothing and it's driving me crazy." Lei chuckled. "Okay, so maybe the first way I offered to help was a bit extreme, but I want to help, nonetheless."

"If you're offering to help her, it must be something serious," Simone decided.

"Right, because when she said she was coming, she made it clear she didn't want to have anything to do with them."

"It's... definitely serious. I wouldn't be able to face myself if I didn't do *something*. Even if I can't do anything right now, when she's ready, I'll be there."

Releasing that did help lighten Lei's load. The conversation shifted, and she was able to stay focused until they were done eating. When Destiny asked if they were going to go shopping or to grab drinks, Lei declined.

"I would love to, but I'm so drained, y'all. I really just want to go to the hotel and nap before we get back on the road."

"That's understandable, I'm sure you've had a long day," Simone said.

"Well, at least we can look forward to hanging out again when y'all move back to Memphis. That's exciting," Destiny added.

"I know, right? And I'll be back before then too. Now that I've stepped foot in the city and faced them, I feel a lot lighter. I can handle it now."

"Good," Simone said before hugging Lei. After Destiny did the same, Lei called Londen to let him know she was ready to go.

While she caught up with the girls, he'd done the same with a few people from around the way. Though she insisted one of them could take her back to the hotel, Londen wasn't having that. He told her he'd be at her in about fifteen minutes, and that gave Lei enough time to decompress. Though Simone and Destiny wanted to stay with her until Londen arrived, they also knew she loved her solitude and needed time to herself after engaging with people. As close as they were, her oldest best friends weren't immune to that.

"Aye, lil mama." At the sound of Londen's voice coming from behind her, Lei's eyes closed as she grinned. "You sexy as fuck. You got a man?"

"I might, but what that got to do with you?"

"I'm just tryna see what obstacles I might have to get to you."

Lei pulled hair behind her ears as Londen sat next to her. Between his lustful glare and how sexy he looked licking his lips, Lei was tempted to give it to him in the bathroom of this restaurant.

"Babe, I missed you too much for all this roleplaying bullshit. You can have my pussy right now."

Londen's laugh was hearty as he stood and helped her do the same. "I'd love to be inside you, but you look a little tired, honestly. You sure you feeling okay?"

Lei shrugged as their fingers connected. As they walked out of the restaurant, she said, "It feels like I'm about to start my period but it's late. I'll just be glad when it comes so this will be over."

His steps slowed as he looked down at her. "Your period is late?" The grin that spread his lips caused her to playfully roll her eyes. Londen's hand lowered to her stomach. "Baby got a baby in here?"

"I considered if that could be the case, but I don't want you to get your hopes up."

"Why wouldn't I get my hopes up?" Londen asked as he opened the door. "This is what we want, right, or have you changed your mind?"

"It's... everything I want right now, babe."

His tone was uncertain as he asked, "Then why wouldn't I get my hopes up?"

Their movements stopped when they made it outside. "Because this isn't the first time I've missed a period." Lei ran her fingers through her hair as she sighed and briefly looked away from him. "I really wasn't planning to have this conversation like this."

"Then let's go to the hotel."

Lei nodded, following his lead as they walked away. A woman gasped at the sight of Londen, dropping her purse and phone as she muttered, "Oh, my God."

Londen stared at her intently before chuckling and shaking his head. "Felicia."

"Lo-Londen... what are you doing out?"

"Good behavior."

Not bothering to respond, the woman frantically looked around. Lei's eyes followed her, landing on a man and younger boy that looked a *lot* like Londen.

"Londen, I thought you were going to be gone for a, a longer time. I..."

"What's wrong with you?" Londen asked.

Lei grabbed his hand and shook before pointing toward the boy. "Um... babe." Lei looked up at him to gauge his reaction.

Lei saw the exact moment Londen's heart stopped beating, causing his chest to deflate. His lips pressed together tightly before he ran his hand over his mouth. Raised eyebrows hovered over watery eyes that stared without blinking. It wasn't until Lei softly called his name did Londen seem to return to the present moment.

"I'm only going to ask you this once, Felicia, and I need you to tell me the truth."

"Yes," she cried. "He's yours. But please, don't say anything about this in front of him. I promise I'll explain everything in private. Just please... don't scar my baby for life with this truth."

Londen's hand covered his mouth as he chuckled, but Lei could see the veins protruding in his forehead. His legs were planted wide, chest thrusted out.

"You're asking me not to scar my son by telling him I'm his father, but you didn't take into consideration the ramifications of hiding the fact that I even had a son. Fuck outta here with that bullshit, Felicia. You're going to introduce him to me as soon as they get over here."

"Londen, please..."

The stern look he gave her silenced Felicia.

Lei could feel the heat radiating off her body from nervousness. She was visibly shaking.

"Is everything okay, Felicia?" the man asked, making his way to her side. His arm wrapped possessively around her waist.

"Londen," Lei called sweetly, and at the sound of his name, the man's eyes almost bulged out of his head.

"Oh, you know me? So I'm the only one that's out of the loop then?"

"Baby," Lei called. "Not here." Londen's jaw was clenched as he looked down at her. Their eyes remained locked for seconds on end while Lei stroked his chest. "I got you, and I'm with you. Let's do this privately."

With flaring nostrils and watery eyes, Londen conceded. He nodded before wiping away a quickly fallen tear.

"Meet me at the Peabody lobby this evening at six," he told Felicia, not even bothering to look her way. He did, however, look at his son for a few seconds before shaking his head as he walked away.

Lei sluggishly followed him, unsure what the hell to do.

fifty

Londen

5:30 p.m.

AFTER PRAYING for him and affirming him, Lei gave Londen space, and he appreciated that. He needed time to process the fact that he had a son. It didn't take him long to lace together a scenario of why Felicia kept the truth about her pregnancy from him. As hurt and upset as he was by that, it was her body and her choice to make. Now that he was out, Londen was going to do whatever he had to, to make a place in his son's life. He wasn't sure how easy that would be, but growing close to the person who was half of him would be worth it.

He had so many questions about his son, the first of which was what was his name? Did he like sports? Was he healthy? What was his favorite subject in school? Did he like girls yet? Was he aware of Londen in any way? How was he being loved and nurtured? Could he fight? What was his favorite food?

Massaging his temples as his elbows rested on his thighs, Londen rocked back and forth. He wanted to call his parents and share the news with them, but they'd have more questions than he'd have answers to. Though he'd calmed down a bit, Londen was still hurt more than anything. There was a whole little person out here in the world with half of his makeup, who probably knew nothing about him. Every time that thought crossed his mind, his hurt would be replaced with anger.

Standing, Londen made his way out of the bedroom and into the living room area. Lei was stretched out on the couch reading "Atlas of the Heart" by Brené Brown. At the sight of him, she set the book down and sat up to make space for him on the couch.

"You okay, babe?"

His head shook though his mouth said, "Yeah."

"Is there anything I can do?"

"You can tell me how you're feeling about all of this."

The blank stare she gave him made Londen smile. "What do you mean? How I feel has no weight right now. I'm concerned about you."

"How you feel does matter. You're my woman. We are

heavily in the process of shaping our futures together. Now... I have a son. How does that make you feel? Does that change anything for you? For us? Or is it too soon for you to tell?"

She scratched her nose and sniffled before closing her silk robe over her gown, and the gesture wasn't lost on Londen. There was something in her heart that she wanted to close him off to. They'd made a hell of a lot of progress getting Lei to open herself up to him. Was him having a son going to change that?

"I feel hurt and angry for you more than anything. In my mind, I know Felicia had the right to do what she did, but in my heart, I hate she kept something so special and beautiful from you. I'm sure she had a good reason, but... I don't know. That just hurts me. Maybe because of how much I want my own child. To know that you've had one all this time and had no idea... that's foul. Personally... I feel like this was a wake-up call."

"How so?"

Her gaze shifted as she carefully considered her words. Looking down into her lap, Lei huffed out her annoyance before calmly speaking again.

"We've been in this fairytale bubble since we met, and this is reality. We haven't known each other for a full six months and we're talking about marriage and babies. On top of you adjusting to being out. Training and a big move. It's a lot already, and now you have a son. I just think we should have gone a little slower. A baby is the last thing you need right now, and now that you have a son..."

"Let me stop you right there," Londen said quietly, though his thoughts were screaming. As much as he was trying to contain his hurt, that was getting harder and harder to do. "Whether we've known each other for six months or six millennias, I'm in love with you, and I've meant everything I said I wanted in this life with you." Londen took her hand into his. "Me having a son does not take the place of the family I want to have with you. I've missed out on everything with my son." His voice broke and head dropped. Londen wasn't the kind of man who shied away from expressing himself, but being emotional and crying was simply something he didn't do. He pulled in a shaky breath and dried his eyes, and when he looked into hers, they were wet. "But I'm honored to have a chance to be in his life now. Still, I want to be there with you every step of the way. I want a hand in it all. And I hope you never allow yourself to think anything different."

"I really needed to hear you say that," she confessed. "I didn't want to bring it up because you already have so much on your plate and my overthinking had me paralyzed. All I could think about was how premature us trying to get to our happiness felt. Life seems to have so many things in store for you. I just... don't want to get lost in the shuffle of that."

"Baby..." Londen chuckled softly and pulled her onto his lap. "I don't give a damn what life has in store for me. We're controlling our own fate. I need you by my side every step of the way."

Lei nibbled her bottom lip before nodding and giving him a kiss.

"I love you so much," she whispered, tears finally cascading down her cheeks.

"I love you too. And I'm still as committed to our life together now as I was a few hours ago."

She laughed softly as he wiped away her tears. "So... are you excited to meet him? I know it might not be this evening, but, babe, you got a mini you out here. I'm genuinely happy for you."

Sitting back in his seat, Londen held her close. "I'm excited but I'm also concerned about how this transition will go. Now that I've calmed down a lot, I don't want to disrupt his normal because the last nine years of his life have been taken from me."

"So, what was up with you and her before you went to prison? Were you in a relationship or what?"

"Well, we were together, but we broke up when I was arrested. She didn't want to leave me, but I wasn't going to let her do that time with me. Now I question if she didn't tell me about my son because I broke up with her."

"If that was the case, that was horrible. Even if you wanted to spare her from that, she still should have told you. But I still get it. If you didn't want her to witness that cycle of your life, she probably didn't think you would want your son to either. It's bad no matter how you view it."

"Speaking of cycles..."

Lei chuckled and shook her head. "No, Londen. There is enough going on right now. We can talk about that later."

"I'm cool with that, but I want to know if you're pregnant now."

"How about we wait at least until we get back home? Right now, all I want you to focus on is this meeting with Felicia and potentially your son. Are you going to be okay if she's alone?"

"Yeah, I think that'll be better. At first, I wanted to see him tonight, but like I said... I don't want to mess up his normal. Once Felicia and I are on the same page, then I'll see him."

"That's very fatherly of you already, doing what's best for your child. I'm proud of you."

"I'm proud of me too, because it took everything inside of me not to handle this a different way."

Though Lei laughed, Londen was dead serious. He was seconds away from blowing up Felicia's whole world. If Lei wasn't there to help him calm himself down, things would have gone a hell of a lot different.

fifty-one

Lei

6:00 p.m.

FELICIA WAS BEAUTIFUL, that Lei wouldn't deny. Her skin was light with a red undertone. Curly hair rested at the top of her head in a pineapple updo. She had round eyes and lips, and a medium-sized curvy shape.

"Are you sure you want me here?" Lei asked as they

headed toward the set of chairs by Felicia. "I can wait for you at the bar."

"I don't want you drinking until we know if you're pregnant or not, and I need you close to keep me calm."

Not bothering to respond, Lei stepped a little closer to his side. When Felicia spotted them, she swallowed hard and stood. Cupping her hands, she twiddled her thumbs.

"Hey," she spoke.

Londen's head bobbed as he helped Lei take her seat, then sat in the seat next to her that was across from Felicia.

"Why didn't you tell me?"

Felicia chuckled nervously as she sat back down. "You'd been sentenced to twenty-five years. You told me you didn't want me to do that time with you. I figured it would be best for my son if he didn't know you."

"Did you not want him to know me because I was in prison, or because I broke up with you?"

"Honestly, both. In the beginning, it was spite I can't lie. If you didn't want me, you didn't want my child. With time, I realized that wasn't the image I wanted him to have. As soon as I knew I was having a boy, my perspective changed. It wasn't about you or me; it was about him. I wanted him to grow up in a healthy, loving environment with good influences..."

"Not a father who was in prison." Felicia didn't confirm or deny. "So who was the nigga that was with y'all earlier, because he knew me even if my son doesn't."

"That was Da'Mir." She smiled just at the mention of his name. "My husband. I met him right after I had Landon."

"Landon?" Londen repeated with a scoff as his leg began to shake. Lei placed her hand on it, and it immediately stopped shaking.

"Yes, Landon." Felicia cleared her throat. "We were in the grocery store, and I was about to have a meltdown. I felt so alone. I wasn't getting any sleep or help from my family because they didn't agree with me not telling you. They are in my son's life now, but the beginning was rocky. Anyway, I was on the baby aisle and both me and Landon were crying." Her eyes watered at the memory. "Before I knew it... Da'Mir appeared out of nowhere like an angel. He took Landon out of his car seat and soothed him, giving me time to see to myself. Once I was composed, he held Landon while I grabbed everything I needed. We exchanged numbers and started a friendship. I didn't tell him about my situation until I felt I could trust him, and he stepped up and helped me. By the time Landon could talk, we had decided Da'Mir was the only father figure he would have, so Landon started calling him Daddy. We were married about a year after that and... the rest is history."

Londen's head bobbed once as he looked away. "He's happy?"

"Very. And very healthy. Like I said, my family is in his life now and, of course, Da'Mir's family is too. I apologize for not telling you, but I did what I thought was the right thing to do."

He released a quick chuckle. "For everyone except me."

"Londen," she called softly, reaching forward to grab his hand, but he quickly pulled it away. "I'm truly sorry. And I know this is a big ask, but I was wondering if you could just... stay away."

Londen's head jerked in her direction. "What did you just say to me?"

"I don't want to confuse him. Da'Mir is his father."

"Except he's not."

"He... legally is. Da'Mir adopted him."

Londen released a bark of laughter before almost yelling, "How is that even fucking possible, Felicia? Wouldn't I have to sign over my rights for you to do that shit?"

Her head hung. "Well, yes, but there are special circumstances where the court will suspend rights in order for the adoption to go through."

"And what picture did you paint of me for that to happen? Or was finding out I was in prison all it took for them to help you take my son from me?"

"Look, Londen, I know this might be hard for you, but you have to believe me when I say my son..."

"He's *our* son," Londen roared. "Regardless of what you and this nigga got going on, that's my blood."

"Okay," Felicia agreed with a shaky voice, hands lifted in surrender. "Our son is good. Please don't come and disrupt his life."

Londen cupped his hands over his mouth. Lei held on to the silence as she waited for him to speak.

"You're out your motherfucking mind if you think I'm going to live in this world knowing another man is raising my son. First, I'm going to sue the state of Tennessee for letting you do this, and you better hope I don't sue you and your weak ass husband too. Then, I'm going to regain my rights to my son and start to establish a relationship with him. It will be a gentle, slow process and I'm going to make sure he has all the resources and help he needs for this adjustment, but I'm going to be in his life, and there's not shit you can do to stop me."

Londen stood and walked away, and his steps were so long and fast Lei could barely keep up. As they made their way to their private floor in the hotel, Londen was on the phone making several calls to attorneys and private investigators, giving orders to ensure Felicia was watched and not able to run away with his son.

Lei gave him space and took that time to call her parents and let them know they wouldn't be returning today. From the sound of it, Londen had a lot to do, and Memphis was where he needed to be.

fifty-two

Londen

THREE DAYS Later

I*t was* their last day in Memphis, and Londen couldn't wait to get home. He'd made a lot of moves as far as regaining his rights to Landon, but it would still be a lengthy process. First, he'd have to win his lawsuit, and with the way courts were, they weren't going to expedite that process. Though

Londen was anxious to be in his son's life, he was patient. This would have to be done the right way. As much as he wanted to send a crew into Felicia's home and leave no one but his son alive, that would frame him as the monster Felicia tried to make him out to be. So as hard as it was to leave Memphis without seeing his son again, Londen had to find peace with that.

Lei had been a gem... there when needed, giving space when not, keeping him focused on what was right instead of allowing his hate and ego to rule him. If there was any doubt in Londen's mind that Lei was the woman for him, she'd proven it on this trip to Memphis. He had something very special planned for her when they made it back home, but for now, there was still a matter of importance that they needed to handle themselves.

After having room service delivered, Londen placed the pregnancy tests he'd gotten on the tray, then took it into the bedroom. Lei was in the middle of the bed, channel surfing. They had another three hours before they needed to check out, and she was taking full advantage of the rest. Londen loved this carefree side of her and wished she'd allow him to bless her with the ability to experience it every day, but Lei insisted on working, even if she didn't have any new clients right now.

"Aw, aren't you just full of sugar. Thank you, babe."

Chuckling, Londen reminded her, "I've told you about calling me sweet."

"Yeah, yeah. Bring me my food."

Lei's smile faded at the sight of the pregnancy tests on the tray. She bit her bottom lip and looked up at him with puppy dog eyes that almost made him want to continue to let her avoid this.

"We need to know, Baby," Londen reasoned softly, sitting in bed next to her.

Her chin trembled and head tilted as she huffed. "I know. I just don't want to take the test and it be negative."

"Well, if it is, that'll just mean we have more time with each other. It won't be the end of the world if you aren't pregnant, Lei."

"I had fibroids," she blurted, avoiding his eyes. "They came right after I moved to Rose Valley. I felt slight differences, but it wasn't until I missed my period for three months straight that I went ahead and made an appointment with my gynecologist. She wanted me to wait until I was ready to start my family to have them removed, but I didn't want to risk getting more or letting the ones I had get bigger, so I had the surgery about six months after that. She couldn't guarantee me they wouldn't return, and even though that was a long time ago, I'm scared that's what this is. I don't want to get my hopes up thinking I'm pregnant and it turns out the fibroids are back."

Londen knew all about fibroids because his mother had them. She couldn't start her family until she had the surgery, and Harem swore that was the best decision she'd ever made. They had severely diminished the quality of her everyday life, and Londen couldn't imagine the pain of what any woman with fibroids or hormonal and reproductive issues had to go through.

"I'm sorry about that, but I'm glad you made the choice to handle that quickly. If these tests come out negative and the fibroids are back, we'll handle that. But we need to know what is going on either way."

"You're right," she almost whispered. "I'll go ahead and take them after we eat."

With her agreement, Londen scarfed down his food as

quickly as he could. Lei laughed because he already ate fast, but it was even worse this time around. She took her time eating, laughing at his annoyance with her pettiness. Still, eventually, she completed her breakfast and headed for the bathroom.

Time slowed down even more as he waited. Regardless of the outcome, Londen reminded himself it would be okay either way. Knowledge was power, and he had to know what was going on with his woman. It was her body, but he'd committed himself to taking care of her for the rest of her life. Seeing her sluggish and in so much discomfort broke his heart. Whatever the reason behind it, Londen needed to know so he could help her take care of it.

Lei opened the bathroom door with a smile. "I don't want to look."

"You want me to?"

She laughed. "Yeah, unless you want to call Keith."

"I'll call Keith."

As Londen reached for his phone, Lei laughed even harder. "Londen! Do *not* make that man come up here to look at this test." She walked over to him and took his hand. "Come on. Let's look together."

They both took slow steps toward the bathroom. She had a roll of tissue paper in front of the tests, and he couldn't help but laugh at the sight of it.

"You really didn't want to look, huh?"

"I'm scared."

"I got you, Baby." Pushing the tissue away, Londen looked down at the tests.

He stared at it, blinking back tears.

"What does it say?" she asked, tugging his hand. "Are we pregnant?"

The laugh that Londen released was so happy and light,

he'd never heard a sound like that come from himself. His head flung back as he palmed his face.

"Babe!"

"Yes," he answered, licking his lips as he smiled. Her eyes watered as she stared into his.

"Yes?" Lei repeated.

He nodded. "Yes."

"We're pregnant?" Her voice was low and shaky as she squeezed his hand.

"We're pregnant."

Saying the words brought tears to his eyes. Lifting her into the air, Londen sat her on the sink counter as she squealed and sobbed.

"Oh my God. I'm really pregnant?"

"You are," he confirmed, cupping her head and placing a kiss to the center of her forehead. He couldn't resist lowering his hand to her stomach. Though she wasn't showing at all, just knowing their baby was in the same room as them had his tears falling. "You are."

"Londen," she almost sang, hugging his neck tightly. "We're really going to have a baby?"

Londen chuckled, unfazed by her disbelief. Shit, he was in disbelief too. This was definitely what he wanted, but he wasn't expecting God to bless him to actually have it so soon.

"Wow," he muttered, placing a kiss to her neck before chuckling.

Londen was so consumed by what he was leaving Memphis without, and now... he had a gift to take back home.

epilogue

LEI & Londen
Back in Rose Valley Hills

"Um... what's going on?" Lei asked at the sight of cars in her driveway.

"I had your mom to give my staff the key so they could put something together for you, for me."

Her head shook in disbelief as she chuckled. "With everything that was going on in Memphis, you took the time to do something here for me?"

"I did. Let's go."

Lei didn't have to be told twice. She was so excited she didn't bother to wait for Keith to open her door. Londen looked on in pride and amusement as she rushed toward the front door. As excited as she was, she still waited for him to make his way to her side.

"Can I have a hint?"

"Nope. Just go inside and see."

With a bob of her head, Lei stepped into her home after he opened the door. A gasp escaped her at the sight before her. An aisle had been created out of tea light candles and rose petals. They led the way to the living room, where Londen had a hibachi chef and her favorite sushi rolls already waiting.

"Ah! This is perfect!" she yelled happily, not even bothering to see what else he had.

"There's more."

"Really?"

"Yeah. Let's go out back."

As they walked out, Londen's heart raced. Up until now, making this choice was so natural he felt calm. The weight of the situation had settled within his heart. Though he was confident Lei would accept his marriage proposal, he was still nervous about doing it. Saying she wanted to spend her life with him was one thing, but agreeing to it was something else. Now that he knew for sure that she was pregnant, there was nothing stopping Londen from taking that next step.

Outside, a professional photographer waited to capture the moment.

Lei bounced up and down at the sight of the custom rose gold Lamborghini Aventador he had waiting for her. He'd started the process of getting the car for her months ago, and it just so happened to be ready right before they left for Memphis.

"Sheesh," Lei mumbled, walking around the car. "This is... *so* freaking beautiful, Londen. Is it really mine?"

"All yours. The keys are on that tray."

Lei's head turned to the left, focusing on the tray that held not only the keys to the car but her engagement ring and a love letter as well. The ring was something he'd gotten her mother's help with. Though Londen believed he had a good enough idea of her style, he wanted to make sure both her engagement and wedding rings were all she had ever dreamed of. With Cashmere's guidance, he'd purchased a ten carat, emerald-cut diamond that was just as elegant and classy as her everyday style.

Her hands shook as they lifted. Lei took small steps back as her body quaked. Covering her mouth, she began to cry. After giving her a few seconds to process the full weight of this moment, Londen walked over to her. Even with the flashing of the photographer's camera, all Londen could focus on was Lei.

Taking her hand into his, Londen got down on one knee. "This was in the works before we found out you were pregnant, but now that we know, I wanted to do this sooner. I want you to be my wife before you become the mother of my child."

Lei wiped a few tears, and just as quickly, more flowed.

"From the moment I saw your picture, Lei, your soul was connected to mine. I didn't know what it was about you I was so drawn to, but I was determined to find out. Even with a simple Hi, you spoke to my heart in a way that no other woman has. I've been falling in love with you, more and more, with each day that passes by. It would be my highest honor to have you as my wife."

Londen grabbed the ring. "Lei Armani Fifer, will you marry me?"

Nodding adamantly, Lei's body swayed slightly as she laughed. "Yes, Londen. Yes!"

She did a little jig as he put the ring on her finger that made Londen laugh. He licked his lips as he stood, not wasting any time pulling her into his arms. Londen's kiss was tender, his embrace sure. Lei trembled in his arms, as if the sheer need of his kisses overwhelmed her senses.

"Babe... really?" Before he could answer, Lei was kissing him again. "You've made this the best year of my life, and it's not even over yet."

"There's so much more to come, I hope you know that."

"I want to read my letter now."

Londen laughed as she removed his arms from around her waist to turn and retrieve the letter.

"We're in the middle of my romantic proposal and you want to read a damn letter?"

"Absolutely." She eyed him as if she couldn't believe what he'd just said. "Not only do I love your words, but ten years ago, I ran away from Memphis filled with nothing but hurt and anger. I was to the point of suicide. It felt like every time I found the courage to live, someone I loved stabbed me in the heart. I never thought ten years later that love letters from Memphis would be the final thing God used to heal me. You've not only restored my faith in humanity, but you've rekindled my desire for love and marriage and babies and a happily ever after. So yes, I love the material things and what this ring symbolizes for us, but your love letters will always reach me in a way that nothing else ever could."

Londen was so taken aback by her words that he couldn't immediately respond. Lei hadn't said them for a response; she said them because they were her truth. She'd started to open the letter and read it when he finally found his voice again.

"I'm happy to provide that for you, and I'm going to spend the rest of our lives making sure you know just how worthy you are of true love."

"And I promise to do the same for you. I love you, Londen Graham, more than I ever thought was possible."

After making love to her lips, Londen left her with the letter so she could savor it. He went back inside to make sure the chef was ready to prepare their meal and checked his phone notifications in the process. He had it on Do Not Disturb, but someone had called back-to-back so their calls would go through. At the sight of Mercedes' number, Londen frowned. They didn't have the type of personal relationship where she'd be calling him just because. Something was wrong.

Quickly dialing her number, Londen made his way out of the living room so he could have some privacy.

"Londen!" Mercedes yelled as soon as she answered.

"Where do I need to be?"

"Seated in a chair for this."

Her words stopped his stroll, but he didn't sit down as she suggested.

"What's up, Mercedes?"

"It's Noah. He's coming home tomorrow."

Londen's body swayed slightly and hit the wall. That news was bittersweet. It made the night even better, but it also deeply concerned Londen. With Noah being released, he'd need to make sure he and Lei were established in Memphis sooner than later. Noah was his brother, but they were on two different paths. As soon as he touched down, there was no doubt in Londen's mind that Noah would hit the streets harder than he ever had before.

The moment his father found out, he would be even more adamant about Londen getting back into the family business. Now that he had a fiancée and two children to consider, Londen was even more dedicated to living a legit life. If Noah was about to be out... shit was about to get real in Rose Valley Hills.

~~The End~~
The Beginning

To follow the new secret society and next couple in Memphis click here. (Lei and Londen are mentioned, but this is a new couple.)

To follow Noah, Mercedes, & the rest of the crew as things get gritty in Rose Valley Hills, click here. (Lei and Londen are secondary characters but will return with their full story in July.)

P.S. Yes, you're going to have questions about Tussi, Yandi, Landon, and probably some other stuff too. This is the beginning of a series, so trust me, I got you 🙂.

As always, if you enjoyed this read, please leave a review on Amazon/Goodreads and mark it as READ on Goodreads.

Tag me in all of your five-star reviews @authorblove.
I appreciate you always 🖤

True lovers of B. Love, click here for details on how you can show your support and receive exclusive, limited-edition B. Love books and merch!

For paperbacks, click here.

Sign up for B.'s mailing list here https://bit.ly/MLBLove22 and make sure you confirm your subscription via email.

For release day text messages only, text BLOVE to **(855) 718-0381**

afterword

Follow B. on Amazon for updates on her releases here.

Subscribe to B.'s YouTube channel here.

We hate errors, but we are human! If the B. Love team leaves any grammatical errors behind, do us a kindness and send them to us directly in an email to emailblove@gmail.com with ERRORS as the subject line.

True lovers of B. Love, click here for details on how you can show your support and receive exclusive, limited-edition B. Love books and merch!

also by b. love

Also by B. Love

Standalone Romance

Love Me Until I Love Myself (Christian Romance)

Give Me Something I Can Feel

Saving All My Love for You

To Take: A Novella

In Haven

Weak: An Irresistible Love

The Ashes: The Medina Sisters' Story

Just Say You Love Me

If You Ever Change Your Mind #1

Coffee with a Side of You #1

If He Loves Me #1

In Due Time #1

Will You Still Want Me? #1

If You'll Let Me

Til Morning #1

I'll Be Bad For You #1

Just Love Me (Shenaé Hailey)

Due for Love (Shenaé Hailey)

Til I Overflow

Flesh, Flaws, and All (Christian romance)

Make it Last

Straddling His Soul #1

Fingers on his Soul

My Love Wasn't Meant for You

The Preying Pastor

Everything I Desire

Someone She Loved #1

Give Me Love

Love Me for Christmas

Trapped Wishes #1

Yours to Have #1

Unequivocally, Blindly, Yours

Brief Intermission

But Without Haste #1

Last Chance to Love #1

Strumming My Pain #1

With His Song #1

Held Captive by a Criminals Heart #1

Fans Only

To Protect & Swerve

Now Playing: Reel Love

Faded Love

Just Like I Want You

Lie in It

April's Showers

The Mourning Doves

Finding a Wife for My Husband

In The Lonely Hour

Ours for Hours

Loving the Lonely

A Valentine for Christmas

The Love Dealer

The Love List

Santa's Cummin' to Town #1

The Boss Babe Series

Tampering with Temptation

Hungry for Her

Seducing a Savage

The Hibiscus Hills Standalone Series

A Picture Perfect Love

The Mister Series

Mister Librarian #1

Mister: The Mister Series Prelude

Mister Jeweler #1

Mister Concierge #1

Mister Musician #1

Mister Teacher #1

Banking on Love Series

60 Days to Love

The Business of Lust

Majority Rules #1

Romance Series

Love Me Right Now (1-2) #1

To Take: Crimson Trails series (1-5)

Send me (part 1) I'll go (part 2) #1

***The Love Series – The Love We Seek, The Love We Find, The Love We Share**

Harts Fall Series – With All My Heart, With All My Trust, With All My Love (Shenaé Hailey)

Her Unfaithful Husband, His Loyal Wife, Their Impenetrable Bond (Shenaé Hailey)

Love is the Byline

Love's battleground

Love's garden #1

Standalone Urban

To Be Loved by You

His Piece of Peace #1

Her Piece of Peace

Her piece of peace: The Wedding

Hunter and Onyx: An Unconventional Love Story

Thief #1

A Hustler's Heaven in Hiding

His thug love got me weak

If I Was Ya Man

A Gangsta's Paradise #1

LoveShed

Kisses for my Side Mistress

Set Up for Love

Promise to Keep it Trill

Her Heart, His Hood Armor

Her Gangster, The Gentleman

Her Only Choyce

Let it H*E (Constance)

Yours to Keep

Black Mayhem Mafia Family Saga

In His Possession

Her Deep Reverence

A Heart's Rejection

Under His Protection #1
A Father's Objection
In His Possession 2
A Heart's Connection
Indiscretion #1
Succession #1
Resurrection #1
Interception — exclusive paperback only.

Gucci Gang Saga

I Need A Gangsta
One Love

Urban Series

She Makes the Dopeboys go Crazy (1-2)
Caged Love: A Story of Love and Loyalty (1-5)
If You Give Me Yours (part 1) I'll Give You Mine (part 2) #1
Loved by a Memphis Hoodlum 3
It Was Always You 2
The Bad Boy I Love 2
No Love in His Heart 3
My Savage and His Side Chick 2
So Deep In Love
Faded Mirrors

Holiday Novella Set Box

Bloody Fairy

A Thug in Need of Love

Holly's Jolly Christmas

Beginning Career Titles

(Series are separated. Characters are overlapped. These titles do not have to be read together, but if you'd prefer to know what stories everyone is from, you can read them in this order. Power and Elle and Rule and Camryn can be read alone without reading anything else.)

Kailani and Bishop: A Case of the Exes 1-3

Alayziah: When Loving him is Complicated 1-2

Teach Me how to Love Again 1-2

—

Power and Elle: A Memphis Love Story

Rule and Camryn 1-4: A Memphis Love Story

Femi (Spinoff for Rule and Camryn)

—

Young Love in Memphis 1-3

But You Deserve Better

Printed in Great Britain
by Amazon